David Wilson was born in London, and was educated at the London School of Economics and the University of Leeds. He now lives and works in North Yorkshire. *Love and Nausea* is his first novel.

'A stylish debut ... Wilson's romance is punchy and satirical'
Julie Myerson, *Mail on Sunday*

'A comic *tour de force* ... clever, funny and romantic'
The Times

'A sharp, funny novel about growing up smart somewhere on the North Circular'
Maxim (Top Ten Books of the Year)

'This is a lovely book which succeeds in being both hilarious and deeply serious'
Bernice Rubens

'An ironic *tour de force* from a wickedly talented writer'
David Profumo

LOVE
and
NAUSEA

DAVID WILSON

An *Abacus* Book

First published in Great Britain by Abacus 1995
This edition published by Abacus 1996
Reprinted 1996 (three times), 1997

A CIP catalogue record for this book
is available from the British Library.

ISBN 0 349 10780 7

Printed and bound in Great Britain by Clays Ltd, St Ives plc

Abacus
A Division of
Little, Brown and Company (UK)
Brettenham House
Lancaster Place
London WC2E 7EN

Author's note

I'd like to thank Penguin Books for their kind permission to quote from *Nausea* by Jean-Paul Sartre, from which most of the chapter head quotes are taken. (*La Nausée*, copyright © Librairie Gallimard 1938, *Nausea* translation by Robert Baldrick, copyright © Penguin Books Ltd., 1965.)

Penguin also gave me permission to quote from *The Prime of Life* by Simone de Beauvoir, translated by Peter Green (Penguin Books 1965, copyright © Gallimard 1960), and *Memoirs of a Dutiful Daughter* by Simone de Beauvoir, translated by James Kirkup (Penguin Books 1963, copyright © Gallimard 1958).

My thanks to the Estate of Simone de Beauvoir for permission to quote from *The Second Sex*, first published by Gallimard 1949, translated by H.M. Parshley, copyright © Jonathan Cape 1953. The quote from Simone de Beauvoir on page 205 is from *McCall's Magazine*, quoted in the biography of Simone de Beauvoir by Claude Francis and Fernande Gontier (Sidgwick and Jackson, 1987).

I am grateful to HarperCollins for permission to quote from *The Female Eunuch* by Germaine Greer, published in Paladin by HarperCollins, 1970, 1991.

I'd like to thank David Profumo and Bernice Rubens for

their generous advice and encouragement, Charles Walker of Peters, Fraser & Dunlop, without whose guidance the book would probably have foundered, and Richard Beswick and Abacus, for invaluable editorial comment and support. My thanks, also, to Charlotte Allen and Pat Clayton for their helpful comments.

Finally, Susan Aitken gave me perceptive advice and support throughout the writing of the book. To her, and our children, Sophie, Luke and Rosalind, my thanks and love.

Prologue
1986

Robert was outdoors. At a party. More specifically, he was halfway along a concrete path to a friend's private swimming pool, and had just noticed that his left testicle was protruding, like a brown giblet, from the side of his trunks. He was embarrassed but unsurprised. His body always sabotaged him in some morose way. He shielded himself with a book, prodded the offending half-organ back inside his trunks and plodded forwards into the heat.

A glistening young woman lay across his path. She glanced at him with a frowning expression that he assumed was disgust. He clutched his book tightly, as a token of a different world, as emblematic of the fact that he couldn't be fully defined by his body. She'd probably seen the testicle at twenty yards' distance.

Robert didn't care that much anyway. Beneath the Factor 15 sun-protector that he'd laid on his thinning crown, as thickly as cream over strawberries, his mind was tenderly nursing bigger issues than stray testicles, like how to spend the rest of his days, and who to spend them with, and whether or not to go and see Eva again: Eva, the most intense, exciting, hurting relationship of his life. After seven years, he'd heard from her: a cryptic message saying she needed to see him, followed by a letter.

He scuttled along the side of the pool towards the main group of guests. He was not at his best naked. The shock of hard sunlight against his skin made him look translucent, blue, Martian. He'd have preferred to get to know people by exchanging CVs or handing out copies of a newspaper questionnaire asking him how he wanted to be remembered, or, best of all, a *Desert Island Discs* transcript. Swimming pools were simply not his genre. The feel of the concrete slabs and the smell of chlorine took him back to how he felt when he was fifteen, at his local swimming pool, which had had a whole class structure based on suntans. Bronzed and golden people strutted like gods closest to the water; people like him went to the furthest corner – there was grass there, hot and sticky with sweat and spilled ice-cream. Once he had stayed by the pool, face down. 'Blimey, look how white that bloke is,' someone had said. It was followed by an irritated 'They shouldn't be allowed in, people as white as that' comment, and lots of laughter.

Eva didn't give a toss about things like suntans. She was about intensity, soul, directness. And danger, too. Did he really want to go near all that again?

His friend Stephen, whose house-warming party it was, came towards him, ruffled and blinking, as if he'd just woken up and wandered straight outside. It must feel great, thought Robert, to be this natural, to be so at ease in the world. He'd never understood how it was done.

'Christ,' said Robert. 'Fancy you buying a house with a swimming pool.'

'We just needed a bigger house for all our kids,' said Stephen. 'The pool was incidental. What do I want a bloody swimming pool for?'

As if to emphasise the point, Stephen was wearing thick

cord trousers and a long-sleeved shirt buttoned up to the collar.

'What's the book you've got?' asked Stephen.

'*Nausea*, by Sartre.'

'For God's sake,' said Stephen, 'you're not still a bloody student, you're in your thirties.'

'It's an important book to me,' said Robert. 'I'm reading it again. You once lent it to me, remember? You used to think it was great.'

'You've got to study what's happening to the Eastern European economies,' said Stephen. 'That's the only thing you need to understand right now.'

They were joined by Marshall, Robert's employer and sometime friend. He was handsome in a worn, lizard-eyed way. His swimming trunks were several sizes too small, so that they kept sliding between his buttocks and transforming themselves into what *Sun* readers would call a Thong. Knowing Marshall, this effect would have been carefully calculated.

Marshall poked Robert's stomach. 'Christ, you're getting fat,' he said. Robert looked down at his stomach: it spread out below him, white as veal, with red horizontal lines where the skin folded, glistening with yellow rivulets of sweat and sun cream. He wouldn't have been surprised if some psychopath had appeared and started carving it for lunch.

Stephen started to talk about Ronald Reagan, but Marshall interrupted and asked how much a house like his was worth.

'No idea, I'm not interested, said Stephen. 'It's just a house.'

'My place is putting on two thousand a month at the moment,' said Marshall, speaking more loudly than was necessary and flexing his buttock muscles.

'Mine's gone up twenty per cent in ten weeks,' said Robert. It was like talking about some mysterious growth in the size of his penis.

Robert's wife Deborah lay on a sun-lounger a few feet away. Her long, bony body had an all-weather tan courtesy of the Electric Beach salon in Edgware Road, and her legs were shaved and waxed till they gleamed. Her legs cost more a year than servicing the car did.

'Robert's stepfather's gone up thirty thousand in six months,' said Deborah. 'It's given him something to live for since Robert's mother died.'

Stephen, impressively, looked bored and wandered away. Robert fetched a cup of coffee and joined Deborah.

'You're letting yourself get terribly seedy,' she said. 'You might have made an effort for Stephen's house-warming. To lose weight or get a tan. You knew he had a pool. And you should get a hair transplant: I'm willing to help pay for it.' Deborah generally treated Robert as a consumer product. He'd often thought she would be happier if he could be deep-frozen or machine-washed.

'Well, your swimming costume is designed for optical illusion,' said Robert. 'It's cut away to make your hips look less prominent.'

'At least I'm not fat.'

'But you should be taking more care in the sun. There was another article the other day, incidence of melanoma doubling every ten years. And what about your friend getting secondaries at the age of thirty-two?'

'Jesus. This is Hertfordshire, not Honolulu,' said Deborah.

It was a typical conversation. They generally intervened into each other's lives in such a way as to promote average states of being, quick to knock down any real signs of joy or power, but propping each other up with a few, homeopathic words of encouragement if they became too depressed. He sometimes imagined what it would be like to die in the presence of Deborah. She'd have no interest in understanding him but the Man-size tissues would never run out.

As if to reinforce his point about skin cancer, Robert began to smear himself with an array of different grades of sun cream: Factor 7 on the bumpy surface of his legs and over the folds of his stomach, then Factor 10 on his face, and a further dollop of Factor 15 on his frayed, £1-a-square-yard head.

He stirred his coffee slowly and rhythmically, without touching the sides. It was one of Eva's gestures and one of the things that brought back a sense of her; brought with it, as her name wandered like a ghost through his psyche, the feel of her, the way she lifted the cup so smoothly to her lips, the calmness of her pale blue eyes as she looked at him, and the black eyebrows that could arch with irony as if putting everything she said in inverted commas.

Deborah rolled off the lounger and walked towards the swimming pool with the careful hip action of someone who knows she is being watched. Robert wasn't going to bother with the pool. It just wasn't the same as swimming in the cold, transforming sea; it was tame to paddle along in this water that was as warm as mother's milk.

He leaned back and closed his eyes. But he found it hard to relax in the hot sun. The sun no longer tanned his skin: it bombed and mined and corroded it.

Marshall sidled up.

'Deborah's looking in good shape,' he said. 'Very sexy.'

'Best screw I've ever had,' said Robert. 'Always dying for it, just loves to get straight down to it, no messing about with foreplay.' This was a lie. Deborah's main preoccupation in making love was, in fact, achieving high standards of hygiene.

Robert wanted to be on his own. He stood up and wandered as far away from the others as he could. He sat under a pine tree and looked at the silver light on the surface of the pool, and the red geraniums glowing against the white walls of the house. It was a beautiful day. You ought to be happy, you bastard, he said to himself. I'm trying, for

Christ's sake, some part of him replied. He was, after all, thinking about Eva making contact after all this time. Eva of all people, talking about needing him. He hadn't seen her for seven years, but he thought of her every day. Psychically she lived next door to him. And now she had got in touch, powerfully and decisively.

'At last an adventure is happening to me.' It wasn't his phrase. It was Sartre's, from *Nausea*. Sartre had been kicked into touch a good few years ago, but the book was important to Robert, nonetheless. It was a book that had always seemed to mirror the operation of his own mind, and to dream some sense of himself into existence. And within its pages and silences, more than any photograph album or record collection, it held his relationship with Eva.

How much he'd once identified with Jean-Paul! The phrases in *Nausea* still collected him up, surged him forwards. It was crystal-clear once more that Jean-Paul would have felt the same as he had at the local swimming pool, would have staggered out of the changing room, short-sighted, flabby, white as paper. Robert saw the scene clearly – the eyes: red-veined, opaque, blinking; the breathless, waddling walk; the navy swimming trunks pulled up almost chest high; and yes, of course, Jean-Paul was exactly the sort of bloke who'd have a testicle peering out of the side of his trunks. He spoke for you. He'd have walked on, angry at the suntan fascists, contemptuous of the stupidity of it all. He'd have gone to the grass in the corner with the spilled ice-creams and savagely indicted the bourgeoisie while Simone de Beauvoir calmed him down and took the odd note. She'd have tucked the testicle back in and they'd have discussed how it was a token of him being invaded by his own existence.

And it was strange, too, how much like Sartre he looked. Robert had his stooped shoulders and a body tending towards plumpness. Like Sartre's, Robert's body looked better fully clothed, in a polo-neck and trenchcoat, slouched, pen in hand, across a table, close to a café crême, notebook and ashtray. The body had to support an unfashionably large head, with a lot of face, thick lips and very little hair.

The ambiguity of Sartre's appearance, the fact that this small, apparently ugly man could succeed with beautiful women, had always been a source of consolation and mystery to Robert. Like Sartre, photographed from the right angle, Robert's face could look powerful and intense. But, in contrast to Sartre, Robert had beautiful eyes, grey-green like the sea, eyes that had always been complimented. Perhaps no one would ever crawl tearfully across a room to play Roberta Flack songs about the first time ever they saw his face, but he had had his moments, nonetheless.

Robert had the beginnings of a plan. He'd plead heat exhaustion, go home early, read *Nausea* again, and write to Eva. He'd ask Marshall if he wouldn't mind running Deborah back at the end of the party, if he wasn't too pissed.

Robert went into a toilet to wash the sun cream off his face. He glanced into the mirror, hoping, maybe, to see reflected back a look of empathy, a mandate to take charge of his life and be happy. But a white blob with suspicious eyes glared back at him. It asked him what he bloody well wanted from his life.

Ah, thought Robert, I want modest little things: to be loved, saved, healed, transformed.

'Tosser,' said the white blob.

Robert splashed cold water on to his face.

Did he really want anything to change in his life? Shouldn't he just settle for the goalless draw?

He looked into the mirror again, worried that he'd find his face empty and soulless.

Did he and Deborah believe in anything other than
steadily rising house prices and the occasional bonk? And
why did he have to be going grey as well as bald? What sort
of universe was this? And, oh shit, was that a mole or a
melanoma on the side of his face?

Robert crept out of the toilet and thought about Eva.
Was the sense of yourself you had with another person – a
sense of freedom for example, or of being able to trust
life – created by the relationship or could you take it away
with you and make it yours?

He looked inside his copy of *Nausea*. Phrases were
underlined, in different coloured pens, from the various
times he'd read the book. They seemed to offer a safe
route back into the past, like marker flags across a
crevassed glacier. And the book stored so many experiences for him, previous self-states: it would help him, as it
always magically did. One phrase stood out in particular:
'Forty-year-olds would like to make us believe that their
past isn't wasted, that their memories have been con-
densed and gently transformed into wisdom.' Well, he
wasn't forty yet, and, of course, thank God, Jean-Paul Sartre
had seen right through that sort of bourgeois crap. Only
Sartre had managed to do it for himself – the books and
the wisdom. And 'bourgeois' was such a quaint word now,
wrinkled, past its prime, empty of energy . . .

Part I
1967–1971

'Everything I know about life, I have learned from books.'

Robert had been waiting for Eva from the moment he read *Nausea*. He was in his last year at school when his friend Stephen lent it to him, along with Camus's *Outsider*. They were the first books he'd read voluntarily since *Biggles*.

At lunch one day he'd sat in an unusual place at the refectory table, on a boundary between his normal conformist friends and Stephen's little group. It was a boundary occupied by one or two social isolates, like Jonathan Creighton, with his pimple-covered moon face and unfocused eyes, the school's outstanding musician and the most chronic of its chronic masturbators, whose leg moved to and fro beneath the table with the relentless mechanical efficiency of a metronome. Stephen and his friends sat apart at the bottom of the table, like a small but cohesive political party, an unofficial Opposition. They did strange things like opposing apartheid and playing postal chess with people in New York and Prague; they avoided cross-country runs because of vague conscientious objections and won scholarships to Cambridge.

Robert was received with curiosity, like an MP who had sat on the wrong bench. They were discussing books.

'Have you read any good novels ?' asked Stephen. 'Like *Nausea* or *The Outsider* or *Steppenwolf* ?'

Robert hadn't. Stephen and his friends talked about Penguin Modern Classics with the enthusiasm other people reserved for all-night parties or football matches. Stephen promised to lend some to Robert.

Robert took the books home in some excitement, smuggling them shyly upstairs like a first girlfriend. You had to take Stephen seriously. Stephen had made love, screwed, got his end away. And he was a Marxist. Robert had seen Stephen's father once, sitting in an armchair watching *Grandstand*, a huge cigar in his mouth, completely impassive. With his black beard and mid-European voice he seemed like Karl Marx himself, a literal descendant of Marx in an Old Testament 'begetter and begat' sort of way. According to Stephen, he'd seen it all – fascist gangs beating up Jews in the East End while the police just looked on, the D-Day invasion (sitting on top of a tank wearing a CP badge and a Star of David – not that he believed in God: it was simply a defiant gesture), and the liberation of concentration camps.

Robert sat on his single unscrewed-in bed opposite his Spurs poster and began to read *The Outsider*, starting with the quotes on the back. He liked what they said about Camus making 'savage indictments of bourgeois hypocrisy', and 'holding up a disquieting mirror to modern reality'.

Robert read. From the first line about Mother dying, to the last, he gulped it in. How zealously he walked with the Outsider along Algiers beach, his eyes blinded by the sunlight off the blade of the Arab's knife, his mind sapped by the heat of the sun hammering on his temples. Muswell Hill Broadway would never be the same again. He would walk along it now with eyes narrowed, poised, whatever the weather, for the menacing solitary figure walking towards him from Macfisheries, for the flash of an Arab's knife from the doorway of J. Sainsbury's.

Robert felt outraged at Meursault the Outsider's trial and execution. He stood at the bathroom mirror and practised the look of supreme indifference he'd have if ever he had to await execution and listen to the crowd's howls of execration. He wasn't exactly sure what howls of execration were – maybe the sort of thing the crowd gave at White Hart Lane when the referee failed to spot an off-the-ball incident on one of their players.

Robert wondered if he might one day run along Algiers beach, tanned and muscular, and swim in the healing sea, and sleep with girls 'one strand of whose hair was worth all the bourgeois certainties'. How he longed for a girl like this.

But then he looked in the mirror and knew he'd never be Camus. Albert seemed too far away, too beautiful, too Mediterranean, heroic and athletic: someone to be admired but impossible to copy.

Jean-Paul Sartre had come next. *Nausea*, with a Salvador Dali picture on the cover showing an arch of green rock with a stone clock fixed to it, and beyond this a pale, empty beach. The book flowed into him easily, milkily, even if he didn't understand some of it in a conscious way.

As Robert read about the lead character, Roquentin, he felt a sense of joy and recognition. He knew for certain that what he read was the idiom of his own mind. Roquentin, like Robert, was lonely and alienated, he struggled with the meaning of existence, hated the bourgeoisie, and didn't like what he saw when he looked in the mirror; and he was trying to 'understand himself before it was too late'. Yes, yes, yes, thought Robert, this guy is just like me. Robert was even certain that at some forgotten point in the past he had had the same semi-mystical experiences that Roquentin described in the book.

But (and it was a delightfully big and pretty 'but'), this character who looked and thought the same as Robert wasn't sitting at home with his parents in North London watching *Sportsnight* with David Coleman. He was free! He was having a ball! He was spending his time in wonderful cafés which shone into the night 'like ships and stars, and big wide eyes'! And in those cafés there were women: sleazy *patronnes* who took him into the back room for a quickie, or beautiful, sensitive women like Anny, the woman of his dreams, the woman who would save him, with her mysterious, intelligent spirit.

Roquentin had travelled the world, 'crossed seas, left women and cities behind him'. Roquentin had thrilling philosophical insights and direct experiences of the Mystery of Being; he'd try to pick up a pebble and suddenly realise he was no longer free. Roquentin didn't just walk along a street, he 'wandered along at random, calm and empty, under this wasted sky'. Bugger the Arab with the knife, thought Robert: this was exactly how he wanted to walk along the Great North Road.

Robert felt his life had suddenly been unstuck, freed. He knew what he wanted: the mysterious insights, the cool sense of freedom, the night-time cafés in unknown foreign towns; above all, Anny, the wonderful woman who would love him. Robert had fallen towards the book and the book had held him. He would never be completely alone again.

'The Nausea seized me.'

Robert decided to treat the book like a manual for his life.
If he followed the basic injunctions, the rest would follow –
the philosophical insights, the women, the travel.

The blurb on the back cover referred to Roquentin having found the Key to Existence. This seemed a handy
enough place to start. The Key to Existence was to have an
experience of Nausea, which was when you felt your mind
was being engulfed by Existence. And you could, if you
were really lucky, get engulfed by Existence through staring
at chestnut trees in your local park.

Robert spoke the word Nausea with reverence; it was a
mystical, transforming experience that seemed to confer
instant, almost pop-star, status. There appeared to be a
simple cause-and-effect relationship between Roquentin
being overwhelmed and disgusted by the pure facticity of a
chestnut tree's existence, and being swept into a back bedroom by the local café *patronne*.

Robert prepared the following Sunday to go to the local
park. It had been transfigured in his imagination. It was no
longer a rather suburban, ordinary place with blackened
trees, a bumpy football field, rusty children's swings and a
wooden Lyon's Maid kiosk. Rather, it had become the

place where the doors of his perception would finally be flung open. Sartre was a genius: he provided LSD in book form.

Robert was careful that lunchtime not to have second helpings of his mother's roast lamb or treacle sponge pudding. He avoided *Two-Way Family Favourites* on the radio, and retreated to his room to take deep breaths and reread key sections of *Nausea*. He had to be in just the right frame of mind.

He'd marked particular passages with lines and asterisks and ticks and 'very goods', as if he were a teacher marking an essay. The big thing was to stare at the roots of a chestnut tree and wait for the meaning of things to disappear. The tree would stop being a tree and become a 'black, knotty mass'. He might see the bark as sea-lion skin or tanned leather. And then he would have a mystical revelation. Everything would dissolve into a disgusting, oozing jelly. He would suddenly know what it meant for things to *exist*. His stomach would heave, and he'd experience Nausea, right there, in the local bloody park. He'd know that his life was superfluous, contingent, arbitrary. Things would never be the same again. At school on Monday lunchtime, they'd say, 'What did you do at the weekend? Any good parties?' (Jonathan Creighton would use some nasty phrase like, 'Get the tits off anyone?' And to Stephen and co., quietly, with dignity, he'd say, 'Nausea. Local park. Yesterday. Like Jean-Paul.' And it would be downhill all the way. He'd tell Fiona Duvalle, 'Nausea, Fiona.' 'Oh Robert,' she'd say, and she'd melt into his arms.

Robert read the chestnut tree passage, which talked of worlds collapsing, and the park emptying through big holes, and did indeed have a troubled feeling in his stomach, as if something mysterious and frightening lay just behind the surface of the words. He knelt by his pale blue candlewick bedspread. 'Dear Lord, please let me go to the park, and be plunged into a terrible ecstasy, just like Jean-Paul.'

It was a warm late spring day. His hands felt a little sticky as he got to the first chestnut tree. It was a good-looking specimen, with leafy branches reaching right down to the ground like a floor-length skirt. It was cool and dark inside. The roots . . . well, yes, like Jean-Paul's, they plunged into the ground. And some images did come: one root was folded back on itself like a giant knee. And the bark looked, not like sea-lion skin, but definitely like the hide on an elephant's bottom.

He closed his eyes and leaned against the tree. He heard the thud of a leather football being well struck, shouts from the children in the playground, and 'Greensleeves' gonging out from an ice-cream van. He wondered whether ice-cream vans in Paris played 'Greensleeves'.

Nothing happened. He decided to try another tree. He passed, at a careful distance, a woman sunbathing in a bikini. He found an older, bigger tree. It was covered in splendid blossoms the colour and shape of ice-cream cones. Each cone had tiny flowers intense pinks and oranges and yellows. The tips of their stamens were coral-coloured.

'Stop. Calm down,' he told himself. 'Be patient, you can't rush Superfluity and Absurdity.' He breathed deeply, waiting to be disgusted and overwhelmed by the sheer facticity of the tree's existence, to see it dissolve into maggoty shapes and sinewy writhing forms. He stared at the roots, hoping to see them as 'steeped in Existence', but this phrase only conjured up images of his mother's treacle sauce. He waited. The woman in the bikini wriggled on a pair of pink shorts and hurried off. He looked up into the heart of the tree and saw layer upon layer of dappled green light. The tree smiled down at him. He felt extraordinarily anxious.

He hurried to another tree, near the playground. It had gigantic leaves, a foot and a half long. They felt like a clammy plastic mac. He heard laughing and squealing. A woman was pushing a little boy on a swing, higher and higher. As Robert kept looking it seemed as if the motion of the swing was taking place inside his stomach. He started to feel giddy. Then he glanced down and saw some pink paper, and realised it was covering human excrement. A wave of disgust surged through him. Here we go, here we go, he thought, at last, *La Nausée*. But the feeling passed. He took a deep breath and felt humiliatingly normal.

Robert was worried. It was his third chestnut tree and this one was no better than the others. Maybe it was the wrong time of year: Jean-Paul had gone to his chestnut tree in February. But that was just an excuse. It was pathetic. He should by now have been suffocating inside • the obscene jelly of Existence. Something inside him was stopping him having the experience. He started to feel horrified by the extent to which life in bourgeois North London had conditioned him.

Robert blamed his family and his school. He remembered a headmasters report. 'Satis.,' it had said in hurried blue Quink. 'Satis.,' his stepfather said in his quiet voice that had lost all its testosterone many years before. 'All the effort we've made to support you, and all they give us is a "satis.".'

Robert leaned against the side of the tree away from the toilet paper, and imagined a different sort of report from a school run by a headmaster like Jean-Paul Sartre.

'Robert is having a very satisfactory final year at school,' it would say. 'He is developing towards the highest state of revolutionary consciousness, ready to take armed struggle to every corner of the globe (and yes, if necessary, to Finchley, too). He is learning to transcend narrow identifications with class and race, and preparing himself to wage permanent war for the international proletariat, through his contribution as an existential Marxist intellectual.

'He mustn't give up on his practical philosophical

studies. Maybe he should try experiencing the Mystery of Being in a different location, such as Hampstead Heath or Regent's Park Canal? He needs to develop his appearance, let slip bourgeois conformity, Dunn's sports jackets and cavalry twill trousers, grow his hair, wear faded jeans. If he could possibly acquire an Afghan coat? And, frankly, we were disappointed that it was merely tobacco that he was smoking in the village cake shop when teachers last visited at break-time.

'Sexually, a disappointing year. He must redouble his efforts. I urge him to make the most of his teenage years. It may seem unimportant now, but it is very hard to make up for lack of application during this crucial time. Learning opportunities were not taken, for example with Christine Hardy on the night of the school dance. He must realise that life is sometimes about having a quick grope with whoever's available, rather than waiting for the perfect person to come along. He is possibly a little over-cautious, lazy even, when it comes to the sexual department. We would like to make him a prefect during his last term, but must await further progress before this is possible.'

Robert had almost dozed off against the tree trunk.

He heard a voice saying 'Oi,' and felt a hand on the lapel of his jacket. For a second he was unsure where he was, and thought it was his stepfather trying to wake him up for school.

A park-keeper came into focus as Robert opened his eyes and blinked against the bright sunlight. The keeper was wearing his navy blue jacket and peaked hat, despite the warmth.

Robert mumbled something.

The keeper pulled him upright.

'You can bloody clear off,' he said, 'or I'll call the police. We've had a complaint.'

Robert didn't have a clue what the man was talking

about, but had roused himself sufficiently to sense that it was not the best moment for a discussion of French literature. He scuttled off.

'And don't come back,' shouted the keeper. 'I've had enough of creeps like you lurking behind trees.'

It had been a disappointing afternoon, but there was plenty of time. The future was endless, full of day-dreamy possibilities for what he might do and whom he might become. Jean-Paul would understand.

'Lead melts at 335 degrees Centigrade.'

Robert came home from the park. Home was a thin-walled modern house fourteen feet from the A1, detached by six inches from its identical neighbours. He sat in the lounge and read a favourite passage in *Nausea* about a good bourgeois town where people believed the world obeyed fixed laws which repeated themselves every day. 'Bodies released in a vacuum all fall at the same speed, the municipal park is closed every day at 4 pm in winter, at 6 pm in summer, the last tram leaves the Town Hall at 11.05 pm. Lead melts at 335 degrees C.'

Jean-Paul had been deadly accurate in seeing how the bourgeoisie operated. Robert felt that he, too, saw things more clearly now, and was able to add laws he observed from his own family life: Fortis Green Woods closed at sunset, and a bell was rung a quarter of an hour beforehand; his stepfather left home every morning at 8.10, to catch the 8.19 tube; his pension scheme accrued by one eightieth of his salary every year; it was best to stick with a job that offered a secure pension; it was more hygienic to be cremated than to be buried; life was about more than happiness; Conservative governments were better than Labour governments; wearing jeans was a common, working-class habit; tight jeans, like tight Y-fronts, created problems of infertility; things didn't just drop into your lap: you had to work hard and make sacrifices; you wouldn't get promotion as quickly if you combed your hair forwards like The Beatles, or wore a beard; people with beards, like immigrants and Japanese cars, weren't to be trusted.

Robert now looked at the lounge through the cool eyes of Sartre. Robert's mother and stepfather had a penchant for sets of things in descending sizes: a nest of tables, a row of copper jugs, a family of elephants holding each other's tails. They liked order: when his stepfather had hung the gilt-framed mirror in the lounge he had spent the whole morning finding the precise centre of the wall.

There was a large china Alsatian dog on top of the TV, which was dusted every morning, and a souvenir ashtray with a picture of the Harwell Atomic Energy Station. Robert wondered what on earth these things were there for and why the *Radio Times* had to be put in a leatherette cover.

The objects in the room conspired to produce a sense in Robert that his life ought to be balanced, incremental and dull. Time would go by slowly, drily, methodically. If he worked hard for twenty years then he too could have a china dog on top of his own TV.

The only thing he loved in the room was a technical manual for Gypsy Moth aircraft. His mother had flown the planes as a delivery pilot during the war, and he used to marvel at the pages of engine diagrams and specifications, covered with black oily marks, his mother's fingerprints from a different life.

Robert decided that The Rolling Stones were best equipped to release him from the room's oppressive hold. He reached into the pit of the radiogram, and wobbled the stylus on to the first plastic grooves of 'Let's Spend the Night Together'. He crouched down, closed his eyes, and pressed his ear hard against the grille of the speaker. Even here, on this late Sunday afternoon, in his parent's lounge, after the disappointments of the afternoon, he could feel dreams and saliva fill his mouth as the first drumbeats raced into the room.

Like most of his friends, Robert responded like a Pavlovian dog to that moment late at a party when 'Let's Spend the Night Together' came on. All light would be blacked out, and people would start jumping desperately up and down, like shipwrecked people trying to attract the attention of a passing plane. Even virginal girls dancing together with minimalist movement suddenly felt required to strut and pout like 'gin-soaked bar-room queens from Memphis'. It was not a question of whether or not one liked the music, more one of social or even religious obligations to be fulfilled, a moment of witness as sincere in its way as a nun kneeling to receive communion or a flagellator lashing his back. It was a moment to sip from the chalice of your generation, say which side you were on, and affirm that the future belonged to you.

And Robert, stranded and white-faced amidst the party-size beer cans in the neon-lit desert of the kitchen, would feel renewed hope and courage, and stagger into the pulsating room, and draw near to the giant organism of the dancers. And he too would start a wild jerking movement, as if he was engaged in the last throes of copulation with some invisible person. He even believed in the magical, transforming power of the dancing; that it was not totally impossible that it would lead him into a wordless encounter with an unknown woman. But then the drums would fade, some light would seep back into the room, and he'd be left stranded once more, exposed, like a voyeur or hanger-on. And he'd shrink back, like Roquentin, to his own consoling inner world.

There was a tap on the top of his head.

He pretended not to have noticed. The music had

reached its soaring, inspirational climax. Let's spend the night together NOW.

NOW. The emphasis was peculiarly satisfying. His mother's view would have been that Mick and whoever the young lady was should postpone things for several years, wait till Mick had gone back to college and they'd saved for a house, and had a white wedding, and . . .

His mother prodded him again.

'Turn that off,' she said. 'You know we don't want our Sunday afternoons filled with Beatles music.'

He was staggered that she couldn't differentiate between The Beatles and the Stones. Or was she just pretending? Even with songs like 'Strawberry Fields', the Beatles songs were so utterly different, so much more benign. If The Beatles had appeared at the door they would have made a few irreverent remarks and smoked a joint or two; but then Paul would have blushed, they'd have had tea, pulled his mother's leg a little, and thanked her for the scones. The Stones would have leaned their liberatingly ugly heads against the wall, taken acid, sworn at his stepfather, knocked the Alsatian off the TV, screwed their groupies with confectionaries, and then pissed into the rosebeds. How could his mother confuse The Beatles and The Stones? How could she not feel the difference?

She reached past him and turned the volume down so low that the rhythms of the music were reduced to a series of cheap metallic vibrations .

'Why can't I play my music?' said Robert. Of course he knew what the reply would be, but he wanted to confirm its mechanical predictability.

'Because it's not the done thing to have pop music blaring out of our house on a Sunday afternoon.' Her voice was tight and high-pitched, each word and syllable carefully enunciated. It always seemed an invented voice, out of keeping with her green eyes and the soft, beautiful face of the mother he remembered as a child.

'Mum, do you believe existence precedes essence?' Robert said. Stephen had explained something about this one day at school. 'I mean, do you believe we're free to create our own way of living, rather than having to do the done thing?'

'I don't understand,' she said, blinking in confusion like a child.

'Mum, can you remember a time when you felt free to choose what you did with your life, a time when you didn't have to do the done thing?'

Even as he said this, it sounded rather silly, as if his mother had never been young or in love.

'Please don't upset your mother,' said his stepfather. His eyes were worried, pleading, as if Robert was some dangerous intruder rather than his own stepson.

Robert looked at his stepfather's bloodshot blue eyes and the vast slopes of pink skull that surrounded them. He looked at his checked Viyella shirt and stained medical school tie. How many time, he had wished that his stepfather was 'a gamblin' man down from New Orleans' rather than a somewhat elderly company medical officer.

'But Mum, you must like some pop music, songs like "Yesterday" or "She's Leaving Home", and you must like some pop groups.'

'I'm afraid I find them all rather coarse,' said his mother.

She stroked her throat as she said this. It was as if she feared that her life might be engulfed by people and things that were coarse.

The opposite of coarse was cultivated. Jean-Paul Sartre might or might not have been seen as cultivated. It would have depended on his clothes and fingernails and whether he stood up when she entered the room. His mother regarded their neighbour Mrs Duvalle as the epitome of cultivation: her husband had been to Winchester School, she smoked cigarettes with gold rings round them and she didn't let her daughter Fiona wear jeans. 'Jeans may be good enough for Princess Anne,' she'd say, 'but they're not good enough for my daughter.' Robert's mother had given up trying to stop him wearing jeans, and merely resorted to ironing a crisp crease into them, as if they were Daks after all.

He took the record off the turntable. In the end he did what they wanted. He was the boy who didn't give them a minute's bother. Sartre would probably say that more than anything in the world he needed to give them a minute's bother.

'It wasn't The Beatles anyway ' said Robert. 'It was The Stones.'

'But they've got the most terrible complexions,' said his mother. 'And they're so vulgar.'

Robert picked up a scone and smeared butter on it. His mother immediately relaxed. He dipped his knife into a pot of strawberry jam, knowing his stepfather would be watching to see how much he took, as if searching for evidence of Robert's character.

Robert and his stepfather found each other more or less incomprehensible. His real father had died when Robert was three years old: he had the vaguest of memories of being with him in a park, and a stronger, maybe imagined, memory of his mother being frighteningly upset, and of her disappearing for a while. Robert and his mother had lived on their own for nearly eight years, and then she'd met and married this man who was so much older and tireder than she was. Robert couldn't for the life of him understand why.

Robert let a large glob of jam slide from the spoon on to his scone.

'Look at Jonathan Creighton,' said his stepfather, staring at Robert's jam. 'He's reached his Grade Eight piano, and he's a dab hand on the organ, too. He'll be playing in the Festival Hall when that man Jagger is back on the dole.'

Robert looked again at his stepfather's sad shoulders, his mother's scones on the double-decker cake stand, and the sprinkler playing on the mildewed rosebed. It was a few minutes to six. The radio would go on, and they'd lapse into a respectful silence while his stepfather waited for the pips and the latest news of a terrible fire in Brussels. Robert had a sudden fear that his mother and stepfather would grow older but not wiser, have nothing to pass on.

He abandoned thoughts of putting on 'Have You Seen Your Mother Baby Standing in the Shadows'. In truth, he wasn't sure how much he liked Stones music. And how would he have really felt if they'd turned up at the house? He'd have been intimidated, he'd have withdrawn to his room and the cool spaciousness of *Nausea*. If he had to have a soundtrack for his youth he'd have preferred it to be provided by someone like Jimi Hendrix or Bob Dylan. But you hadn't got a completely free choice about what played inside your head: songs lived in you mysteriously, like dreams. And, disappointingly, there were times when he couldn't stop his mind filling with the high-pitched voices of the Righteous Brothers and Roy Orbison, singing about unrequited romantic love, and wearing, he imagined, the cleanest and whitest of neatly ironed Y-fronts.

'... but it was really out of politeness.'

Robert's second experiment from Nausea took place the following Friday evening. Ultimately, what he wanted was to experience the Mystery of Being and to have a lifelong love affair with a woman like Roquentin's Anny. But in the meantime he could experiment with being a cool existential intellectual and, more specifically, he could experiment with the type of casual sexual encounter which Roquentin had with café *patronnes*.

'I had to fuck her, but it was really out of politeness.' This magnificent and shocking phrase had writhed and wriggled in Robert's mind from the moment he'd read it. The words posed a puzzling, alchemical question: how did politeness turn into desire; how did niceness become lust? The word 'politeness' until that moment had meant things like giving up his seat to elderly people on the tube. My God, thought Robert, if fucking *patronnes* is politeness, then count me in – I'll be a paragon, a fanatic. It was revelatory. All he had to do was experience Nausea, and understand a concept like 'existence precedes essence', and he too could take his place in the world of cafés and *patronnes*.

Robert considered the nearest thing to a Parisian café within striking distance of home. The Express Dairy Café at the top of Highgate Hill? The East Finchley Wimpy Bar? The Lyon's Corner House at Crouch End, if it still existed? (He'd always enjoyed their individual trifles in white oval-shaped bowls with a cherry on top of the bright yellow custard.) Maybe the Hampstead Garden Suburb Cake Shop with its milky Nescafés? But none of them served alcohol. In the end he settled on the William and Victoria pub in Muswell Hill: when it was warm, people had been known to drag a couple of bar stools out on to the front steps, and look at the traffic passing along the Broadway two feet away. And he'd heard that a barmaid had once let someone sit there with a Penguin book and an empty half of bitter and had asked them about the book rather than asking them to leave.

He'd arranged to meet Stephen at eight, but arrived a clear thirty minutes earlier. He was wearing his new black polo-neck sweater. He had felt a sense of transformation as he put it on, his head squeezing through the dark tunnel of the neck and out, via a small shower of dandruff, into the light.

The nearest thing to a *patronne* was a barmaid in her early twenties. She had deep purple lipstick and blonde bouffant hair. She wore a V-neck top that seemed to be made of black string; Robert was almost certain, even allowing for his untrained eyes, that she wore nothing underneath. She looked exactly right.

He hovered near the door for a few moments before drawing renewed courage from the thought of Jean-Paul out there somewhere in the world of Left Bank cafés. Remember, Robert said to himself, you're different now: you didn't just walk to this pub, you wandered towards it, calm and empty, under a wasted sky.

He got to the bar. A few bloated regulars leaned against

it with their pints, their hips thrusting outwards like flying buttresses. He moved to a space as far from them as possible, and stood at the bar, holding *Nausea*, the Salvador Dali picture uppermost, like an advertisement for who he really was.

She came across, slowly, her breasts moving importantly inside the black knitted top, flicking softly To, and then suddenly back Fro. She was looking down, but then suddenly, almost insolently, she held his eyes as she came opposite him.

There was a short silence. Her eyes ratcheted down to the book, and then, he thought, down to his trousers; he glanced for a fraction of a second into the angle of her top. He looked away, only just in time, as her eyes came up to meet his. She smiled at him. On the blurred edge of his field of vision, he was almost certain that she placed a hand briefly on one of her breasts: to relieve a slight itch, possibly, or maybe to free a nipple that had got momentarily entangled in the matrix of black string. His tense, wired cheeks heated up with the speed of a toaster.

She looked at him without blinking. 'Yes,' she said, in a way that seemed suspended between an answer and a question.

Robert had experienced sufficient semi-mystical events in his life (feeling the living presence of God as he stared into a starry sky, melting with praise as choirs sang 'Morning Has Broken', prayers being answered, that sort of thing), to retain a childish sense of being special and a belief that the moment could open up in front of him like a dazzling, miraculous flower. Could it all be as simple as this? Was she about to ask him out of politeness?

'Please can I have a glass of red wine,' he said, wishing he hadn't said 'please can I' but something tougher, like 'I want' or even 'give me'.

'I'll have to see if we've got any: there's not much call for wine in here.'

She glanced at the book.

'Mmm. *Nausea.* What's that about, then?'

Say something, you bastard, thought Robert.

'It's about the meaning of existence, and, er, it's got a lot of scenes set in bars and hotel rooms.'

'Oooh,' she said, in a way that used several syllables and octaves; her eyelids clicked down then back up again.

She came back a minute later, with a glass of red.

'There we are, we did have some,' she said, and gave an uneven, possibly sly, or even teasing, smile.

He should offer to lend the book to her, say something inspiring.

A regular was tapping his empty glass at the other end of the bar: there wasn't much time. 'Purple Haze' floated in from a distant jukebox. Robert wished that the spirit of the song could fill him up, take him over. His mother thought Purple Haze was a type of air freshener.

The barmaid touched the book with a painted finger, then looked at him.

'Mmm,' she said. 'Anything else?'

Robert paused bravely. He felt slightly giddy. 'Anything else' might be one of those ambiguous, barber-shop phrases. Quick, he had to reply, find some words that would play with the uncertainty of the moment and shape it into something poetic, sensual and beautiful.

'A packet of Cheese Specials, please.'

Fool. Idiot. He'd blown it, his first go at being like Roquentin with a *patronne*. The phrase 'a packet of Cheese Specials' had very little scope for double meaning, and was unlikely to create a sudden magical fusion of art and love.

When she came back he thought that her fingers rested a shade longer than necessary in his hand as she took the money but she never looked at him again. Fool.

He gulped down his wine. Maybe a little incident like this didn't matter: it was just another minute or two of his life passing by. But he was deceiving himself. Events like this revealed who you really were. He'd been unable to flirt, to be spontaneous, to live in the moment, without rules. He'd killed time.

He glanced at his face in the tarnished mirror and saw a look he hadn't seen before – older, more disappointed. Maybe he was kidding himself when he thought he was like Sartre. He felt suddenly hungry and crammed all three Cheese Specials into his mouth at the same time.

Stephen strolled in. He wore a white sweater and looked dark and cool. Despite a small queue at the bar, he got served immediately, and had an easy laughing conversation with the barmaid.

Stephen swivelled a gold ring on his fourth finger as he listened to Robert describe his attempt in the park to experience Nausea.

'You're just a mixed up liberal,' said Stephen. 'Don't get self-indulgent. You need to read a bit of solid Marxism, maybe the Manifesto, or the German Ideology, or a couple of Maurice Cornforths.'

'But they're great books,' said Robert 'the ones you told me to read. *The Outsider* and *Nausea.*'

Stephen looked at Robert with eyes that were almost black, and framed by luxuriant masses of dark hair.

'Listen,' he said, 'they're just literature. They're great books, sure, but only a fool would try to imitate them. The way to take on the bourgeoisie, as you call them, is through Marxism, through working with the CP, not sitting next to trees in the local park. Nausea is anti-historical, my father said so.'

They left early. Robert had to be in by eleven, and

Stephen wanted to go via his house to lend him the Maurice Cornforths. Stephen drove him in the splendour of his father's new Rover 2000.

Stephen's family were exciting, but a little frightening. As he went into the hall Robert could hear shouts and heated arguments, swearing and laughter, from their sitting-room. Stephen's brothers and sisters and parents and friends would be in there. Their house pulsated with visitors – Russian industrial attachés, Greek resistance leaders fresh out of jail, North Vietnamese negotiators, beautiful American hippies. You could argue about anything – psychoanalysis, Spurs' midfield problem, Stalin's reputation, which pubs had the best beer, who fancied who, anything. As long as you weren't boring or right-wing, it was an open-door, welcoming house.

It seemed to Robert that Stephen's room had as many books as the upstairs section of the public library: shelves covered every wall, and books were also stacked on the floor, in precariously balanced towers. A line of novels stretched for fifteen feet, contrasting painfully with Robert's two Penguin Modern Classics. Stephen also had a double bed, and could take girlfriends home. His mother would let him lie in till lunchtime, then take them fresh coffee and toast. Robert had once rung Stephen at noon on a Sunday and been told by his mother that she didn't want to wake him up, he needed his rest. Stephen had probably been breastfed for at least the first three years of his life.

Stephen tugged out *An Introduction to Dialectical Materialism* from under a pile of clothes, and they hurried back to the car. Robert looked through the windows of the sitting room. He could see people laughing, and hands gesticulating, and in the middle of it all Stephen's dad, massive, impassive, watching late-night football, the whole of the twentieth century in his magnificent historian's grasp, a thick Havana cigar stuck between his lips, probably despatched by Fidel himself.

Robert's own father would have been impressive, too, but in a different way. He'd taught languages, and liked jazz, and kept a personal diary. He'd have been more of a Roquentin.

On Sunday Robert took the Maurice Cornforth down to the park, and sat under the shade of a chestnut tree in the very remotest corner, by a fence where tube trains rumbled into a tunnel and the grass was long and unmown. He was struggling to memorise a technical definition of materialism when he suddenly heard a voice coming from the long grass.

'No, of course it's private,' the voice was saying. 'No one comes up here.'

The voice was impatient and higher-pitched than normal, but definitely Stephen's.

There followed some difficult-to-interpret grunts and groans. Robert couldn't stop himself peeping round the side of the tree. He recognised the partly obscured figure of Fiona Duvalle, her dress pulled up in a far from cultivated way. Robert withdrew his head quickly, but retained an intense image of Stephen's gold-ringed finger stroking the inside of Fiona's thigh. Fiona started to gasp and groan. Right on cue, a tube train plunged into the tunnel, and the tree roots trembled beneath them. Robert felt shocked, giddy, slightly sick even. The tree didn't seem like an ordinary tree any more, but alien; the bark didn't look like bark but blackened, boiled leather. The pool of saliva in his mouth felt strange, disgusting even. As he walked home later, after a full hour spent hiding behind the tree, he realised that it was the nearest he'd yet come to experiencing the shock and existential overwhelmingness of Jean-Paul's Nausea.

*

Stephen rang a couple of days later after school. He was driving down to a party in the country with a stunningly beautiful friend of the family from San Francisco. Why didn't Robert come? He had the Rover 2000.

'There are no such things as perfect moments.'

In truth, Robert wasn't particularly bothered about a meaningless relationship with a café *patronne*. What he really yearned for was someone like Anny in Nausea, the intelligent, passionate woman who talked mysteriously about perfect moments.

Stephen told him that Anny was based on Sartre's companion, Simone de Beauvoir. As a young woman, Simone was achingly beautiful yet doubted her own attractiveness; she had the most penetrating philosophical intelligence of her generation, and she was sensual to the point where she worried about being driven mad by the intensity of her desire. She also wrote Penguin Modern Classics in French cafés, effortlessly indicted bourgeois hypocrisy, and happily stayed up all night talking, laughing, drinking and dancing. It was, for Robert, a list of qualities that would do to be going on with. But, so far as he could see, Simone de Beauvoirs weren't exactly plentiful in Finchley.

It was with some wonder, therefore, that he gazed at Julie.

She was a friend of Stephen's American cousins. Her hair fell in thick golden streams down her back, She had bright blue eyes and the most brilliant of smiles. She wore a very short tent dress. It was so loose that when she lay down on the settee and hooked a bare brown leg over its arm, Robert could see nearly the whole of her body. This was Eros and Civilisation! This was the Revolution in the Revolution! This was the Dialectics of Liberation! This was the Post-Scarcity Society!

They were in the sitting room of a large oak-beamed cottage in Kent, surrounded by middle-aged people drinking Chardonnay and arguing about politics. Stephen's father told them that Paul Sweezey, author of *Monopoly Capital*, was coming along later. Simon and Garfunkel's 'Mrs Robinson' played silkily on a quadrophonic sound system.

Julie told Stephen and Robert about life in San Francisco. She wore a bell round her neck on a red ribbon and said that making love was a beautiful experience which one should not be possessive about. She described at first hand things that for Robert had become iconic TV memories, like placing flowers in the barrels of soldiers' guns.

Robert agreed with her every word, and managed to nod and maintain a watery eye contact. If she'd suddenly proposed the re-introduction of hanging for children who stole apples or expounded a theory that Stalin was really just the first hippy, he'd have wistfully nodded in agreement. He wished he could say something like Sartre might say, that would be magical, that would reveal things in their true meaning and show the juncture of art and love. He gazed at a small puddle of spilled wine and softened his focus, hoping that he might go into a live and spontaneous experience of Nausea, swooning and giddy, seeing colours spin around him, emerging occasionally to utter a poignant ontological truth. But the most he could find to say was a repetitive 'That's beautiful.' She gave a shining, generous smile, then, suddenly, rose and swayed towards him.

'I want to hug you,' she said, and opened her arms wide. She held Robert warmly and closely, and said it was lovely to meet him. Robert closed his eyes and wished he looked more like Che Guevara.

Stephen looked decidedly like Che Guevara – dark and swarthy, with long sideburns, gleaming brown eyes, and tanned legs encased in long Cuban-heeled boots. And he had a mid-European father and a Ukrainian grandmother.

'You're talking nonsense,' said Stephen to Julie.

Robert winced. How could he treat this beautiful person so contemptuously

'All this hippy peace and love business is just nonsense from rich white kids,' said Stephen. 'It ignores the objective conditions. It's an irrelevant little diversion to the main struggle. I mean, look at Vietnam. What you say has got no fucking relevance to what really matters.'

Robert remained sympathetic towards Julie. He gazed at her lovingly. But her eyes were on Stephen. She protested, her eyes gleaming and her cheeks flushed. Stephen argued back. She leaned forwards, her long hair closing like a curtain across her face, and touched Stephen's thigh to emphasise a point. Stephen gripped her arm as he elaborated a criticism. She laughed and said, 'No, no, no, you've not understood what I'm saying,' slapping his thigh in unison with the words.

Robert began to understand more of the Maurice Cornforth book. He could see the dialectic moving between them, thesis, antithesis, synthesis. Marxism in action, material and dialectical. The bastard.

The three of them walked into a meadow next to the cottage. It was appropriately strewn, with daisies, red poppies and blue forget-me-nots. Robert thought Julie was the most attractive person he'd ever met. She picked flowers and threaded them laughingly into the boys' hair. Her own hair brushed against Robert's cheek and he knew it was worth more than all the bourgeois certainties. A minute later her hands were stroking Stephen's face and then she and Stephen were rolling on the ground kissing like hungry dogs at bowls of food.

Robert experienced the feeling he knew so well from parties: of sitting there pretending to be cool whilst dying of disappointment inside. He muttered that he'd get another glass of wine. Julie looked up and smiled.

Robert stood by the side of the house and watched them kiss and sway across the meadow to a field beyond. For the next half-hour he went into intense and lonely ideological reflection. Maybe there was something about American society that he'd never be able to get along with. For the first time in his life he seriously considered the benefits of living in the Soviet Union or China. In his imagined Communist society, a positive advantage of it in fact, a lot of this awful sexual competition would not exist. Anyone would have a more or less fair chance of anyone else. Maybe people as beautiful as Julie would have to undergo a nose uglification or a drug to make them fat – while the likes of Robert were given thousands of pounds' worth of state cosmetic surgery and hair transplantation. And men like Stephen would be given drugs that caused permanent hair-loss and halitosis. Or perhaps women like Julie would be required to sleep with men from different classes of sexual attractiveness, so many from each class per year. Or perhaps everyone would wear veils and regulation Maoist underwear in bed, or have to use exactly identical phrases in chatting each other up ('What, comrade, are your three favourite military bands?'). Robert felt grey and disciplined, ready for Five Year Plans and stern social controls.

The flowers in that field were so beautiful: red poppies shimmering against the ripening corn, the scent of roses curling in from the garden. Robert could hear Julie's hippy cries from the far corner of the field, and Stephen's deeper Stalinist grunts. He remembered a section in *Nausea* where Roquentin was kissing Anny on a river bank; she explained later that her thighs had been getting stung by nettles, but that it had been her duty to try to help create a perfect moment. Eventually she came to the conclusion that there were no perfect moments in life: the mind or something else always got in the way. Robert hoped fervently that Stephen was getting stung by nettles, but it seemed bloody hard to believe that they were having anything other than a Perfect Moment.

Stephen and Robert had a quick pint together just before Stephen dropped off Robert at home.

'Is Marxism true?' said Robert. 'That's my question.' He asked it with considerable force and passion.

'It's an odd question,' said Stephen.

'Well, alternatively, is it right or good?' said Robert. 'What I was thinking was how come you had Julie and you've got Fiona as well? It just isn't fucking fair. Maybe there's really a Darwinian thing going on and we're all just kidding ourselves about equality and justice. And who's to say that a middle-class bloke without a girlfriend doesn't suffer more than a working-class lad with one?'

'My father says that Marx's position on justice is very hard to sort out. One moment Karl is condemning capitalism as immoral, the next he's saying that it's perfectly just for its given relations of production.'

'You know what I'm trying to say,' said Robert.

'But you're not getting hold of it at all,' said Stephen. 'Marxism is not particularly about morality, it's about the unfolding logic of history.'

There was silence. They both sipped their pints.

'Is you making love with Julie part of the unfolding logic of history?' muttered Robert.

Stephen laughed, and wiped a bit of beer froth from his

lip. There was a sickle-shaped love-bite on the side of his neck.

'I don't think you'd have slept with Julie if we'd been living in China,' said Robert.

'You're daft,' said Stephen. 'Look, I know it must have been a bit tough on you, but that's just how it is.'

'I don't suppose there were any nettles,' said Robert. They both laughed.

'Julie's incredibly beautiful,' he went on. 'She was out of my league anyway. I'm just a member of the lumpen proletariat when it comes to women.'

'Don't put yourself down,' said Stephen. 'Sure, Julie's beautiful, but she goes to the bog each morning just like anybody else. Don't forget your dialectical materialism. And remember people like Rasputin, who was the ugliest man in Russia.'

'Well, thanks very much,' said Robert, inwardly wincing at the thought of Julie going to the toilet: it was an impossible image, unthinkable.

Late that night, Robert sat up in bed, comforting himself with some relevant sections of *Nausea*. He read the part where Sartre asserted that there were no perfect moments – they were an illusion imagined by onlookers: the actual participants in an event never experienced it as perfect. And it was reassuring how Roquentin found sunny days extremely threatening – the light shone on you with a 'pitiless judgement'. He preferred wet, dark, cloudy days. He couldn't have handled Californians.

There was a passage, too, about seeing mirrors as dangerous traps. You got caught by them and couldn't move away. Every room in Robert's house had a mirror, each with its own distinctive reflection of who he might be. A merciless south-facing mirror in the spare bedroom exposed every skin blemish and pimple: his life seemed to dissolve in front of it. In contrast, a round misty one in the bathroom provided glimpses of possible happiness. The full-length mirror in the hall was handy for rehearsing expressions before opening the front door. And a hinged three-piece version on his mother's dressing table gave the most neutral scientific light, and could be used to assess the risks of hair loss from a side profile.

In a drawer of the dressing table was a locked metal box containing his father's diaries. Ridiculously, Robert was not allowed to see them.

Another phrase from *Nausea* . . . 'A quarter of an hour would be enough, I am sure, for me to gain a feeling of supreme self-contempt.' God, Sartre understood: he'd served his time in front of mirrors and behind chestnut trees. Robert had looked in the hall mirror on returning home. Sure enough, the sun had brought out a rash on his neck and a flake of crusty yellow crud was hanging off his lower eyelid.

He noticed and underlined another telling phrase from the book. 'A perfect day to turn upon oneself.'

'A perfect day to turn upon oneself.'

On his better days, Robert saw his penis as a subtle onto-logical instrument, as the main representative of his unnamed existential being-in-the-making, as belonging spiritually to the Rue Montparnasse rather than the North Circular. It was a delicate space-probe or bathyscaphe taking him into unknown depths and possibilities of whom he might one day become.

He lay on the virgin bed in the rubbery darkness and thought about Julie. He gripped himself conscientiously. It was late. He should really go to sleep.

It was hard to imagine making love to her.

He could form an image of her face, her shining bright blue eyes, but the image kept dissolving. He forced himself to recall the moment when she had swung her leg over the arm of the settee, the flimsy flower-patterned tent dress, and her skin, which was the colour of – he searched for the right sense of it – the colour of Gale's honey from Sainsbury's or Keiller's Butterscotch.

He saw himself walking at her side into the poppy-strewn meadow, worried and hunched, stumbling slightly like a doomed Camus hero. He tried to get himself, his thoughts and feelings and vision, inside the man walking across the meadow, to imagine kissing her and making love, but it was impossible: he remained on the edge of the field, in his nylon pyjamas, spectating, unable to suspend disbelief. She was out of his league, adorable and unreachable.

A bus came down the Great North Road. It accelerated to a bend just beyond their house, then braked hard, with a piercing scream, and finally revved up hard for the long hill. They looked so unstable, the double-deckers. He was always expecting one to overturn.

He felt hot and tiptoed across the room to open a window. An orange blob appeared suddenly in the dark hole of the mirror: his face, disembodied, lit by a streetlamp.

Well, if he couldn't have Julie, if he was out of his class there, he was going to have Betty, the *patronne* in the William and Victoria who'd served him the Cheese Specials and red wine. He remembered the bits in *Nausea* about the *patronne*: 'She never says "no", she has to have a man a day.'

She had no face, save for a pouting mouth and brazenly leering dark eyes. And no voice. She was crude, sexy, begging for it, common, working-class—

'Cut!' Stephen's voice intruded. 'That's disgraceful , getting off on a sense of her being some sort of inferior working-class servant.'

Robert refocused. 'OK. Scrubber, then? Tart? A classless nympho who votes Conservative, exploits the other barstaff, and isn't kind to animals?' None of the jury inside his head objected.

He told her about being and nothingness. She pushed her pissed, desperate tongue into his mouth. 'Do it to me,' she said, 'if only out of politeness.' The music was loud as she rubbed herself against him. The rest was quick and vulgar. He would have hated Julie to know he could be like this. It would have taken someone like Jean-Paul to understand.

'Nothing. Existed.'

Things happened in the long months between his day in the country with Stephen and Julie and the night he met Eva. Bourgeois things, like not getting good A level grades, and Stephen getting into Oxford while he could only manage an obscure London poly. And other things, like becoming friends with Marshall, a postgraduate student who looked a bit like the Sundance Kid and was obsessed with sex, statistics and shoplifting.

Of course, Robert knew more now.

He knew the main causes of the French Revolution, but not quite well enough to have got into university. And he knew two psychoanalytic theories about Hamlet. He had changed the clutch on a Ford Anglia. He could tap out the cowbell start to 'Honky Tonk Woman' and give a plausible account of the debate over vaginal orgasms. And he knew that, whatever his teachers said, the Vietcong had strong support among the South Vietnamese, and that London bobbies were quite capable of kneeing demonstrators in the groin.

He understood more of *Nausea* now, and had even got closer to the experience itself. He was reading a passage which began with Roquentin looking at his hand, and seeing it as alive; watching the hand lie on its back and show him its fat underbelly; dangling it at his side and feeling the gentle pull of its weight on the end of his arm. Wherever he put it, the hand went on existing; he couldn't suppress it. Roquentin realised that it was equally impossible to stop himself thinking; the thoughts went dully on and on. The passage continued for page after page, the only punctuation being little dots. The words created a menacing rhythm inside Robert's head, and a sense of secret explanations trying to force their way out. He began to feel that if he didn't stop reading he was going to throw up. It was a relief for once to go downstairs and watch TV while his mother's spaniel lay snoring in front of the fire.

His sense of rapport with Sartre grew stronger than ever. He acquired a pipe to suck on while talking, and started to memorise quotations from existential literature and philosophy in the knowledge that it was essential to him ever being truly loved or desired. He studied Sartre's notions of consciousness, and how Nausea was the fundamental sensation that revealed the existence of the body to the mind.

Of course, he would have liked to have been the sort of man who drove women home on a Norton Dominator, their fingers digging into his groin as the bike revved up, who could excite women merely by grunting from under the black visor of his helmet, who could take them by the wrists and kiss them hard, and get their eyes glittering with animal desire while they told him he was a bastard and that he cared more about the Party than he did about them. But it was useless to even dream about this – he was too small, his hair was all wrong, and he didn't even have a moped, let alone a Norton Dominator.

And, equally, he'd have loved to have been a cool rock musician, dressed in crushed velvet and satin, and so stoned that boundaries between his body and hers dissolved in cosmic oneness. Or to be the type of man who had a torso and phallus, some sort of D.H. Lawrence character living in a world of elemental forces of yin and yang, the kind of man who, at just the right time, had rainbows of light play on his naked torso, and who attracted women who said, 'Let me see you' in an intense, hoarse voice, and then wriggled his trousers down over his hips.

But he realised such dreams were useless. The only possibility that still seemed to fit was to be like Jean-Paul Sartre. He could imagine himself inside the person in the photos he liked to look at, sitting in a café, in his black polo-neck, a coffee at his elbow, his eyes staring into the middle distance as he explained some ontological insight to someone like Simone de Beauvoir. Her look back towards him would be full of intelligence and irony.

Robert had even been to Paris briefly, for a couple of hours with his parents, en route to Belgium. He'd spent half his money on a small, hustled beer in the Café Flore. He thought he saw Albert Camus sitting at an upstairs table and was so excited that it was several minutes before he remembered that Albert had been dead for at least eight years.

Increasingly, he came to see himself as some kind of existential being-in-the-making. It had a nice ring to it. It was not the sort of thing you put down on university application forms, but it seemed to fit. His favourite stories had titles that consisted of the definite article and a singly symbolic noun: The Room, The Wall, The Castle, The Trial, The Fall, The Outsider, The Rebel, The Idiot.

Robert liked to think of himself, as he stood at the isolated far end of tube-train platforms, as a doomed existential hero struggling to find meaning in an alien world. All he needed was the right situation: a drowning person he could feel guilty about not having rescued from a canal, a pregnant girlfriend for whom he could seek out an abortion whilst agonising over issues of freedom and responsibility, a sadistic interrogator trying to trick him into revealing where his comrade was hidden, the motiveless *acte gratuit* murder of a relative like Auntie Janet. He occasionally hoped for a 4 am knock on the door of his home, for a Kafkaesque arrest and trial. He once got cramp in bed and wondered if he might have woken up to find himself an insect. He was even willing to settle for a bog-standard Kierkegaardian leap-of-faith situation, but where were you meant to go? The library? Fortis Green Woods? The end of the Northern Line?

Nothing. Existed. There'd been no major *rites de passage* as yet: no first flat or woman or fight outside a pub. He hadn't even read his father's diaries. Increasingly, he imagined that they might be a little like Roquentin's. Mostly his life was just waiting – to meet someone, for some sort of adventure to happen. He wasn't anything much at all yet. His life seemed to lie hazily in front of him, in daydreams, half-thoughts, possibilities. Who he was seemed tentative and flickering, like a badly tuned TV channel.

But waiting was quite pleasant in its way: he didn't have to think much or make many decisions – it was a bit like being in a well-organised queue. With a bit of luck he'd get there. Eventually he'd meet someone like Anny or Simone, and adventures would finally come.

'At last an adventure is happening to me.'

He met Eva a few weeks before some poly exams, in the sort of place he hated, a packed discotheque underneath the arches at Charing Cross, all heat and noise, and with strobe lights that made it impossible to recognise his friends. He'd been dragged there by Marshall.

It was the very last dance, to Procol Harum's 'Whiter Shade of Pale'. She just swayed into his path, completely drunk or stoned, he muttered something, and then she was in his arms, holding him tightly, the very first person other than his alcoholic Auntie Janet who had ever rubbed her crotch against his. She felt hot and damp, real and substantial, as her breathing rose and fell against his chest. They inched round to 'faces turning ghostly and the crowd crying out for more'. She was extraordinarily relaxed. Robert felt himself tumbling down a slope towards her, and had an uncanny sense of intimacy, as if he was meeting someone he already knew.

A couple of lights were switched on. The DJ interrupted the music to say goodnight. Robert wondered why she was so relaxed, why she let herself fall against him in such an uninhibited way. The strongest possibilities seemed to be alcohol or drugs.

The record reached its final verses.

'Tell me something about yourself,' she said into his ear. She tilted her head back and looked at him. Her hair was stuck to her face with sweat, in a sickle shape across her cheek. It was quite long, probably black.

Robert took a deep breath. He'd prepared for this for years.

'I suppose I'm what you'd call a bourgeois Marxist intellectual,' he said, 'but I agree with Sartre that Stalinist interpretations of Marx have to be modified by existentialism, by its emphasis on individual freedom.' He was conscious of shouting. He had to hurl his words into the thick sweating noise of the discotheque, and the effort accentuated his nasal London accent.

'Do you like to smoke dope?' she said slowly. She looked at him with an unblinking stare and with what he hoped was mock gravity. She was about the same height as him, and the right sort of size, neither too fat nor too thin.

'I think you ought to,' she said. 'It would do you good.'

The lights were switched on, making people look shocked and exhausted, like potholers emerging into sunlight from some underground drama. She had black hair, an oval-shaped face, and smooth skin with a few freckles, quite pale, thank God – he wouldn't have to feel awful about not having a suntan. They still had an arm around each other's waists, but time was running out; people were starting to leave, he had only a few seconds. He had to say something, quickly.

'Can I walk you home?' he said. Shit, what a stupid phrase that was, like a song title from one of his mother's Ivor Novello records. Shit, idiot, she'd felt so good.

She giggled. She had very red lipstick, so smudged that it was difficult to make out the shape of her mouth.

'No, it's OK, I'm getting a taxi,' she said. She smiled. Fuck, he thought.

'I must see you again.' His voice shocked him. It was insistent, desperate, passionate. It was as if a romantic actor auditioning for a part had borrowed his body for a moment.

She stared at him. Her eyes were strikingly bloodshot. It was difficult to tell their colour, probably blue. He was clutching her sleeve now, like a child. There was a stoned confidence about her, about her mouth and her smile, the way she grinned and took her time. 'Ah,' she said. 'OK. We can walk home.'

Great. Wonderful. He had to think of something good to say. Conversation pieces whirled through his mind. This is an existential moment, he thought as she started to put on a white trenchcoat, Jean-Paul, Albert, here I am. As she stretched her arm into the sleeve of her coat he looked at her red mini-dress, dark with sweat, clinging to her like a second skin. Phrases came back from half-remembered books. In the briefest of glances he took in the hollow dimples of her bottom and her breasts, pushing – possibly even straining – against the tight membrane of her dress.

They wandered along the Embankment towards Lambeth. Robert concentrated on looking moodily into the river, with his coat collar turned up like the Outsider. He quoted bits of T. S. Eliot about the river's tent being broken, the nymphs being departed and so on, speaking not in her direction, but in an abstract, preoccupied way towards the dark canyon of the river and the lights of County Hall on the far bank.

She swung round a lamp-post at full stretch, leaning out and giggling. She was full of energy and movement. It was difficult to work out what she looked like, especially when he was spending most of his time gazing at the river. For a moment he thought she was attractive and then an angle would change and he wasn't sure.

'Have you any brothers or sisters?' she said. What an odd question. Her accent seemed to have got stronger. It was difficult to place. Perhaps it was even French.

'No, neither,' he said. 'Why do you ask?'

'Things like that are important,' she said. 'I was curious to see if my guess was right. It was.' And she laughed again. The laughter was wild and semi-private – mainly her own business. Her voice was husky and she seemed very pissed.

He pulled his collar up tighter, lit a Gauloise, and wished again that he looked like Albert Camus or Che Guevara rather than Sartre. But he had to remember that whilst Jean-Paul considered himself ugly, he was almost irresistibly attractive to women when he got animated about some philosophical topic.

'Do you think existence precedes essence?' asked Robert. His voice still didn't sound right. He made Existence and Essence sound like rival toiletry products in some market-research interview.

She didn't seem to have heard. She was swinging off another lamp-post.

He looked over the wall at the black river, and shouted towards her in a rasping voice, 'Sweet Thames run softly till I end my song.'

She stopped and swayed towards him.

'Are you OK?' she said. She looked concerned. She laughed. 'I'm training to be a nurse.' She giggled again. 'But only so I can pay my way as I travel round Asia.' She put a hand on her hip with what seemed like an exaggerated self-mocking gesture.

'Don't you want to kiss me?' she said.

She kissed like a lion. He was mainly conscious of her teeth, which scratched against his, like a fork against a plate. She twisted and turned her head, as though she was trying to eat his mouth. He struggled to keep his end up, to not be hurt by her kissing, or forced to collapse in a humiliating heap on the pavement. Her tongue came into his mouth like a wild wet fish, sweeping away all the careful practice he'd done on grapes and Christine Hardy. He fought for breath as he tried to match her passion. Christ, wait till he told his friends.

She asked him in for a coffee, and he followed her past gloomily lit Victorian buildings to the entrance of the nurses' home where she lived. They tiptoed along a corridor. A security porter dozed behind a desk. A door creaked and he jerked upright. 'Don't you ever take a rest from it?' asked the man. 'You know you can't take people up to your room after ten-thirty.'

Eva shouted insults at him, but he just lowered his eyelids and shook his head. She grasped Robert's sleeve and tugged him back towards the entrance.

She was cursing and almost sobbing with anger. Robert did his best to be animated and said that the man was clearly a neo-Stalinist, but he felt puzzled as to why she should make such a big thing out of a cup of Nescafé at what was, after all, three in the morning.

Her bottom bumped against the tightness of her dress. And then it occurred to him. It had been a close thing. How stupidly naive he was! What drama and danger the moment had held! He had been, for a moment, anyway, an object of desire for her. How foolish not to have recognised the coded words – it would just not have been the same if she'd invited him in for cocoa. He was grateful she hadn't mentioned Horlicks.

They reached the entrance. She swung round and sank against him with such trusting abandon that he had to brace his right leg to avoid being pushed over. He managed to negotiate a second meeting that was a full week ahead, beyond her evening shifts and all but one of his exams. He was massively relieved: like all exam candidates he needed time to prepare. She kissed him again, then suddenly he was out in the street, staggering off in what he hoped was an approximately northerly direction and muttering over and over again, 'At last an adventure is happening to me!'

'Existence precedes essence.'

There was only one area of his life in which Robert did not have complete trust in Sartre, and that, when it came to the crunch, as it did indeed now seem to have done, was sex. Jean-Paul was self-evidently much cleverer than Albert Camus, but was not as good at making love. Sex for Sartre always seemed to involve things like nettles, and flaccid muscles, and sickly white skins and odd things with cats or soldiers, and hunting for back-street abortionists, whereas for Camus it seemed effortless and enjoyable. He'd go down to the beach, and maybe run along it or play a bit of football while the girls admired his bronzed muscular body. He'd watch the sparkling blue Mediterranean and compose a line or two about the passing flower of youth, then sprint across the sand and dive into the glorious water for a Greek-style act of communion. (This contrasted sharply with the experience of Jean-Paul, who saw the blue surface of the sea as an illusion – the real sea was cold and black and full of disgusting animals. Robert could picture Jean-Paul in a heatwave in somewhere like Bournemouth: all his clothes on, at the back of the beach, listening to the 'death-rattle of the sea', and shielding his eyes from the sun as he fought off another attack of *La Nausée* and failed to see a football about to thud on to his head.) Albert would come running up the beach, smile at a girl whose pocket handkerchief just covered her breasts, one strand of whose hair etc., then stroll back with her for a light lunch and easy, graceful love.

Much as Robert admired Jean-Paul and much as he agreed with him that in general existence preceded essence, it was different when it came to sex. Robert was completely convinced that the essence of sex was contained in Chapters 2 to 23 of the Peters and Blackshaw *Manual of Modern Sexual Technique.* This was divided into different sections and subsections, and respectably referenced according to the approved guidelines for international medical and biomedical journals. Whilst he had not been there, sex with a woman was no vague 'dark continent' – it was a definite place and territory, like France or Spain, fully and reliably mapped. Sex was as exterior a knowledge as how to massproduce a Renault 4 or a frying pan, subject to known laws and constructs.

He worked as hard preparing for that second meeting with Eva as he had for any examination. He skipped Chapters 2 and 3 (on Kissing and Preliminary Caresses) and began his preparation, notebook in hand, on Breasts. He tested on himself insofar as he could the eighteen different finger combinations and grips: nipple-rolling between thumb and first finger; nipple-rolling between thumb, first finger and middle finger; under-and-over four-finger flicking; turning and screwing motions; pulling and pushing techniques. Then it was on to lip-to-breast contact: gentle butterfly kissing; blowing; mild sucking; deep sucking; tongue-flicking. This was followed by basic combinations of finger and tongue work, and, finally, advanced combinations of tongue-flicking, lip and finger work.

*

The next evening he laboured through the chapters on Further Caresses and Buttock Technique (which offered suggestions as elegant as his mother's Elizabeth David book on French cooking), and came to a major section on Genital Caresses and Advanced Foreplay. His concentration became yet more intense, the number of double and triple underlinings increased, diagrams in other books were consulted, centrefolds were spread out and studied. It was another full evening before he reached Intercourse – Basic Positions.

Between each session, while having breakfast or going for a walk, he would rehearse and repeat key messages from the book – like the desperately unromantic exhortation to 'USE THE PENIS AS A RASP RATHER THAN A PUNCH', maintaining firm, even contact throughout the length of the stroke; or the injunction – reminding him of Second World War petrol conservation advertisements – 'DO NOT SQUANDER VAGINAL FLUID DURING FOREPLAY'. The Vagina had to be treated as a precious and limited inkwell – fluid had to be rationed carefully and used for essential purposes only.

Robert periodically turned to the Test Your Knowledge section at the back of the book, and scribbled down answers to the questions set. He found some of the multi-choice questions especially difficult, for example:

Question 16. Given the following . . .
1.　light nipple pressure
2.　massaging the hips to provide indirect clitoral stimulation
3.　gentle tugging and squeezing of earlobes
4.　French kissing (medium deep), and
5.　stroking of hairline with tip of index finger
indicate which sequence would normally be most satisfying:
A. 53142;　B. 34125;　C. 21543;　D. 12453;　E. 53412.

*

On the final evening before he met Eva, he did some work on the origins of the First World War, ran through his Peters and Blackshaw *Manual of Modern Sexual Technique* notes, and said his prayers – a complicated affair emphasising Christian Marxist dialogue and asking for success with Eva.

Existence and essence. He tried to remember what Eva looked like. He could remember details, like her eyes or her mouth, but couldn't bring them together into an overall picture of her face. What remained most powerfully in his memory was a kinaesthetic sense of her: her energy, the wet cocky pushiness of her tongue, the encircling warmth of her arms when she squeezed him.

Finally he studied an article on non-verbal communication: if she crossed her legs towards him, if she pushed something like a handbag over the table into his body space, if she smiled and the smile showed bags under her eyes, or she gripped an object like a pen or bottle and rubbed it . . .

'A shock ... she exists.'

Eva's thumb and forefinger moved rhythmically up and down the bottle of barley wine that rested on the table between them. She'd suggested the nearest pub to her hostel. It felt just right: it was womb-like, gloomily lit and almost deserted. It smelled comfortingly of beer, crisps and cigarette smoke. It had dark brown walls, holes in the lino and torn beermats. He was grateful he wasn't in La Coupole or La Rotonde.

He'd wanted to sit next to her, but she'd sat opposite, quite upright, and was now looking at him calmly with pupils that were two-thirds dilated, a reliable sexual signal even after allowing for the poor lighting (Peters and Blackshaw recommended carrying a small exposure meter for such assessments, and had a complicated formula for relating pupil dilation and light intensity). Robert bravely returned eye contact. She was a little different from what he remembered. Her hair was black and straight, and fell smoothly to around the middle of her chest. It was cut across her forehead in a high fringe, making her face look a bit like Cleopatra's in a Carry On film. She had a pale, elegant face, with high cheekbones that tapered into a small neat chin; her nose was what his mother would call prominent, but it was strong rather than big. There was a slight bump that might have tweaked the interest of a struggling cosmetic surgeon, but it was OK, definitely OK. He was bloody lucky, really, to have met someone like this.

'So,' she said. She pressed her lips tightly together for a second, then smiled. There were dimples at the corner of her mouth.

He attempted to hold her gaze. Her eyes were pale blue, nothing particularly special like robins' eggs or anything like that, but they were shockingly still and calm in the way they looked at him. There was a sort of purity about her, or maybe she'd taken some sort of drug. His own eyes felt prickly and watery.

'So,' he said. Stupidly, mimicking her.

She was silent. He had to follow it up, say something quickly to punctuate this eye contact. But he was struggling. It seemed that the whole of his vocabulary had shrunk to a single word. Copulation.

'Where are you from?' he finally managed to say.

'My mother lives in Nancy, and my father in Cambridge,' she said. 'She's French and he's English. I don't see much of either of them now.' Her voice was slow and quite husky, but now had almost no accent.

'I couldn't place your voice,' said Robert. 'I wondered if you were from outside England.'

She flicked a strand of hair behind her ear. No longer plastered in sweat as it had been at the discotheque, it was lustrously black and thrilling – and worth a hell of a lot of bourgeois certainties.

'French was my first language. We lived in France when I was a small child. But for a lot of my life I've lived in England. I was putting on the French accent a bit the other night. I was a bit pissed: I thought you'd like it.'

There was something soft, lisping and nasal about the way she pronounced 'France'. Christ, thought Robert, maybe she knew Jean-Paul and Simone – stranger things were possible. Quick, get on with it. Say something.

'What do you think about Dubcek?' he asked. He was planning to lead into a conversation about Czechoslovakia, and then on towards Hegel's definition of tragedy as a conflict of right and right, which he'd read on the back cover of a Penguin Special, and then on again to a quote he'd read about Sartre's *Critique of Dialectical Reason*. His definition would be accompanied by a poignantly wise ontological look past her face and into the farthest recesses of the bar-billiards room.

She stood up and started to take off her white trenchcoat. She stretched an arm behind her, and Robert saw an orange cheesecloth blouse, and there, definitely, was the curve of her breasts. She saw him looking, and smiled. Fool. He felt his face get hotter and redder. He reckoned she was at least a year older than him. The jukebox started to play 'Halfway to Paradise'. Right now that seemed quite far enough.

'I'm sorry,' she said, 'but I don't want a big intellectual conversation right now.' She put her arms behind her head and leaned back in her chair. Whilst not making the mistake of directly looking, he had an impression of armpits and dark hair. Revealing armpits was another, almost certain sign. Peters and Blackshaw gave it a 90 per cent sex predictability coefficient.

She finished her orange juice and smiled. There was something confident about her, and a sense of fun, maybe mockery. He hadn't even begun to think about whether he liked her. Her lips were neither full nor unfull, rather nice really, with palish purple make-up. And he had kissed them.

'Shall we have one more drink,' she said, 'before we go back?'

Robert would have preferred about twenty more drinks, but they'd agreed to go out for just an hour: she'd been insistent about not wanting to be blocked at the entrance again. She held out a pound note, insisting on paying for them both. Robert's mother would have found this behaviour extremely uncultivated. As he took the money he noticed a small patch of wrinkled skin on the side of her hand: it looked like a scar from a burn.

Robert began the walk to the bar, feeling her eyes on his back, imagining her watching him, appraising him. Maybe she thought he was calm, laid-back, experienced. But his tight back would be giving him away, making him look like an early experiment in robotics, about as warm and relaxed as a Dalek. He tried to loosen his shoulders, and even to wiggle his hips a bit. But the tightness went straight to his neck and head, and his right eye, mercifully out of her sight, threatened to start a sabotaging twitch.

He carried the drinks to the jukebox. It was crucial to work out what to put on: nothing as romantic as 'Macarthur Park'; possibly politics or protest – something like 'Eve of Destruction' could give some leads for smart political comments. He was tempted by Joe Cocker but the stuff about getting by with a little help from his friends might seem a bit too desperate. The Troggs would be too confident and provocative. Ditto 'Light My Fire'. Engelbert Humperdinck was to be avoided at all costs. Shit, he mustn't stay too long – he'd start to look indecisive. He chose 'Lucy in the Sky with Diamonds', and Cream's 'Sunshine of Your Love'.

As he turned to take the drinks back, he noticed her checking her lipstick with the help of a small make-up mirror.

'I've put some records on,' he said. He felt bolder at the prospect of the music. 'Have you ever read *Nausea*, you know, by Jean-Paul Sartre?'

'Yes, sure, I liked it. I read it in my first year as part of my course, before I packed it all in.'

He took a deep breath. 'Do you recall that bit where he

puts "Some of These Days" on the juke box, and he says, "And I too have wanted to *be* . . . Behind the existence which falls from one present to the next, without a past, without a future, beyond these sounds which decompose from day to day, peel away and slip towards death, the melody stays the same, young and firm, like'" – he had to stop himself saying 'breasts' – '"young and firm like a pitiless witness"?' He stopped. His right eye had started to twitch slightly. His voice, infuriatingly, had become rather more nasal as the sentence had worn on.

'That's a lot to digest,' she said, 'but it sounds very interesting.' She leaned towards him, smiled, and stroked his hand. It lay stiffly on the table between them, like a crab.

Things were going reasonably well. Robert heard the opening bars of his music and gazed into the middle distance with a mystical expression. It took a relatively large number of chords, during the course of which he muttered things like, 'This is one of my favourites,' and 'Listen out for the guitar riff,' before he recognised the music as Pinky and Perky's Christmas Special. Shit. He'd either blown the code or some other bastard had got there and hijacked it. There were two spotty, under-aged types giggling, smirking and looking in his direction. He glared at them.

Eva laughed with furious hiccuping giggles. 'I like you. I like your style,' she said. 'That's very funny.'

Robert had a go at a sophisticated, self-deprecating smile.

'It was a shame about the other evening,' she said. 'It's crazy not letting you bring guys in after ten-thirty at that dump of a hostel. Do you have that sort of problem where you live?'

'No, I've never had any problems taking girls back to my place,' he said. Shit, he'd lied, committed himself, in a not very Sartrean way, to having some sort of expertise and credibility. Peters and Blackshaw would have to work, or he'd be shown up. He wished things could have been slower, that he could have got to know her gently and gradually, had a courtship even, but it was out of the question, simply not the done thing. He carried on speaking.

'I believe we have a duty as human beings to understand and make sense of what is happening in Eastern Europe,' he said. But she had closed her eyes and was leaning back, swaying her head to the music. Her face looked different, softer, with her eyes closed. He considered saying 'I am a man of many contradictions,' then thought better of it, and worked hard preparing a piece that would define, like Jean-Paul did, the meaning of the situation they were in, which would fuse art, love and intellect in a magical sort of a way. It would link a comment about 'Lucy in the Sky with Diamonds' to his definition of the difference between being in itself and being for itself. And when she opened her eyes he would be rocking his head sensuously to the music just to show her he wasn't simply a limpid, upright mind.

'You must stand in front of it all by yourself... all the past history of the world is of no use to you.'

The room was small, hot, and painted white. There was a single bed on the far side underneath a window. Robert was relieved to see three shelves of books in her room, including *Nausea, L'Etranger, The Fall, The Castle, Steppenwolf, Dr Faustus* and lots of D.H. Lawrence. Eva was kneeling on the floor licking a Rizla paper and carefully sealing the edges. Robert asked her whether she preferred *The Outsider* to *The Fall.* She lit the joint, sucked in heavily and said she wasn't sure, and anyway she was planning to take most of the books round to the Oxfam shop – they hadn't done her any good. Robert looked at the pictures which covered most of the walls of the tiny room. On one was a black and white photo of the bust of a Roman senator, with taut muscles and swollen stone eyes: it bore a more than passing resemblance to his old headmaster. On the opposite wall, creating some sort of dialectical tension, was a poster showing an Indian goddess with four arms, dressed in blue, green and gold, beside a river and gardens with peacocks, all flattened into two dimensions. The goddess had shining black eyes and a sensuous empty smile. On the third wall, opposite the window, Eva had stuck up photos – presumably of herself at different ages, in rough chronological order – cut into tiny pieces and ending with a big red question mark sellotaped to the wall.

In a surprisingly quick succession of movements, she took off her shoes and socks, lit a joss-stick, pulled an Indian rug off the bed, switched on a table lamp and flicked off the main light. Then she padded across the room, her bottom flicking from side to side in her jeans, and lay back on the bed, her arms behind her head, her face half-turned towards him. He sat on the floor by the bookshelves, in known territory, pretending to read, his head awash in notes and injunctions and key phrases from Peters and Blackshaw. The gas fire hissed.

'Are you comfortable over there?' she asked, raising her eyebrows and giving a slight smile.

The words curved through the air towards him, like a flight of birds, precise, perfectly angled. Her voice was soft yet insistent, unambiguous but ironic.

So this was how it was done. He'd often wondered how one got from polite discussions of Being and Nothingness to screwing each other. He felt the phrase surround him, pull him towards her. Her words changed the situation from something indeterminate, where various outcomes were possible and he could still leave if he chose, to a tight, linear cause-effect sequence of events. Intuitively, he understood something new about history, about how moments got coupled together and given direction, about Marxist determinism and teleology and stuff like that.

His eyes could no longer focus on page 140 of *The Politics of Deprivation*. He laid down the book a short distance in front of him. It was an act that seemed as intimate and defenceless as removing his underpants.

'Yes, but I'd be far more comfortable over on the bed with you.'

His voice when he spoke sounded hoarse and unfamiliar, as if a cold had suddenly got worse. Maybe he could plead illness, produce a sick note from his mother – 'Will you please excuse Robert from sexual activity this evening as he has been suffering from a nasty chill.'

He paused, and tried to give a knowing smile.

'I need to go to the toilet first,' he said. It was a phrase that could carry not the slightest hint of sophistication. Could one see James Bond, as he strode hairily towards the bed, or Mellors, or Clint Eastwood asking to go to the toilet first. If only he'd said something like, 'Where's the can, lady?' or '*Ou est le pissoir?*'

Robert was surprised at the way the toilet seat folded all the way back – clearly it was a women-only hostel. The bathroom had no mirror but there was a reasonable reflection in the door handle. He checked for smudges of the Fast-tan he'd applied that morning. His eyebrows looked a bit orange. He licked a piece of toilet tissue and rubbed at them. He fervently hoped he wouldn't leave orange stains on her pillow. His nose wasn't too shiny nor his eyes too bloodshot. His body looked taut, muscular even. He sniffed his armpits. He'd put on plenty of Mum rollette deodorant, and they still smelled OK.

He took his Peters and Blackshaw notes out of the back pocket of his jeans and repeated key sequences to himself. Then he tore them into tiny pieces and flushed them down the toilet. A few bits of paper needed to be prodded out of sight with the brush. He felt disorientated, unable to concentrate, unreal. Most of him was at home, or somewhere else, waiting for the adventure to be over. Maybe this was how athletes felt at the start of a big race.

He wanted as little of himself in that room as possible. His aim was to be as detached from events as possible, as if he were watching them on telly; to be a cool technician devoid of thought or feeling – someone who wore a boiler-suit with a company logo on it, and carried a little tool kit and whistled tunelessly while he worked; a technical representative who knew the P&B text off by heart, who could go in, do the business, make any needed conversation, then get the hell out of it and back home for his tea.

The first bit was easy. He'd practised Chapters 2 and 3 before. He noticed again the warmth of her skin and the thick organic smell of patchouli. He was still startled by the ferocity of her lion's kiss.

The section on gentle brushing, circling, cupping, etc. of the breasts, combined with continuing preliminary caresses to hairline, cheeks and earlobes, worked extremely well. Her kissing grew even more intense, a thigh rested heavily and powerfully on his for a few seconds, and her breathing grew faster and louder – almost on the edge of groaning. Things were going swimmingly.

Then Robert became aware of a voice somewhere in the back of his head observing him and starting to comment. It was barely audible, but there was a richness and assurance about it. The voice was saying things like, 'He's applying a neat preliminary caress now, note the relaxed hand action and the evenness of finger pressure,' and 'Oh my, that's a really classic French kiss, straight out of the text book, an object lesson for any schoolboys watching who want to improve their technique,' and 'What's impressing me is that he's taken her on in such a positive manner.'

Robert began to feel a deep respect and gratitude for Peters and Blackshaw, and composed the first few lines of an appreciative letter. This was a triumph for theory and modern technique. It confirmed the contribution of intellectuals in anticipating and guiding praxis. As his technical representative conscientiously went through the full range of intermediate caresses, Robert allowed himself the luxury of imagining what it would be like when it was all over. He had a sense of being about to enter, through some strange transmigration of his spirit, a Parisian world where he would soon be gazing down from a shuttered room, leaning on the balustrade, Gauloise in hand, and occasionally glancing back into the room where her sated body lay sleeping on the bed.

He looked at the travelling alarm by the side of her bed.

'Will you take your blouse off?' he said. It was definitely time to move on to Explicit Nipple Contact.

'Yes, if you'll take your jersey and shirt off,' replied Eva promptly.

He sensed his friends in there watching proudly, people like Stephen and Marshall, and Jean-Paul. He had a highly public sense of himself, of an examination being passed, a *rite de passage* being successfully accomplished. He wanted no ambiguity. If Eva had handed out a certificate or signed affidavit, he would have clutched it gratefully.

He glanced across and out of the corner of his eye saw her take off the cheesecloth blouse, and there they were, definitely two of them, not as big or sharply delineated as his centrefolds, but actually there, in three-dimensional space, with weight and mass. In Existence.

He pulled his jersey over his head and stayed inside it for a moment, savouring its dark, woolly safety. Then he undid his buttons very slowly, using each button to rehearse finger and thumb movements from the chapter on Breasts. As he reached his fourth button, he glanced across at Eva and was startled to see her flicking a pair of apricot-coloured knickers over her ankles. She put the knickers over the table lamp, dimming the light in the room and creating a slight smell of singeing. This was dramatically out of sequence, at least three chapters ahead. Eva was forcing the pace, but he was resourceful enough to stay with her. In a spirit of equality he eased off his jeans and neatly ironed underpants, but in such a way as to reveal as little as possible to her. He was not at all sure whether an erection at this stage was or was not the done thing.

With an almost subliminally brief glance he registered that her body was slender, but with rounded bits in the right sort of places.

'You've got a lovely figure,' he said foolishly. It was the sort of thing his mother would have said.

'Ta,' said Eva, and did a little curtsy. She had lean, strong legs, like a long-distance runner's. Her hair looked dramatically black against her white skin.

Chapter 5 went beautifully. The nipples visibly hardened, grew from small pale discs into definite pink stubs like some mysterious mushroom. This was amazing, a stunning confirmation of theory leading to practice – as revelatory an experience as his first erection, on the basis of which he had sent a quasi-scientific letter to the editor of the *Daily Telegraph*. Her tongue, as predicted, flashed deeper and deeper into his mouth.

The inner voice was getting clearer now. Robert experienced a brief moment of disappointment that, after his years of reading, it was not Jean-Paul Sartre. The voice was rising in excitement, thickening with emotion, absolutely sure of the value of the event it was describing. It was unmistakably David Coleman, dressed in a yellow V-neck jumper and clip-on mike. As Robert worked through each of the eighteen different finger combinations, the commentary flowed on. 'He's here for one purpose and one purpose only . . . he's on target for an outstanding personal performance . . . she's a very strong and experienced athlete, just look at those thighs . . . oh, and he's switched to oral nipple contact, she's responding magnificently, now that's what I call sensitive timing . . .'

The little bedside travelling alarm, next to 'The Prophet', the box of Kleenex and the KY Jelly, showed it was 12.45, nearly two hours since they'd started. Robert estimated it must be time to move on. The next logical step was to stroke the Clitoris explicitly, all the while remembering to lubricate, but sparingly, and to vary pressure and rhythm every ninety seconds to prevent numbness. Trying, with

his eyes shut tight, to visualise the female front-view diagrams from Peters and Blackshaw, he reached down
through an expectant silence and brushed what seemed an
abundant mass of pubic hair. There was a clear sigh of
approval. He picked up through the heavy haze of her
patchouli another smell, deeper, unambiguously female. In
some barely formed way, he had a sense that he was
representing his country.

The whole of his consciousness was focused into the
explorations of his fingertips, as they searched, like miniature Victorian explorers, for access to the Vagina and his
sunlit future. He realised he didn't know quite where to
push or how hard. The book hadn't said. He felt slightly
fumbling, like a drunk trying to put a key into a door. A
few first doubts came, images of Jean-Paul rather than
Albert Camus. He carried on, trying to find his way. In the
back of his head David Coleman was in a transitional
phase, that moment of uncertainty in an athletics match or
a football game when all the previous data has been used
to support confidence in a good England performance
and contrary signs have been ignored; that point when
first doubts are voiced. 'I'm a bit surprised, Bobby, that he
seems to be putting on the brakes a little . . . maybe losing
his way slightly . . . he doesn't look quite as flowing as he
did a couple of minutes ago . . . perhaps he's paying the
price for a bit of over-confidence earlier on.'

Robert made a bold, quietly admired decision to rescue
the situation by moving on to the oral methodologies of
Chapter 14 (pp. 145–52). It had the advantage of giving
him direct sight of the problem. Surely he would be able to
work it out.

The space between the end of the bed and the washbasin was cramped. He knelt down uncomfortably and
kicked a green metal wastepaper bin against the radiator,
making a sharp clanking noise and spilling out orange
peel and an *Evening Standard* with a headline about the

expulsion of Dubcek from the Czech Communist Party. Eva was very quiet and seemed to be looking straight up at the ceiling. He stroked her thighs and kissed her in what he thought was approximately the right place, tasting mouthfuls of dry hair. He pushed again with his finger, as hard as he dared, but nothing happened. What was the matter? Was the book wrong? Was she some amazing circus freak who actually had her most private parts in some dramatically different location, like under her left armpit, and had cruelly neglected to tell him? He tried ferociously to remember diagrams and finger measurements – what was the angle to the vertical at which the Vagina was meant to slope? Did it slope forwards or backwards? It depended on whether the elevations in the book had been left- or right-facing. He couldn't remember. Fuck.

He crawled across the room to his jacket, pulled out a small diagram from the inside pocket, and crawled back. He opened the curtain slightly but the light wasn't good enough to see. He knelt in the darkness in front of her legs, which were opened like a book, but one written in a language such as Braille that he couldn't understand.

A phrase came to him from *Nausea*: 'If you want to understand something you must stand in front of it all by yourself, without any help . . . all the history of the world is of no use to you.' How much that man understood.

'Come inside me. Come inside me.' The voice came unmistakably from the other end of the bed, accompanied by a groan. It came again, insistent, powerful. He felt like a washing-machine repair man who had the customer's machine in bits on the kitchen floor and couldn't reassemble it.

'This is it,' he thought. Despite this temporary setback, what counts tonight is a bona fide orgasm inside her. He was happy to settle for a scraped O level pass, or even a City and Guilds Certificate, but he wasn't going to give up.

'We're at the point where character tells,' David Coleman was saying. 'He's being asked a very big question. He's going to have to dig deep and gather all his resources for one final push.'

One small detail remained. Robert's lack of sexual desire. He'd been far too busy with the modern techniques to bother about such things. Kneeling down out of sight at the far end of the bed, he closed his eyes and tried to fantasise, to make emergency calls to Betty and Fiona Duvalle. He simulated the odd groan and gasp to match the noises and demands coming from the far end of the bed.

'Come inside me,' she said. 'Please come inside me.'

This was ridiculous. Wasn't this what he'd dreamed about, longed for, this very situation? He started to pray, silently and quickly, but in a good accent. 'Oh Lord, forgive me for the things I have done wrong – for selfishness, vanity, self-pity, cowardice, laziness, ignorance, unkindness and so many other things.'

'Come inside me NOW,' she said. It was an emphatic command.

Robert briefly considered retrieving his underpants, crawling silently for the door and leaving her with a mystery, like a one-act existential play about an *acte gratuit*. But running eight miles in his underpants through Central London, even whilst striking a nonchalant pose and heading for the southernmost tip of Hampstead Heath, was not an attractive proposition.

It was no good. It was as if his body wasn't there. It seemed remote, uninhabited, devoid of sexual desire. He stopped trying to kiss her and knelt motionless by the end of the bed, his simulated groans lapsing into a silence like the one when he had stood up in class and forgotten the words to 'Ode to Melancholy'. David Coleman and his colleagues now sounded for all the world like they'd expected a poor performance all along. 'Oh dear, oh dear, that's not the sort of thing we expect at this level . . . when the call came he simply couldn't respond . . . it's just as we feared, I'm afraid, Bobby, you can do it all in-preparation but you only find out about yourself under pressure. When you start to come apart you come apart completely.'

He crawled up the narrow bed and beached himself beside her. 'There's going to have to be quite a post-mortem,' David Coleman whispered ominously.

It was 2 am. He closed his eyes and buried his face on the hard, unfamiliar pillow, aware of the sweet, rubbery smell of her skin, not daring to look at her or speak. He felt trapped in the room, felt that this moment might swallow his whole life.

She kissed him slowly, lightly, and, it seemed, thought-fully, on the lips. It was as damned near a question-mark as a kiss could be.

'Are you OK?' she said.

'I'm sorry,' he said, mumbling. 'I'm not quite myself tonight. I was thinking about all the problems of humanity.'

'It's OK,' she whispered. 'I'm on the pill.' She giggled and tickled his ribs.

'I mean Dubcek,' he said, then dried up. He made the name sound like a new contraceptive product.

'Let's just lie here for a little while,' she said. 'Maybe have a little sleep.' She stroked his hair. He had a shivery sense of being mothered by her.

A whole parliament of friends and relatives started a debate inside Robert's head. Marshall was first: he couldn't understand it, a bird like that, dying for it: he'd made a right balls-up of it. Stephen was more charitable: Robert had been going well; it had been a near-triumph for social-ist planning and rationality till all his guilt-ridden ideas and religion had got in the way. The subjective conditions hadn't been quite right. Robert's mother had been shocked to discover he had genitals, but deep down knew he was still a nice boy.

Jean-Paul Sartre was the most understanding, telling

him that sex was always problematic, it showed us what Nausea showed us – the uneasy, sticky relationship between ourselves as body and mind, subject and object. It was all good existential experience, part of a great European tradition. But why didn't Robert talk to Eva? Remember the commitment he and Simone de Beauvoir had made to transparency, to sharing their thoughts and experience honestly and openly, whatever the risk. Why not be honest, talk to her?

'What are you thinking about?' said Eva.

'Oh, nothing very much,' said Robert.

The night moved on. On several occasions he felt Eva's silky hair on his skin, the soft pouting pads of her lips on various parts of his body, different scents and smells being unlocked as she squeezed her thighs beneath him, and things starting to happen, exciting new entrances and grippings and muscle contractions, and he revived with the image of himself as a drunken Hemingway being ministered to on his bed while he swigged whisky and denounced bourgeois hypocrisy. But each attempt ended in failure. At 3.30 am he stared at the ceiling thinking with startling clarity about the origins of the First World War and the answer plan he would use: the relative contributions of the Anglo-German naval arms race, and colonial rivalry, and mobilisation plans, and the assumptions Austria made about the extent to which Russia would support Serbia. If only some invigilator had tapped politely at the door and given him permission to sit his exam there and then – how well he would have done!

At 5.30 am he heard the chink of milk bottles and whistling in the street below. Suddenly Eva said, 'I'm sorry but I've got to go to work.' She tiptoed across to a cupboard and pulled out a blue and white uniform, covered in badges and insignia. Pretending to doze, he looked at her through narrowed eyes, at the black hair lying so smoothly against her skin, at the planes and curves of her back. It had been strange: different from books – she had felt more real, he less real. She reached down to pull on her tights and the bumps of her spine showed through her skin. He felt a shiver of longing for her and wished it had worked out differently. She pulled the tights up her legs and wrestled a dress over her head. She checked that her watch and scissors were in place. Finally she folded a complex white linen hat, pulling up the hair from the nape of her neck and stuffing it under the hat before fixing it with a grip. 'Stupid fucking thing,' she muttered, then she walked towards him and kissed him gently on the lips before stiffening her posture and slipping out of the room. The word, after all, had not been made flesh.

'I am free: I haven't a single reason for living left; all the ones I have tried have given way and I can't imagine any more.'

Three days later, and after a less than successful history exam, Robert sat in his parents' lounge eating a slice of Genoa cake. His mother's grotesquely overweight spaniel lay snoring on a rug and beyond this was *Z Cars*. The room was, as ever, desperately overheated, with three radiators and a Magicoal fire all set to maximum.

Robert sat distractedly in front of the blind, friendly face of the TV. For the hundredth time he wondered what Eva was doing and whether there was any point in contacting her. His evening with her already seemed abstract: if he didn't concentrate, it felt like a dream.

He was preoccupied with the idea that he had been unable to surrender to his body and allow nature to take its course. What had happened with Eva had been a failure of trust, in himself, in Eva, in nature. He understood now that his mind was not completely his own, and that it didn't always function in his best interests. He had been so nice and controlled and polite. He had tried to fuck her out of politeness – and with painstaking academic preparation. When it came to sex, he'd been right to mistrust Sartre.

In the warmth of the room, it was almost impossible to keep any sort of mental alertness. The clicking of his mother's knitting needles slowed and stopped, and his stepfather's head rose and fell like a great bell as he tried to resist sleep. Only the dog's flatulence, acting like a whiff of tear-gas, seemed to jerk them, momentarily at least, into a waking state.

'Are you warm enough, dear?' she said to Robert, looking at him over the top of blue-tinted glasses.

'Yes, too warm in fact,' he said.

'Maybe you're sickening for something,' she said. 'You've had too many late nights lately.'

What would it be like to speak freely, thought Robert, to say what he felt? It was what he imagined Eva would do.

'We haven't really heard how your exam went,' said his mother.

He grunted something about it not going too badly.

The exam had, in fact, been a somewhat strange episode. He'd gone to the hall where it was being held and arrived late, dripping with rain and sweat after running uphill. As he pushed open a creaking door, dozens of faces had turned, white and triumphant, to watch the late-comer. A beaky invigilator, with a flapping black gown, had shown him to a seat. He'd turned over the paper and seen the words 'Organic Chemistry'. It was the wrong fucking hall. He'd pushed his body out of the desk and staggered past rows of barbed-wire faces, feeling as he did the threatening subterranean approach of the ecstasy he'd failed to have two days earlier with Eva.

'Have you thought anymore about careers?' asked his mother.

'Careers will be meaningless in a post-scarcity society,' said Robert automatically. 'I want to be free, to travel, to explore life.'

The spaniel was yelping and appeared to be having an orgasm. In some faintly heroic way, it seemed to be having one for the whole family. His mother swallowed some tea with a tight clicking noise, and let out a loud sigh. She asked him if he wanted more cake. He hesitated, then said yes. These were the exchanges that mattered, that made her, forever, his mother.

Z Cars was finishing, with its furious pipe-band marching music. The spaniel's rattling snore grew louder. His step-father's sleeping head lay on his chest, exposing his neck, like that of a prisoner waiting to be beheaded. This has made me, thought Robert. This is my milieu. At his age Sartre and de Beauvoir had spent their evenings debating philosophy in the Café des Arts, moving on from there to the Sphinx, where you snorted cocaine bought from the toilet attendant and people thought nothing of you danc-ing naked; they'd wander on from there for coffee at the Flore, maybe chatting to Proust or Buñuel or Modigliani on the way.

And yet Robert realised that he felt more free sitting in front of the TV than he had felt a week before. He had more secrets now, was a little more independent. He'd had experiences that were alienating. He was more of a bona fide outsider. He might not be condemned to an ordinary life. He might even, like Roquentin, had done, stab a penknife into the palm of his hand in an attempt at a liberating penetrative act.

The electronic sounds of the 8.50 News bleeped into the room. His stepfather jerked upright. In the manner of a South Sea Islander waiting for a Cargo Cult plane or a pilgrim in front of a statue at Lourdes, his stepfather lis-tened to, or watched, a dozen news bulletins a day, with a mystical sense of expectancy, apparently hoping that the TV might bring some news so dramatic and miraculous that it transformed his life. Something like a news flash that he'd been picked at random to be the next secretary-general of the United Nations, or that his unit trusts had climbed 800 per cent on the day, or an important announcement that God was letting everyone start all over again.

But it was yet more Vietnam. B52s, bombing, body bags being carried into planes. Robert felt his eyes start to prickle with tears. He leaned over the side of his chair, sheltered from his mother's glances, and picked up imaginary crumbs dropped from his plate.

They watched in grim silence as the world spilled for a few seconds on to their new Axminster.

At the end of the news, Robert said, 'It's terrible, it's got to be stopped.'

'I know,' said his mother. 'It's awful, I feel for all those people too, but you don't want Commonism to take over the world, do you?' She pronounced the word with the same frown and intonation as she used when talking about pop music.

'Of course I do,' said Robert.

'Oh dear,' she said. 'It looks as if we've brought you up to be working-class.'

'Well, I'd at least like to be in the intellectual vanguard,' said Robert.

The TV weatherman was fixing magnetic clouds on to south-east England, which meant Robert would get wet on the factory picket he was going on with Stephen and Marshall the next morning.

'I suppose you'd want us shot,' said his stepfather, quietly and with a certain degree of humility and resignation.

'Only after a revolutionary tribunal.'

Monty Python was about to come on, and Robert wanted to keep his feelings more to himself.

His stepfather's eyes looked dazed.

'It's OK, I'm only joking.'

They insisted on watching *Monty Python* with him. A charlady called Mrs Sartre was going on in a squeaky voice about her Jean-Paul. His mother's and stepfather's laughter seemed forced, part of an effort to emphasise their similarity to Robert, that deep down they shared the same values. I blew it, he thought, I blew it with Eva. What a farce it was, all those notes and techniques. He suddenly missed the father who might have made his life more relaxed, more trusting.

There was no Vietnam demonstration that weekend, so his mate Marshall had suggested that they leaflet a factory near Southgate. It was rumoured that the company made electronic components for the American defence industry. It was believed by some of the poly's political cognoscenti to be a likely flashpoint for the imminent crisis of late capitalism – the fact that it could be conveniently reached on the Piccadilly Line was meant to be purely coincidental. Stephen was down for the weekend and was coming along out of curiosity.

It was good to see him again. Robert was surprised at how little pain he felt as Stephen talked of Oxford and the women he was seeing in addition to Fiona and Julie. There was something about his natural, free way of being in the world that made Robert feel admiration rather than envy.

It was drizzling as the first workers arrived for their shift. The ink on the leaflets started to run as the rain grew heavier. In the cold light of day the pamphlets were less impressive than they'd looked at the polytechnic: it was harder to understand the connections being drawn between the food in the poly canteen and the struggle of the Vietnamese peasants.

Marshall shouted out, 'End links with American imperialism!' and thrust leaflets at people's chests.

A raw-faced mate of Marshall's called Jim kept saying, 'General strike now, innit,' in a flat Brummie accent. It sounded like a commiserating comment on the weather, and some workers looked at the sky and nodded sympathetically in agreement. Jim was genuine Working-Class: he had been to pubs in the Midlands where men fought rats with their bare teeth.

Robert decided to quote a favourite line from the

Evénements in Paris: 'Let the workers take the flag of battle from the frail hands of the students,' he said to a burly man in an Arsenal bobble hat.

'You should be fucking studying,' said the man, and pushed him aside.

'False consciousness, that's your problem,' shouted Marshall.

The man spat in a perfect proletarian parabola and trudged on.

Most of the leaflets ended up in the gutter. Soon there were only a few latecomers hurrying by. They decided to go to a café.

Robert watched the café owner intricately picking his nose while he slapped bacon on to slices of bread. They were lucky: they'd stumbled on an authentic workers' café.

Marshall's blonde-haired girlfriend sat impassively next to him: she kept her head and eyes very still as if she were constantly posing for some invisible camera. Her role in the revolution was mainly to fetch tea, tell Marshall how clever he was, and sleep with him. Marshall had reduced the longed-for synthesis of Marx and Freud to a quick shag in his greasy bed before going off to a sit-in or demo.

'False consciousness,' repeated Marshall, 'that's the problem with those buggers. They're fucking alienated and they don't know it. I mean, objectively speaking, they're on lousy wages, they have to get up at five every morning, and they spend all day pushing a button. Then they go home, watch telly, screw the wife and think that's freedom.'

Marshall spoke with the authority of someone whose room contained the finest collection of shoplifted social-science books in London. But paradoxically his words created in Robert a painfully attractive vision of a relationship with Eva that didn't involve long trips to discotheques, endless cigarettes, dozens of hours swotting up notes, agonising self-examination in mirrors, and soul-grinding débâcles.

'I think you've oversimplified Marx's view of freedom,' said Stephen to Marshall.

Marshall fingered his chest hair. He looked aggrieved. His girlfriend stroked his thigh and glared at Stephen.

Challenged to define what he meant by freedom, Stephen munched his bacon sandwich and said that a person was unfree if he was prevented from achieving significant purposes. Robert listened with the careful attention of someone to whom that had happened twice in the past week.

He remembered Eva's hair, the slightly salty taste of her skin and the smell of her patchouli; he thought about Roquentin saying that he was free because he had no reasons for living left. That seemed a bit romantic and mystical now.

'Marx,' said Stephen, 'thought that significant purposes were those to do with someone developing and using their full potential as a human being. The tricky bit is when you start saying that what someone wants isn't really in their interests, that it's been put there by indoctrination or advertising or parental pressure or whatever.'

Robert remembered how he had wanted to study psychology. But his mother and stepfather had said that he wouldn't get a job if he studied psychology, even as a school teacher.

Marshall ordered his bird to get him a cup of tea. He had been subdued during Stephen's Oxford-educated comments, and lifted his spirits now by eating the rest of his girlfriend's bacon sandwich and telling them how good she was in bed. Robert felt quite sorry for the girlfriend, but then again, she barely bothered to pass the time of day with him: she, too, had her purposes and made her choices.

Stephen said that what stopped people fulfilling

themselves could be external things like unemployment or internal things like inhibitions.

'You mean things like sexual repression,' said Marshall, and winked, rather coldly, at Robert.

Robert was frightened that Marshall was going to ask him about how he'd got on with Eva. He decided to change the subject.

'Sartre said, "It's time to put the imagination back into politics,"' he said. 'He talked about breaking free of old structures like hierarchy and patriarchy.'

'What the hell does that mean?' said Marshall and Stephen more or less simultaneously.

Oh shit, Robert didn't know what it meant. He might as well have said Pinky and Perky as hierarchy and patriarchy.

He smiled at them nervously. Here he was, with his friends, but he didn't feel free and he didn't feel equal. His politics were false, a front.

He wandered home again, lonely and alienated, under a wasted sky.

'We are to ourselves our own work of art.'

It was hard for Robert to ring Eva, but he thought that if he didn't see her, he might give up on the whole love business as just too intellectually demanding and emotionally draining.

It was the afternoon and she wanted to meet outside the hospital and go for a walk. Robert took this as a worrying sign. It was the first time he'd seen her in daylight. He was surprised, and rather disappointed, to discover how attractive Eva was. He trudged along the pavement with the dogged commitment of someone about to resit an examination.

Eva wore the same white trenchcoat and flowed along at his side, the sunlight and wind playing on her long, black hair, still holding all the questions he wanted answered, still holding the key to the world of lovers and screwers and shaggers. Her cheeks had small pink circles from the cold wind, which seemed to have sucked all the colour out of the rest of her face. He noticed how proudly she carried her head – very upright, possibly tilted back slightly, in a way that made her look independent, haughty even, as if she'd come through some defiant struggle. His own head tended to be too heavy for his neck muscles and to be always dropping detumescently forwards or leaning wearily to one side.

On the tube between South Kensington and Turnham Green, Eva held the gaze of a long-haired man opposite who looked like Ray Davies of The Kinks. Robert feared that at any moment she might get up and leave the train with him, or remove all her clothes and climb on to the man's lap. He glared at the man, and tried to talk to Eva above the demonic noise of the train. He realised that Eva's attractiveness was not just a matter of things like her long hair and pale blue eyes. It was subtler and more mercurial: it lay in the way she held her head, and made eye contact and used her hands while she talked. There was something free and exciting about it all.

Eva was delighted to reach the park and ran laughing and skipping through the autumn leaves. She closed her eyes and turned with a beatific smile on her face towards the sun. Then she hugged a chestnut tree and lay her cheek against it. 'Isn't it wonderful, that all this is just given to us?' she said to Robert, rather poetically he thought, and he was shocked to see that she had tears in her eyes. He felt a little embarrassed, as if he was accompanying an attractive but slightly unpredictable mental patient on an outing.

He walked a hundred yards ahead of her on the towpath, like Roquentin, an untipped Disque Bleu hanging from his mouth, the collar of his navy blue donkey jacket turned up. He'd decided that his only option for the afternoon was to be indifferent and alienated, to be a man who belonged to a serious, deeper, more angst-ridden world where people stayed up all night tortured by ontological doubts, a world which people who enjoyed the useless sexual baubles of life could not possibly understand.

He stopped and waited for Eva, gazing moodily at the dark river and willing a novelistic event to happen – if only someone could fall into the water, or drop off that bridge;

if only a tree could start ostentatiously oozing Existence, or an Arab walk towards them out of the sun with a gleaming knife. The space between Eva and himself closed relentlessly, compressing and tightening all the time.

Her lips were pressed together, if anything turned down slightly. She was probably angry at him for walking on ahead and ignoring her. She muttered that she wanted to sit down somewhere and climbed over a fence into a small clearing of grass surrounded by brambles and nettles. Robert followed and tore his trousers on a strand of barbed wire. Much to his relief his leg was bleeding: it was a useful diversion. She dabbed the graze with her handkerchief. He wished it had been a more substantial cut.

'These nettles remind me of the scene in *Nausea* where Roquentin and Anny, who are really Jean-Paul Sartre and Simone, are lying down and where he has a great time kissing but she says afterwards that she was lying in nettles all the time, and Jean-Paul says there are no perfect moments,' said Robert. It came out in a breathless nasal rush.

'He should have smoked more marijuana, or taken some acid,' said Eva, rolling his jeans back down, 'or done some meditation – there are plenty of perfect moments.' Her voice sounded husky, faster than usual, a bit impatient and matter-of-fact.

'And anyway,' she went on, 'the character Anny wasn't Simone de Beauvoir, she was named after Sartre's cousin Annie, and her character was taken from another Simone, Simone Jollivet. Sartre had an affair with her before he met de Beauvoir. And he didn't like to be called Jean-Paul – not even Simone de Beauvoir called him Jean-Paul.'

'Christ,' said Robert. 'How do you know all this?' He felt a sense of retrospective embarrassment at all the things he must have said. It was the intellectual equivalent of the time when his Auntie Janet had told him that his flies had been undone all the way through his first communion service.

'I read it for work I had to do at college, before I packed it in.'

Robert started to re-edit all his one-liners and conversation pieces.

'About the other night,' she said.

He looked towards the river, hoping desperately for a rowing boat to sink or a Boeing 707 to fall in flames from the sky or a small invasion by Russian paratroopers.

'It was absurd,' he said, hunching his shoulders and continuing to look away from her. It was all he managed of quite an involved explanation.

Suddenly she stood up and faced him. She stared at him with intense unblinking blue eyes, and gripped the sides of his arms. For a moment Robert thought she was going to head-butt him.

'I must feel something,' she said fiercely; her body was trembling. 'I'm sick of all this.'

She put her arms round his back and pulled him into her. The front of him felt squashed against the warmth of her body, in a sub-tropical micro-climate different from the cold drizzle on the back of his neck. The buckle of her coat dug into him at a point dangerously near his groin. She squeezed him so hard that she forced most of the breath from his lungs. She kissed him in a semi-continuous French kiss for what Robert became increasingly confident would be an almost unheard-of length of time. He was conscious of the light slowly starting to fade, of the rain increasing, of a Top 20 show on a distant transistor radio moving from number 14 to number 5, of a black mongrel dog coming back for a second and third time to sniff at their legs, and of words like 'darling' and 'love', improbable as it seemed, coming from her mouth when she occasionally paused for breath, turning her mouth briefly to one side in the manner of an expert swimmer doing the front crawl. He felt warmed and flattered and shocked by her intensity and passion. Was it anything to do with him, or was she like this with everyone – all the boyfriends, patients, tutors, passing Jehovah's Witnesses, double-glazing salesmen? Did everyone have a chance to play opposite her in the same passionate role?

But this was too cynical. As they staggered apart – with Robert thinking he'd kept his end up, batted pretty well, so to speak – he knew she'd given something, put the whole of herself towards him, and made herself open, in ways that created subtle shifts in power and vulnerability.

They slumped down into the long damp grass. Neither spoke.

Robert could only stand a maximum of twenty seconds' silence before he began to tremble, go red, and sense the imminent disintegration of his nervous system. He had to say something.

'Tell me something about Simone Jollivet,' he muttered.

She grinned. 'She was quite infamous, one of the ladies who chased after famous writers and artists. And she was very beautiful, with waist-length hair. When she was a teenager, she used to climb out of the window of her parents' house and go to the local brothel. Her favourite way of greeting clients was to be leaning against the mantelpiece absolutely naked reading aloud from *Thus Spake Zarathustra.*'

'You're joking,' said Robert.

'She and Sartre had a very torrid affair. She used to do things like give him lampshades made out of her sexiest knickers.'

'Blimey,' said Robert.

'A small pair in purple cotton trimmed with lace,' said Eva, giggling.

'Your recall of detail is remarkable,' said Robert. 'I could see a whole new product line in this, for someone like Marks and Spencers. They could make a fortune, especially if they got famous people to endorse signed copies of their knickers, a Brigitte Bardot or a Marianne Faithfull or a more sedate Queen Mother product.' He would have been giddy if he'd tried to stand up.

They lay on their backs and stared up at the darkening sky. 'When I lived for a summer in Amsterdam,' she said, 'I knew this guy from Paris. He thought he was really clever, a real intellectual. He looked a bit like you, he had your frown and nice green eyes. His way of being angry with me was never to say it straight but to argue more cleverly about something than I could – politics, books and things. He made me feel really bad about packing in my courses. And when it came to making love, you know, screwing, he liked to do the same sort of thing as Simone Jollivet, to be standing up reading some philosophy book to himself. I was to knock on the door and come in very quietly with a tray of tea and some honey. Then, while he read the book, I was to kneel down, with the honey, and do, you know, verbal sex with him. He didn't touch me, or even look up from the book.

Robert was stunned. The only sounds he managed to utter were a couple of weak 'tuts' with his tongue feeling sticky against his teeth.

'It was OK, actually,' said Eva. 'And he used to do the same for me sometimes. No, it wasn't that which used to piss me off about him, it was how he used to screw.'

Robert took a deep breath and crossed his legs.

'He'd like me to lie face down, propped up on some of his favourite books,' said Eva. 'Whatever way, it was all over too fast. I was a fucking idiot to stay with him so long. It's just that I was very much in love with him, I suppose. But I thought it would be nice if he occasionally got turned on by kissing me or something strange like that. And he never washed his feet. They really stank. He wanted all that from me, and he couldn't even be bothered to wash his fucking feet.'

Robert could feel her breath on his cheek, smelling of eucalyptus chewing-gum. He looked through the mist towards the grey river. A man walked along the towpath carrying a radio from which sounded the pips of the six o'clock news. His stepfather would have just switched on the telly. Robert felt cold and shocked and excited. He had an image of Eva standing naked by a mantelpiece, her silky hair falling in long black streams down her pale back, nonchalantly reading some existential classic. What should he say? Should he correct her minor mistakes with language, or were those deliberate little jokes? Should he just keep silent?

'What were the names of some of the, er, books he liked to read?' He couldn't help the question jumping out: it had bypassed his brain and come directly from the region his old headmaster called the scrotum.

'Shit, I don't care what the books were. One was something by Sartre, I think – you talking must have reminded me – one of those big ones like *Being and Nothingness*. What does it matter?'

The rain eased. Robert realised that Eva wasn't completely naked in his image but wearing a pair of glossy high-heeled shoes, much like Mrs Duvalle's or Betty the *patronne*'s. He felt a helpless victim of *Penthouse* copy and Reader's Letters.

'I read somewhere,' he said, 'that *Being and Nothingness* in its original edition weighed exactly one kilo. It was used a lot in the war for weighing fruit and vegetables when they didn't have proper weights.'

She began to giggle, and tickled him. They both started laughing.

'You're kidding me.'

'No, it's true. Straight up.'

'Listen,' she said, 'the only reason I was telling you all this was because of the other night.'

Oh God, thought Robert, feeling a trickle of rain slide down his forehead and accelerate into his eyes.

'I thought you were into something like Tantra,' she said. 'You know, the yoga of sex, going on for as long as possible, until you have a kind of inward-turning reverse orgasm. It all took so long, I felt really respected. Your hand was so cautious and smooth.'

She was stroking his arm lightly. Robert was gobsmacked. He held his breath. He could think of nothing to say, not even the pretence of a glimmer of understanding about Tantric yoga. The nearest he'd come to how he felt at this moment was at a corner during a football match when he'd run towards the goal and out of nowhere been struck a painful blow on the bridge of the nose. As he'd blinked back tears and wondered who had hit him, people had come rushing up saying, 'Perfect, pure magic,' and he realised he'd scored his first headed goal.

'What happened to the guy from Paris?' he asked feebly, but with the look, he hoped, of someone who knew one end of their Tantric yoga from the other.

'One day he left the apartment before me: he had some job at the university. And I had the place to myself. I like snooping around, and I found he'd written all these notes about the things we did in bed, as if he was going to write some fucking play. I thought what a bloody narcissist. There was a white sheepskin rug on the floor and I was going to pour a bottle of ink on it, but then I thought, why bother, so I just burned his notes instead.'

He leaned towards her, and they started another long kiss. It was getting darker, and he could see the headlights of buses and cars crawling slowly up Richmond Hill.

She broke off suddenly and said: 'I wondered if you found me unattractive . . .'

'No. Just the opposite.'

He could still make out her face: there were beads of

rain on her eyelashes and her eyebrows against her white skin were like long perfect brushstrokes of black ink.

She curled her soft wiry arms around him. Two dissonant ideas were coming together from opposite sides of his head. One was mainly represented by the image of Eva lying naked with *Being and Nothingness*. The other one, as simple and warm as new bread, was the idea that he really liked her. This was his Anny, but also his *patronne*. The ideas came together across some kind of Checkpoint Charlie in his mind.

They hugged each other. Again there came, from somewhere close to him, long groans and words like 'love', and 'darling' and 'I want you'.

You must be joking, he thought, that's impossible. My hair looks ridiculous when it's wet and you haven't heard my critique of Sartre's concept of freedom. But this was silly. He felt welcomed and accepted by her in some relaxing way, invited simply to be himself, whatever that was. He had a sudden vision of making love without reference to the Peters and Blackshaw *Manual of Modern Sexual Technique*, of their own love-making, deliciously imperfect and free, conforming to no one's expectations, created by them. Existence before essence.

Struggling back over the fence in the dark, he bashed his leg again, and more blood oozed through his trousers. Eva did her best impersonation of a bossy nurse. Then she was dancing and skipping at his side. She seemed celebratory, and was singing and laughing and suggesting they went for a drink on the way back to Lambeth. He was thrilled with how attractive and intelligent and exciting she was.

He had a sudden intense sense of the importance of this day and this place, and a dangerous rush of lyricism to the head. He realised that this particular bend on the river, holding this particular afternoon, would be his place, where he might come in future years with flowers or grand-children, a place where, whatever else happened in his life, these two people shivering now against the cold had met and welcomed each other. He wished he'd brought his Zenith.

Back in the room, as he made love with Eva, Robert felt mystically at one with the music of The Troggs which grunted through from the room next door. Indeed, from within his state of triumph and ecstasy, he felt a sense of rit-ualistic *rite de passage*, unity with all men, with Camus and Clint Eastwood and D.H. Lawrence and Stephen and the million or so who must have been doing the same thing as him at exactly this moment. But above all with Jean-Paul.

Eva's groans and cries grew louder and louder, more and more drunken and delighted. She would undoubtedly be heard by dozens of people in the nurses' home and hospital. Robert casually wondered about junior doctors twitching as they gave delicate injections, and patients hav-ing to be given sleeping-pills by annoyed night staff.

He was not surprised, then, to hear a sharp knocking on Eva's door. Whilst he expected some annoyed senior nurse, he would not have been unduly shocked if it had been David Coleman with champagne, or even his mother with a cup of Darjeeling and a box of man-size Kleenex.

'Eva, Eva. Are you all right, my dear? Shall I get help?' It was a woman's voice, sounding very concerned.

'It's the nurse from next door,' Eva whispered. 'She's a nun.'

They carried on. Eva gave another loud groan.

'Eva, I'm going for a doctor,' the nun said firmly. 'Hang on till help arrives.'

They resumed making love, and Robert felt at last like a Penguin Modern Classic, felt magically close at last to a white bed in a Parisian apartment room with shuttered windows and a balcony with a wrought-iron balustrade, from which he'd look down, briar pipe in hand, on the café where afterwards, when she awoke from her sated sleep, they would laugh and sip wine and talk. They rocked and rolled and pushed and pulled in and out of a future that seemed deliciously sweet and free. Or maybe they were simply having what Marshall would call a really good screw.

Afterwards he noticed that there was blood on the sheets, from his cut leg, which seemed appropriate for a Hemingway reader, and he thought of Che and Tania, of Jean-Paul and Albert, and of other pleased friends, and he rehearsed, in an idle sort of way, what he might tell the likes of Marshall. They hugged each other warmly, his hand cupped against her soft breast, and he wondered if, after all those lonely nights, the complex Outsider he had imagined himself to be was really destined for a simple, ordinary story of love and happiness.

She bent down and kissed and sucked him gently. That hadn't been in the Post-Coital Etiquette section of Peters and Blackshaw. A sudden thought occurred to him, a dim sense of the contradictory nature of some of the things she had said by the river.

'Was all that stuff you told me by the river true?' he asked. She smiled, and shrugged a strand of hair off her shoulders.

'I never believed much in examinations,' she said. 'They kill the imagination; that's why I got fed up with my course. It was all true in its way.'

Seconds later, and rather mysteriously, she started to cry.

'I am astonished at this life which is given to me – given for nothing.'

And so, overnight, life became good. The Age of Aquarius dawned. Robert no longer walked along the Great North Road poised for the flash of an Arab's knife, nor calm and empty under a wasted sky, but harvesting happiness. The objects in his parents' house – the china Alsatian, the rose in a specimen vase, the elephants holding each other tails – suddenly stopped emitting evil signals and regained a type of innocence. He became, at a stroke, someone who could make changes: he rang Marshall about renting a room in his house, and talked to his tutor about switching from history to psychology. Every pop song played for him: he had met her on a Monday and his heart had indeed stood still.

He had a sumptuous, Lotus-eating time getting to know Eva. Every weekend was spent in her room. He'd always viewed Mornington Crescent tube station as the boundary between the boring and exciting bits of London and travelled through it now with a ceremonial sense of joy, as if he was crossing the equator.

The most obvious sort of getting to know Eva was sensual. Weekends typically started with him tiptoeing in and finding her meditating by candlelight, naked except for a

pair of silk knickers. Her room looked like a small temple:
filled with Indian tapestries, Buddhas, prayer bells, joss-
sticks, massage oils and books on Tantra. The room
smelled of the sweet, spicy scent of patchouli. It was a smell
he'd always loved: it dreamed into being a sense of intimacy and warm skin, a world where spirit and flesh met. It
was a wonderful Bohemian contrast to a life spent with
lemon-scented toilet fresheners.

She'd be sitting cross-legged facing the fire, her long
hair dramatically sleek against her back, the candles send-
ing fingers of orange light across her skin. She'd give the
slightest of smiles. He'd sit for as long as an hour while she
did her slow breathing, savouring the sensuality of life lived
in the present, the televisionlessness of it all, the amazing
fact of her actually being there.

Eventually she'd stand on her head, her legs taut and
sinewy with effort, like a diver poised on a high board.
After a few minutes, he'd slip off her knickers. There'd be
ι beam on her face, quickly suppressed, and he'd sit watching her, in sweet anticipation; then she'd open her eyes,
pad across to him and seconds later they'd be making love.

Sex was incredibly important to her. It wasn't just fun, it
was a route to personal transformation, a route to God.
There were times when she seemed to disappear as they
made love: she'd start speaking in tongues and talk afterwards about states of bliss and ecstasy, and how close she'd
got to the ultimate life-changing orgasm. The noises she
made were plentiful. He'd never heard a sound in the road
his family lived in, not even in the hottest heat waves when
everyone had their windows open. Eva grunted and
groaned, whimpered and yelped, ooohed and aaahed,
cried and screamed. She was not remotely ashamed or
embarrassed.

She showed him the variety of sexual experience: dramatically quick and intense couplings, and long, slow
afternoons of massage and exploration, loving in the bath,

against the wall, and with various types of drugs and music; times when she was menstruating and he'd come out of her covered, almost ritualistically, in blood; and a wonderful afternoon spent decorating each other with paints, creating identical psychedelic bodies, and then making love.

Robert treated all this as excellent education. After fifteen years of school and college and long nights poring over books like *Being and Nothingness*, it was a pleasure to be in a type of learning situation that didn't require a pad of A4 paper and a dictionary. It was a relief to leave abstract issues behind and concentrate on grown-up questions like how many times he could manage to do it next weekend.

There was some odd learning, too. For example, one day he thought it high time they used a woman-on-top position: they'd done all the male-in-charge ones. He waited his chance then rolled over and pulled her on to him. She was as outraged as she would have been if he'd brought a donkey into the room and suggested interspecies troilism. She talked later about yin and yang, about how the man should be in the dominant position: Robert was, after all, the one with the phallus. It all sounded terribly important.

When they weren't making love, they looked into each other's eyes until they saw faces behind their own faces, smoked joints, talked about God, wrote poems, did drawings of each other, and slept locked together as tightly as lovers in a Rodin sculpture. They discovered the various ways in which they could make each other laugh – the voices, impersonation and games. Sometimes, when they were in bed, they pretended to be the Queen and Prince Philip, or Jean-Paul and Simone. Robert as Jean-Paul would insist on wearing his vest while making love, stop frequently to make notes and see any leaking bodily fluids as horrifying reminders of our contingent existence.

Occasionally Eva would talk about intellectual things,

but usually only to convey something else: she might use a quote from de Beauvoir to talk about how she felt, or a criticism of Sartre as a teasing bit of foreplay.

She spent a lot of time meditating. He tried some of the techniques, like counting his breaths from one to five, and watching candle flames. Meditating next to a beautiful naked woman had certain subtle advantages over morning C. of E. services at Muswell Hill, but for the first time in a long while he acknowledged a part of him that had sometimes been overwhelmed by beautiful hymns or starry skies. Sometimes Eva quoted gurus who said things like, 'The only thing we have to lose is our expectations.' 'Try telling that to Vietnamese peasants,' he'd feel a need to say. Eva would fling up her arms and start shouting that he was trying to score a cheap point rather than to understand her.

She was phenomenally intense. Intensity and passion were at the core of her being. It was nothing for her to cry, shout, shake, pound the walls. Robert assumed this was all natural enough: he took it for granted that women cried after making love and wanted to cling to their man for hours; that they talked about their cruel mothers and how wretched they felt at times, and how some bloke in the past had made them suicidal. It was sometimes hard, though, to imagine how she managed to walk out on to the wards and do normal, everyday things: it just didn't seem possible.

He could find big words to describe Eva, words like intense and passionate, but as often as not it was the little things that thrilled him: the slow, graceful way she stirred her coffee, almost as a meditation; the soft, sad, lisping way she pronounced the word 'France'; the sudden skipping movement she might make as she crossed a room. Maybe, he thought, the essence of a person was contained in these small idiomatic things.

*

Robert was often surprised at how different his life felt now that he knew Eva. And if he was completely honest, the most surprising thing of all was what the hell she was doing with him.

And this most surprising thing of all came to a climax on one of the very few occasions they ventured out. They had his stepfather's car, and went, of all places, to Bognor, on a whim of Eva's (at 2.00 am in the morning) to be close to the sea.

'In each privileged situation, there are certain acts which have to be performed, certain attitudes which have to be assumed, certain words which have to be said.'

They reached the coast at sunrise: a grey winter's day with a few pools of lemon light out to sea. Eva started to do a chanting meditation while Robert hung around feeling embarrassed. Then she had her clothes off and was running into the sea, her bottom red from the stones on which she'd been sitting, her body a beautiful combination of soft dimpled curves and lean, springy legs. He wondered whether to join her, thinking about Nietzsche and the Need to Overcome, but also about how cold the water was and his less than perfect underpants. He took off his nylon socks, sniffed them and thought about washing them at the water's edge. She swam in close to the shore, then suddenly stood up, shivering and joyful, like someone emerging from a baptism. He waded in in all his clothes and hugged her to him. It was the only thing to do.

They found a café, where the owner refused to let them use the toilet because they hadn't had a full English breakfast. The coffee came out of a bucket-sized tin with 'catering only' stencilled on the side. Was this all southern England could fucking muster? thought Robert. Was this Bognor's answer to La Rotonde or the Café Flore?

Eva took out a packet of contraceptive pills and began

tracing her finger along the complex arrows on the foil. The woman behind the counter glared.

'I left home when I was sixteen,' said Eva. 'My mother just went round finding fault with me the whole time. She turned from a mother into a policeman, going round asking why wasn't I wearing a petticoat under my dress, and saying I couldn't go out. She found the pills one day in my drawer, and said either the pills went or I did. She was always sniffing round my room looking for evidence about what a slut I was. There was no privacy at all. It was awful.'

It was raining hard outside. She had started to cry. Marshall would have said the tears were pissing down her face.

Robert admired Eva's capacity to feel: words came from inside her, bloodied, umbilically attached, unchallengeably personal.

'This scar on my hand,' she said. 'When I was thirteen, my mother screamed at me for taking some of her makeup. I put my hand in the fire.'

Robert felt various fluids and colours drain from his face.

'What about your father?'

'Oh, he buggered off when I was twelve. We were very close when I was young, and then he fucked off with some girlfriend. That's when my mother turned into the policeman. And she did as little as possible in the house: it was her revenge.'

The irises of her eyes were strikingly blue against the reddening that the tears had brought. She stared ahead without smiling, scarcely blinking. Her skin had purple and orange patches from the cold. He held her hand across the table, with a mixture of love and fear. Her hand looked sadder and older than his own. It had nursed people dying of cancer and been thrust into fire.

'So I left home,' she said. 'It was an easy choice. I worked as a waitress for a bit, mostly over here, then got into college in France, but that pissed me off: all the exams and rules. You've no idea how bad it is compared to England. And then I thought I'd do a nursing course: it's a lot more useful, and you can get work all over the world.'

Eva's hair, wet from the swim, dripped intermittently on to Robert's hand, which continued to hold hers across the table. She had stopped talking and was looking at him with an intensity that made him half wish that the jukebox didn't have an out of order sign on it.

'Tell me about your family,' she said.

He told her the basics. That his father had died in a car crash; that his mother had remarried when he was ten; that his stepfather was boring and fossilised but otherwise OK.

She squeezed his hand and looked concerned.

'What was your father like?' she asked.

'I barely remember him,' said Robert. 'I have a sense of holding a big hand and of being pushed on a swing in the park. But maybe those are imagined things. Most of what I know is based on what my mother says about him.'

'What sort of things?'

'Oh, that he taught French and German and played a bit of jazz piano, and kept a diary. My mother won't let me see it.'

'That's crazy,' said Eva.

There was a pause.

'How do you *feel*?' she said. Robert tried hard, but struggled, in the manner of someone with empty bowels expected to defecate. At that precise moment he had no particularly strong feelings about his family. Besides, he wasn't that good at talking about how he felt. He was better at intellectual talk: it was more impersonal, with its own logical machinery. One day he might even have a Rolls-Royce mind. But he'd never express feelings like Eva did, never be quite as alive.

'You look sad,' she said. 'You can say anything you like to

me, you know. I don't want you to feel any restrictions about anything: the only thing I ask is that you're completely honest, just like Sartre and de Beauvoir. I am, of course, madly in love with you.'

Robert almost looked over his shoulder to see who she was talking to. He felt disorientated. It was like a scene from a film.

'You look like I've just told you I've got the clap or something,' she said loudly. The woman behind the counter tutted and sighed.   ·

She's in love with me, said Robert to himself. A Red Sea had parted in his life. At a stroke his life had been turned from contingency to necessity. Everything that had happened now had meaning: those lonely nights at home watching Bruce Forsyth, reading *Nausea*, studying Peters and Blackshaw – who was to say they hadn't been precisely essential in creating exactly this person, Robert, whom Eva loved? A beautiful, retrospective light shone into his life. And of course he now had a much more accepting, almost playful attitude to the spot that had recently sprouted on his face like an unwanted nipple. She was in love with him.

'I'm in love with you too,' he said. It was necessary. It would have been impossible to say anything else. He remembered a scene in *Nausea* where Anny talked about feeling obliged to do and say what was necessary to create perfect moments. This was clearly such a situation. The story demanded it. He was, indeed, in love with her. Though he had a strange feeling, too, of wanting to put his arm round her in the way he might comfort a child who was ill or hurt.

'Its been better with you than with anyone I've known,' said Eva. 'For a start you're the first person I ever had a decent orgasm with.'

Robert's arm twitched and knocked over his cup. The coffee went in a slow but unstoppable stream over the edge of the formica table and on to the chipped lino floor.

'Let's go home,' she said. 'It's going to rain all day.' Home. She hadn't called it home before.

As they drove round the South Circular he glanced at himself in the mirror and saw not just Robert, but Robert who was Eva's lover. For the first time in his life he saw himself in the third person, as a definite character, Eva's lover, in a story. He felt both happy and unsettled. He felt that he didn't inhabit his life in quite the same way he'd done before.

Back in Lambeth, they stripped out of their wet clothes and had a bath together, giggling noiselessly as other nurses came and washed. She cooked him a spicy Indian omelette while he lay on her bed listening to 'Fresh Cream' and feeling tiny drops of seawater slide from his ear on to the pillow. The gas fire hissed. Their clothes were drying on the radiator. The curtains were pulled tight against the cold and rain outside and two incense-sticks burned. Neither of them had to work the next day.

She leaned over him, warming the air and filling it with the smell of patchouli. Her hair fell over his face in a heavy black curtain, still slightly wet and salty.

'Perfect moments,' she said, and giggled. 'I suppose you'd say today was just average.'

'Forcing the people she meets to keep on inventing.'

Their relationship didn't take a turn for the worse until the day they went to visit his mother and stepfather after almost a year of good times. He was never clear why, but Eva was increasingly persistent in asking to meet them. Apart from this, she never wanted to go out. Their relationship took place on a desert island, and he was happy to keep it like this, uncontaminated by the outside world.

They walked to his home through the local woods on a beautiful early autumn day. She wanted to mess about on the swings, and he was suddenly one of those rather intimidating adults who play in children's spaces. She put on a pretend mothery voice and started to push him. It was a strange sensation – the surprising, jerking power of the shove forward, the sense of lightness at the top of the arc, the gaining weight and momentum as he came back. She pushed him higher, and his insides started to move with a sickly counter-motion of their own. He wanted to stop, but she shoved him harder. He jumped off the swing and thumped painfully on to the tarmac, barely suppressing an urge to burst into tears.

They walked on, and he pointed out the chestnut trees

where he'd tried to experience Nausea, and told Eva about his foolish belief that some ontological experience had been waiting for him there. She laughed and said that Sartre had probably been stoned on mescalin when he'd had his experiences of Nausea. He'd spent months thinking that he was being followed by a giant lobster. Robert, however, thought *Nausea* had been written long before all this.

'Maybe you came here a lot with your father when you were a little boy,' she said. 'Maybe it's got some sort of special association for you. I think places hold a lot of memory.'

She often went on like this. Robert tolerated it all with a good grace: it was just part of how Eva was. In truth he wasn't particularly bothered about his father or Nausea right now. He was much more concerned about what Eva was going to be like with his mother.

It was an hour before Eva said 'fuck' for the first time. Things had gone well at first. She didn't faint with the heat of the lounge – four bars wasn't too bad considering it was a warm September day. She patted the spaniel, which, thus encouraged, hooked its paws round her and, with its tongue sizzling like a rasher of bacon, attempted to have intercourse with her leg. 'Don't worry, Eva,' said his mother. 'He's a very friendly little dog.'

'I guess he has to get it where he can,' said Eva.

His stepfather sat in his blue recliner and said nothing. He looked at Eva with total unfamiliarity, as if she were a passing aboriginal hunter-gatherer who'd just dropped in to demonstrate some alien skill such as blowpipe-making.

Eva talked quite seriously about her work. So far, so good, thought Robert. What did he want her to be? Did he want her to role-play a kind, polite girlfriend, or to be as honest and intense as she normally was? He didn't trust her to say or do the right thing. She really did believe in honesty.

His mother left the room, and a few minutes later the door opened and a wooden trolley creaked through carrying a double-decker cake stand with lace doilies, the best china, and a teapot in the shape of a car with RUOK4T on its registration plate.

'My own mother never did things like this,' said Eva. 'She was always horrible to friends if I tried to bring them home. She'd never have dreamed of giving us tea and cakes.'

His mother erected herself a few inches taller and started talking about Entertaining as if she were some sort of avant-garde hostess who presided over soirées for Europe's leading intellectuals.

Eva put her arms behind her head. Her nipples stood out as clear dark buttons underneath her white blouse. The luxuriant hair in her armpits was clearly visible. She was sprawled across her seat. She talked with her mouth full of scone. No, she said in reply to his mother, she hadn't watched *Steptoe* or heard of Bruce Forsyth. She put her little finger in her ear, then suddenly pulled it out and inspected it as if she'd caught something. It was awful.

She started talking more and more about her mother. What the hell is she up to? thought Robert. Had she been at the ward drugs cabinet? Did she even know she was talking so much?

'Your dog farts a lot,' said Eva.

'Breaks wind,' said Robert. 'We say "breaks wind" in our family.' He spoke slowly and emphatically and for some reason rolled his 'r's.

'You should try giving him bran in his food,' said Eva. 'It'll help bind things together a bit more.'

Robert's mother smiled politely and said nothing. No one spoke for a few seconds. He was grateful that *Grandstand* was on in the background.

'How private is your garden?' said Eva. Robert felt waves of panic sweep over him. Was she going to propose meditating in the nude? Was she going to insist, at the risk of ending their relationship if he refused, on making love in the centre of the lawn? Was she going to offer to give his stepfather a Tantric massage, or the spaniel an enema?

'Down at the bottom dear, yes,' said his mother.

'I think I'll do my meditation for a little while,' said Eva.

'The quiet one, please,' said Robert.

'Don't worry, darling,' she said, 'I'm not going to embarrass you.' As she left, she leaned over and stuck her tongue between his lips. His eyes met the glazed blue eyes of the china Alsatian. The spaniel let out a soft howl.

Robert understood in a new way that Eva didn't bother much with rules and conventions, with politeness and the done thing. This meant that anything was possible: he couldn't predict what she was going to say or do next.

He'd had enough of the tension this created. As soon as her meditation finished he said he wanted to drive her home. But his mother, appallingly, fetched a photo album showing the various stages of niceness in Robert's life. Eva wanted to see a photo of his father. She thought he looked interesting, and a lot like Robert, with his nice eyes and ironic slightly hidden face.

And then, in response to a question of his mother's, Eva started going on about the food in the nurses' home, how fucking shitty it was, how depressed she sometimes felt. His mother was confused: she was disapproving and supportive in the same coiled tense gestures.

Eva asked to see Robert's room. It was embarrassing showing it to her: it seemed suddenly dominated by the El Cordobes poster and the plastic Vulcan bomber on top of the wardrobe. He told her how stressed he felt.

'You should let yourself go a bit more,' she said, 'be more natural with your mother and stepfather. They're nice. You don't have to keep your life in separate compartments.'

As if to emphasise this last point, she took off her clothes
and stood at the net curtain, which blew in the wind like a
flimsy bride's veil. She bent down to kiss him. He saw, in
slow motion, the rolling curve of her upper lip, how it
almost curled back on itself, like the ridge of a wave, as she
came towards his face.

'If it wasn't for you, I don't know what I'd have done this
past year,' she said, 'I was feeling so lonely.'

He could hear a rumble of voices downstairs and an
audience applauding on the TV. He heard the slow, tired
sound of suburban hammering that he always heard
whenever the sun shone. He looked at *Nausea* on the
bookshelf, gratefully, and marvelled that Eva was here, in
this room.

She kissed him with a mouth that felt like the sea.

The football results were being read out on the telly.
His mother shouted something about supper being nearly
ready. A toilet flushed, with a nauseatingly familiar pattern
of whooshes, gurgles and drips.

Robert felt he was being asked to choose between the
world of his mother and stepfather and Eva's honesty and
intensity. Have a little courage, he thought. It would take a
lot to get them away from the early-evening news. Take a
risk. Live a little. He started to undress.

He felt he was making love with her spirit more than her
body, with some unvanquishable spirit that reminded
him, as she moved beneath him and he felt the clean rush
of her breath, of the sort of rugged small boat that could
sail round Cape Horn and into the blue calm of the
Pacific.

He heard a door or window somewhere in the house
banging in the breeze.

His fingers were on her warm silvery back as a tube train
accelerated out of the station. It was a sound as familiar as
his own voice. The bed knocked against the wall. A book

fell off the shelf. Camus. Mother died yesterday, and all that stuff.

Was that his parents banging on the ceiling, or a noise in the central-heating pipes? Was that the television or a call from his mother?

Eva groaned loudly. The pushing movements of her body grew stronger and reminded him for a moment of being on the swing. And then she started, oh god, to yelp like an injured dog. He kissed her mouth, trying to dampen the noise. He realised that he was not so much making love now as trying to achieve what Stephen would call a wishy-washy liberal compromise.

Mr Webster started up his motor-mower. It was blissfully noisy.

Part of Robert wanted to be filled with sweet reckless desire for Eva, but mainly he was filled with a desire to get her to a climax before Mr Webster finished his pathetically small square of lawn.

'Never leave me,' she said, as Robert tried every Peters and Blackshaw trick he could think of to speed things up.

Then Mr Webster's motor cut. This was it. Crucifixion. The moment of truth. He didn't stop. He knew that if he stilled the sound of his breathing and of the blood rushing in his ears, he would hear the voices of his mother and stepfather saying, 'In our house, in the afternoon, too, with the windows open and neighbours out in their gardens – we'll never live it down.'

As he came, wrenchingly, the front door was slammed with the force of something being destroyed. Robert lay as stiff as a corpse on the bed.

'It's so secure and orderly in this house,' said Eva a moment or two later. 'I really like it.' And then she told Robert that he was the only person she'd met to whom she could ever imagine being married.

*

'I've made you some scrambled eggs,' said his mother when they went downstairs. 'I hope they aren't too cold.' Robert hadn't a clue what she was feeling or thinking. All he knew was that various exchanges had taken place and that it had been one of the most hauntingly stressful days of his life.

'That "I" ... a dough which goes on stretching and stretching.'

When he wasn't with Eva, Robert stayed at Marshall's house, a battered villa in Maida Vale that Marshall shared with five other blokes. He'd moved there a few months after meeting Eva.

The house was dominated by Marshall. He was older than the others, doing a postgraduate course in psychology. As a northerner, being in psychology was a matter of some shame. He restricted himself to things involving electricity, pain and rodents, and explained that he'd only gone into psychology because there were more women there than in any other department.

He attempted to run the house as a type of sexual production-line, and kept copious statistics, in notebooks and on wallcharts. He could quote vast tracts of data from Kinsey, and the penis size of every living species of mammal, and the water temperature of each ocean: one of his major ambitions was to make love in all the world's major seas. He'd been married briefly, but his wife had left him following a particularly gruelling episode in the Gulf of St Lawrence.

Marshall was suspicious of Robert because he had switched from history to psychology out of an interest in people, and because he had one steady girlfriend who never came to the house. Marshall had only seen Eva once. He was always prying into what she was like and what positions they used, so that he could enter the information in his records, but up till now Robert had resisted anything more than a few lighthearted generalisations.

Marshall was annoyed, too, that Robert had not been to any of the parties he masterminded, which were held without fail every month. Even though Robert tried to make up for it by buying them extra-large quantities of beer, Marshall was accusatory. Coming to the parties, joining in, and trying to score was an expected part of life in the house, as much the done thing as putting money into the kitty.

One Saturday night a couple of weekends after the traumatic trip to his parents' house, Eva had a late switch of shift and Robert decided for once to go to the party rather than sit on his own in her room.

Party night. The Stones. Self-appointed Jumping Jack Flashes from Merton and Mansfield leered at pouting girls through the greeny darkness. An oxbow lake of urine covered the floor of the toilet, and two used condoms floated in the bowl. Marshall was disgusted at the fact that the perpetrators had not mastered the basic art of timing the throw of a johnny into a flushing toilet: in the age of the pill he felt it was becoming a dying skill. People covered every step and corner of the stairs. Robert was unclear whether they were involved in some act of coition, or waiting for the toilet, or hoping that the queue led to a secret cache of food.

After one tour of the house Robert made for his room, the smallest in the house. There was a pile of coats on his bed and a faint smell of copulation, like a distant tin of anchovies. He put the light on. A man's head emerged from under the heap of clothes. 'Fuck off out of it,' the man said simply. 'It's my room,' said Robert. 'Fuck off out of it, then,' said the man.

Marshall appeared in the doorway with hard amber eyes, wearing an unbuttoned frilly shirt and fluffed-up chest hair.

'You'll have to go to the kitchen,' said Marshall. 'You'll put people off just hanging around. Anyway, I don't see what you're doing at this party if you're not trying to score. You're letting the side down.'

'But I don't want anyone else. I'm happy with Eva.'

'Shit, you're not thinking of doing anything silly with her, are you? Like being faithful or settling down? I mean, the tits are nice and the face is OK, I'll give you that. But she sounds bloody neurotic, and in any case—'

'You bastard,' said Robert. 'I'm happy with Eva. I don't want to go chasing after anyone else.'

'Christ, you sound about sixty,' said Marshall, and hustled away.

Robert sat on the fire escape for half an hour. He wanted the willowy silence of Eva's room, the books, the sight of her cross-legged on the floor, meditating.

He forced himself to go down to the kitchen. Marshall's mate Jim from the demo was there, dressed, as if for a working-class night out, in a navy blue suit and white shirt. He was inhaling the air with quick, deep sniffs, like a wine connoisseur.

'Fanny,' said Jim in his nasal Brummie accent. 'There's a lot of women here who are dying for it. Just smell the air. I can tell you know.'

You had to respect a man from the proletariat, thought Robert, a man who had tossed a rat into the air with his bare teeth, and who could, no doubt, time to perfection the throw of a condom into a flushing toilet.

'Fanny,' Jim said again, yet more profoundly. 'The air's thick with it. Mark my words.'

Marshall jogged into the kitchen.

'I've found a new hole,' he said, and gave a smile of calm, understated triumph. 'A new hole.'

Jim beamed. 'I knew it,' he said. 'I knew something was in the air tonight.'

'It's at the top of the thighs,' said Marshall, 'like a key hole, if she keeps her legs pressed tightly together.' His girlfriend of the previous three days came to the door in one of Marshall's shirts, and stood there with the blank dignity of a camel.

'Do you want me to show you?' said Marshall, 'Carole, do you mind?'

'It's OK,' said Jim magnanimously, 'I can imagine, ta very much.'

Robert made a coffee, breaking the seal on a new jar while Marshall and Jim made jokes about hymens.

The first drum beats of 'Let's Spend the Night Together' surged in from the room next door, followed by desperate whoops and cries. The volume was turned up to maximum, and the floors throbbed and shook as if the very house itself was approaching a sexual climax. Marshall hurried towards the room as if summoned to prayer.

Yes, thought Robert, he had changed. Or rather, he'd never fully acknowledged that this vision was not for him. He'd never be the sort of person who leaped phallically up and down in front of a nameless woman, and then slunk wordlessly off with her to a spare bit of floor. He'd always want to get to know people as he imagined Jean-Paul would do, intelligently, with wine and magical words. Jean-Paul wouldn't have been seen dead at a party like this.

Robert found a small padlock with which he could secure the door to his room and queued to get into the bathroom to brush his teeth. He edged out, and there, at the foot of the stairs, stood Stephen, Fiona, and Julie. Stephen's arm was firmly round Fiona's shoulder. Julie stood a little apart, smiling with hundreds of perfect American teeth.

Fiona kissed Robert on the cheek with the slight unease of someone who has an intuition she might have featured in a masturbatory fantasy. Stephen put an arm round him, squeezed him, asked how he was and said he didn't think they'd be staying long with a bunch of degenerates like this.

Julie hugged Robert and gave him her bright hippy smile. He felt discontinuously older: postgraduate, independent and equal to her in some new way.

The music had slowed down. 'Try a Little Tenderness'. Julie and Robert had a dance. 'I've brought a present for you,' she said, and giggled. He felt her tongue against his ear, and her lower body pushing dialectically against his.

With the energy of a masturbating baboon 'Let's Spend the Night Together' started out for a second time. Robert glanced across the room and saw Marshall by the record-player, saw his inflated manic face and his right arm opening and closing in the most vigorous of sexual gestures.

'Am I myself not a wave of icy air?'

A week after the party, Robert sat in the William and Victoria, explaining to Stephen that he'd only had a casual encounter with Julie, and trying to tell him some of the things that made his relationship with Eva so special. He meant it to sound lyrical but it sounded more like he was trying to sell something.

Stephen drank deeply at his pint, fitting the glass over his face like an oxygen mask. He thought it all sounded incredibly intense, and that Eva seemed just a tiny bit strange.

'You're missing the best Cup run Spurs have had in ages,' said Stephen. 'You don't go to any political meetings or demos any more. And this is the first time you've been out for a pint in months.'

How much judgement should we surrender to our friends? thought Robert. Once you let an idea into your head, for example, the idea that someone was neurotic or that love didn't last, it could take a lot of shifting.

Eva did seem to be changing slightly: the times when she was unhappy had begun to outweigh the times when she was playful. She was starting to hate her job. She was far too intelligent and anarchic for it. It was restrictive, hierarchical, petty: she was told off for sitting on patients' beds and for holding the hand of a man dying of cancer. She missed shifts, argued with tutors and couldn't be bothered to study. She was as obsessed as ever with her mother and blamed her for the stomach upsets she was getting. She went to meditation groups in search of help. Occasionally she would cry and shake for no apparent reason.

Sometimes she'd tell Robert that she lived for the times when she was with him, that he was all that mattered. When she talked like this, the power balance between them shifted like water suddenly slopping across a boat. In a half-thrilling, half-frightening way, Robert realised that his role was to give meaning to her, love her, save her even.

As if to compensate for saying that she needed him, she was bossier and argued more. One day she accused him of being too nice all the time, of coming in as Mr Nice Guy with his bottle of Rioja and polite manners. Women didn't want men to understand them all the time: they wanted something more dominant and primitive as well. That afternoon Robert tried to make love as he imagined Clint Eastwood would do, cutting out the foreplay crap and thrusting into her without perfect understanding. Eva was remarkably, almost desperately, excited. Afterwards, as always, she wanted him to hold her. 'Clint wouldn't do that,' said Robert. 'He'd have fucked off by now: a last mean stare, on to his horse and away.' He managed to make it sound funny, but for the first time some part of him wanted to be out in the bright puritanically cold winter sun, on his own, or having a laugh with friends. Being in bed in the afternoon, especially now it was sunny, suddenly made him feel as if he were ill, being kept out of school or off games. He noticed that the room smelt musty – a mix of stale sexual smells and damp socks drying on the radiator. He had the strange, fleeting notion of being a prisoner in her room, and the sense that she was trying to mould him into something more substantial than he actually was. She was trying to make him into her perfect lover, someone who knew just how to touch her and how to meditate and when to speak and when to be silent.

One night he dreamed of going with Eva to buy a flat in a Victorian terraced house. They looked at a room together, an attic room, long and narrow, and painted white. Suddenly the room started to change shape so that Eva fitted into it but he had to bend his head uncomfortably. The walls were pressing against him, and the room felt frighteningly hot and airless. Whenever they went to a different room, the same thing happened. He woke sweating, squashed between Eva and the wall, with a feeling of nausea.

The crisis started the next day, with Robert's testicles: he'd always been slightly suspicious of them, so, looking back, it should not have come as a surprise. In the middle of kissing him, she suddenly squeezed them so hard that tears came into his eyes.

'Fucking hell,' said Robert. 'Stop trying to castrate me. That hurts.'

Her body went rigid, motionless.

'Oh shit,' she said, 'I can't even do this right. I can't get anything right. My whole life's a disaster, everything, my job, my relationships, my health, everything. I'm full of bloody problems, I fuck up everything I touch.'

She looked at him, her eyes filling with tears, and moments later she was sobbing. He put his arms round her and she curled up against him in a way that made her seem more like a daughter than a girlfriend. He felt tender but frightened too. This was a moment that demanded real passion, but the more he thought about how much he needed to show this sobbing person that he loved her, the more his mind went into a stratospheric place. He stroked her hair and watched a tear trickle over the small bump in her nose. He was role-playing love and compassion.

You haven't changed as much as you thought, some voice said to him.

He glanced into Eva's mirror and saw the cool detached eyes of Antoine Roquentin looking back.

When she stopped crying, she took both his hands and gave him a glistening, peeled look.

'Thank you,' she said.

She hugged him. Smotheringly. Right at this second she was like a bath that was too warm.

'I'm not sure I'm in love with you any more,' said Robert. The words just came out, known but not thought.

Eva said that he'd been full of stupid romantic notions, that infatuation passed and didn't really matter. She asked him if he had any cigarettes, and he said he hadn't.

'How dare you say you're not in love with me, and then not have any fucking cigarettes,' she said.

She started throwing books at him. He thought it best to let something hit him, and moved his head so that it was caught a glancing blow by *Thus Spake Zarathustra*.

'Has there ever been anyone else,' said Eva later. 'I mean, while you've known me. Not that it's particularly important, I'm just curious.'

'No, nothing very much. I had a bit of a session with this woman Julie. But we didn't screw, we just had a kind of extended grope, then she was so relaxed and mellow she fell asleep. She was a bit soulless, really. And I didn't want to, anyway. I felt too close to you. I love you so much.' The 'so' didn't sound right. It sounded like a careful measure.

'Ha,' she said. 'That's pathetic. I'm disgusted that you didn't screw her. How half-hearted. What difference would it make? We've always said we have the freedom to do what we want.'

*

They opened a bottle of wine, and drank it quietly, unsure of what the afternoon had meant. She sat against the wall looking at him for what seemed like hours, and it was a relief at last when they went to bed and his face, resting against her hair, was free to find its own confused expression.

The next day, sitting in his room at Marshall's, Robert decided to read *Nausea* again. He no longer had a burning desire to experience dread at trying to pick up a piece of paper, or to see Existence oozing out of a chestnut tree. He no longer felt ensnared by mirrors and disgusted with himself, nor did he feel the sun's rays fall on him like a pitiless judgement. He felt calm and independent. Roquentin seemed very neurotic, banging on about understanding himself before it was too late. Robert didn't need this sort of thing anymore.

But for all that, the book still held some sense of the life he wanted. What he loved most about the book now was its cool sense of freedom. He too wanted to cross seas and leave cities behind him; to stand on a railway-station platform, able to go anywhere, do anything; to sit in cafés lit up like ships and stars, and watch the night enter the streets, 'smooth and hesitant'.

Sartre once said to de Beauvoir that the three things that mattered most in his life were travel, sexual freedom and transparent honesty. Robert thought that being honest was probably the hardest but, if he was utterly honest now, allowing the book to help him decide, he wanted to be on that platform and walking into the smooth, hesitant darkness by himself.

The next time they met, Eva told him that she was going to pack in her job – she was about to get kicked out of it anyway. She wasn't sure what she was going to do, maybe go back to France, possibly even overland to Asia.

'But of course,' said Eva, 'I won't go if you really want us to be together. As I've said before, you're what matters most to me in my life right now. I'm sure we can work things out if we give it a try.'

He hugged her to him, feeling like Judas, and kept his mouth shut.

Three weeks later he stayed in her room for the last time, and got up early to give her a lift to Victoria Station. It was hard to say goodbye, to see her room empty, the temple stripped of all its posters and photos, the shelves bare of books. They shared a plastic beaker of coffee made with hot water from the washbasin tap. She put her white coat on. He hugged her.

'We're good for each other,' she whispered into his ear with a voice like the sea. 'We're like Sartre and de Beauvoir. Good for each other. An essential rather than a contingent love. I really do believe that. That time in the nightclub . . . I didn't just bump into you; I'd been watching you all evening. I knew we were special for each other. You should have trusted things a bit more.'

She looked calm and beautiful now. His doubts seemed foolish. But, deep down, he wanted her to go, in the way he wanted to reach the blank white page beyond the end of a book. He wanted to feel what it would be like to be free for a while of her passion and power, to feel the size and shape of the sadness she would leave, and know what it meant.

He was trembling as they got out of the car at Victoria Station. She looked at him with pale blue eyes that were serious and unblinking, daring to see and be seen. She kissed him wildly, squeezing him with all her strength, then she spun round and walked towards a small queue of passengers. Robert waved robustly, waited and waved again. But she walked away proudly and bravely and never looked back. She walked away, he suddenly thought, like an existential heroine.

He bought a copy of the *News of the World* and a bar of Fruit and Nut, uncertain how to spend this day that was now dramatically his own. He climbed back into the car, closed his door and, as Jean-Paul would have put it, the years with Eva collapsed into the past.

Part II
1971–1979

'I wanted the events of my life to follow each other in an orderly fashion: like that of a life remembered.'

For two years after Eva left, Robert felt powerful, free and independent. He did indeed cross seas, make love and leave women and cities behind him. To be precise, six seas, twenty-two cities and fifteen women. The number of women was, for him, quite remarkable, even allowing for the fact that a considerable proportion were on a trip to Torremolinos with Marshall. In addition to all this he managed to get a 2.1, followed by a research assistant post in the polytechnic where Marshall had become a senior lecturer. He was successful.

He missed Eva, but in a vague sort of way. She sent him long letters from France (saying she was missing him badly), from Turkey (where she'd nearly been raped), Iran (vivid memories of the past), and India (where she visited an ashram but was disappointed to find it full of people from Camden Town squabbling over who had used whose coffee). Robert didn't try too hard to chase up the fleeting post-restante addresses. He felt scared that Eva might appear, shaking and tear-stained on his parents' doorstep. Then he received a postcard saying that she was going to the States with new friends and was feeling very good. After that the letters stopped. He was sad but relieved.

As he got towards his middle twenties, his existence, as Jean-Paul might say, started to cause him serious concern. The shared house broke up: Marshall bought a flat; others went abroad or got married. Robert found a bedsit in a brick terrace in Holloway. He had a new double mattress, ninety LPs, a blown-up photo of himself running, almost Camus-like, along a beach in Morocco, a hairbrush thick and greasy with his fallen hair, and two shelves of novels. It was OK but nothing more. If he wasn't careful it was the sort of place where he could lie in bed on a Saturday morning surrounded by piles of dirty washing and wonder about the meaning of life.

Work grew insecure. His research assistant job was renewed for only six months at a time. And he had to get involved with things he didn't much believe in, the worst of these being the self-administration of electric shocks by paedophiles and other sorts of sexual offender. It was hardly the most appealing of fields, but there weren't any alternative jobs. He was trapped underneath a vast intake of people only a year or two older than him who'd been recruited to staff the post-Robbins expansion of higher education.

Women became suddenly less easy to meet. Try as he might, Robert could not entirely resist Marshall's assertion that all the best women of their generation had got married, and that the rest were scrubbers, lesbians, Trotskyists, or people with mental health or personal hygiene problems. In addition, Marshall, who had just remarried, said that for the first time in a hundred years the number of men in Britain was greater than the number of women. There were 151,329 more men than women in the 15–29 age group, enough to fill Wembley and White Hart Lane. It was a stupid statistic, but just the sort that came into Robert's head at one in the morning as he lay in his none-too-clean bed.

Robert had generally assumed that life had stages which followed each other in a reasonably orderly fashion. He'd been through Adolescence and spent quite enough years in the events of Early Adulthood. And now, increasingly, he wanted to put down roots, build a career, find a partner and have a home of his own. He'd always had a reasonable degree of optimism about the future, a sense that the next stage of life would come along with all its transforming power. But now he began to worry that life didn't automatically get better.

Political events in Britain seemed to mirror this view. It was true that there'd been optimistic things, like North Sea Oil, the struggle at Upper Clyde Shipbuilders and the miners getting 35 per cent. But there were uglier events, too, that he would never have predicted, like having to cross the road because of skinhead gangs, and being at the Red Lion Square demonstration where Kevin Gately got killed, and the Birmingham pub bombings. Maybe he'd always seen Britain, and his own life, too cosily. It was possible for things to get worse, to fail, or explode, or simply stagnate in three-day weeks and 50 mph motorway speed limits.

He missed Eva more and more. No one he'd met remotely compared with her. He came to think that his life was being wasted because he wasn't spending it with her. The two years he'd been with her were unquestionably the time when he'd been happiest. Eva grew into his Lost Love, the Real Thing, the Girl of his Dreams, the only person who'd ever really loved him. This feeling was never more intense than on the afternoon he spent on his own in Les Deux Magots, imagining Eva opposite him, with her freeing, intelligent look.

Some part of him knew it was myth, but Eva started to become an alternative story about how good his life would have been if only he'd stayed with her. He would not have ended up in a bedsit with a frustrating, insecure job. He would have had dramatic adventures, made spiritual and personal discoveries, lived with intensity and joy. And then, at the right time, they'd have thought about settling down, about a home and children.

Robert saw now that he'd been unable to trust Eva. He'd been frightened of all her passion, love, honesty and spontaneity. All the things, he thought bitterly, that made her so special. Time and again he wished he'd run after her as she walked towards her train, and said that love was the most precious thing in the world, all we ever really created, that he'd love her forever, that Nausea got it all wrong. He wrote letters to dramatically out-of-date post-restante addresses, but all to no avail. She had disappeared.

Robert drifted, out of loneliness or by default, into a relationship with a girl called Deborah. He'd met her briefly many years earlier, and bumped into her again at a party given by Fiona Duvalle.

Deborah was the sort of person Robert could look at for a long time without being able to decide finally whether she was attractive or unattractive. She had wavy chestnut hair that more might be made of, and hazel eyes, and a body that his mother would call a worker's body, sinewy and functional, but others might see as commendably slim.

Deborah never made love with enormous animation, but tidily, with a sense of polite surprise at her own muted gasps, and at rather infrequent intervals. She was extremely clean, and very concerned that none of Robert's trembling ecstasy should ever leak on to the sheets. Freshly laundered towels and large, four-ply pink tissues were close to her heart and always to hand. After making love she would talk in an animated way about Brent Cross and the Shopping Revolution in the way the political cognoscenti had once talked about Vietnam and Paris '68.

The only thing she was really passionate about was Marks and Spencer. She believed in Marks and Spencer more than she believed in democracy, with an intensity that at first had completely thrown Robert and led them into each other's arms. She'd stood in the kitchen at Fiona's party and started saying that 'only Marx has got it right', and asking Robert whether he'd seen the new Marx yet. He'd been impressed by her certainty and commitment, which reminded him of Stephen's, and it wasn't until they'd been to bed together that he found out she'd been talking about the department store.

Robert felt angrier with *Nausea* now. Roquentin banged on about clinging to the moment with all his heart and how he longed for Anny to save him. But when he finally met Anny again, he was such a cold fish: he didn't even take her in his arms, he let her walk away, all in the name of some philosophical insight into the nature of consciousness. It was chilling to read how Roquentin lived all alone, never spoke to anyone, gave nothing, received nothing, just because of some intellectual insight. He was a fool.

Robert felt stuck. Missing Eva, becalmed in his job and with Deborah, going nowhere. Nothing happened for months and months, and then, out of the blue, one November day in 1977, things changed.

'Nothing. Existed.'

'I want you to go to a weekend conference,' said Marshall. 'It's on advances in humanistic psychology, part of some weird festival of body, mind and spirit. I want you to write a critique of it for a new behaviourist journal.'

'Oh shit,' said Robert, 'do I have to?' It was pointless asking really. Marshall was deputy head of department, and no one else wanted to go, so it was down to Robert, as the reigning and undisputed lowest-status person in the psychology department.

Robert found the prospect of going to a humanistic psychology conference rather daunting. He was not particularly proud of his job, and envisaged finding himself next to people who wanted to talk about the finer points of personal growth. 'And what do you do?' they'd say. 'Oh, I'm in the electric-shock end of the business,' Robert would reply, 'working with various sex offenders, all volunteers. It's harmless enough, really, pretty low-voltage stuff. You just need to keep your terminals clean, remember the KY Jelly and hope it doesn't rain.'

He rang Deborah and told her he'd got to go to a conference.

'But we're going out shopping, and for a meal. What about Us?'

He often saw Us in capital letters, US; it was almost like the United States the way she talked about it – the United States of their two lives, the country to which they owed allegiance. And all this after only a few rather average screws and a lot of post-coital conversation about Brent Cross. He explained that he had no choice, and added, as gently as he could, that right now he didn't want a heavy relationship with anyone.

And so he spent a grim weekend among people who believed in the myth of mental illness and established alternative communities on Greek islands; he danced with dervishes from Tooting Bec, and had a blurred photograph taken of what was claimed to be his aura. He received sales pitches for little glass pyramids to keep razorblades sharp, and for machines that amplified the squeaks that plants made as they were stroked. He went to a serious lecture on humanistic models of man, and followed it with an hour's meditation with the Rajneeshi people in their orange robes.

He called it a day after a final lecture by a Scottish guru who claimed to be bigger than Buddha. In between asking whether anyone had sexual difficulties which they wanted to share, the guru kept going on about Mind, Body and Spirit. Robert wondered how much of any of these he had left. His mind largely belonged, in the best Marxist tradition, to his work: he hadn't read a good book in ages, it was all research papers. His body was, he supposed, OK; he didn't think about it much: it contained all his organs well enough, he presumed, and seemed good enough for the likes of Deborah. And his spirit? Well, God knew what that was or what had happened to it.

It was 4 pm, as early as he could legitimately leave if he was to claim a whole day in lieu.

He edged past some happy, throbbing Rajneeshis and held open the door for a couple of people behind him.

The woman who caught hold of the door raised her long, black eyebrows in a way that wavered delicately between irony and thanks.

And there she was. He recognised Eva immediately – the way she carried her head, like a queen, proud and still, as if it were held by invisible hands; the eyes, calm and powerful, pale blue, slow to register him. Her hair was the same wonderful shiny black, like the darkest and smoothest of black cats, but short, swept behind the ears now, with much less of a fringe.

'God. Eva.'

'Robert, what a surprise! How are you?'

'I missed you so much,' he said. 'I was mad not to go with you all those years ago.' He had to say it. He'd promised himself that. But the words were almost lost in the traffic noise: she barely seemed to hear.

He leaned forward to kiss her, and found his lips straddling an awkward surface between her cheek and her ear. Some friend or colleague was waiting and watching by a taxi.

'I'd no idea you were in London,' he said. 'It must be years since your last card.'

'I haven't been here long. I've been thinking of ringing your mother to find out where you are. It's great to see you.'

She looked towards her friend and said she had to go, but that it would be good to meet him, to catch up on news, she often thought about how he was.

She scribbled down an address and phone number, in Tufnell Park, for God's sake. He looked at her hands. All ten fingers were magnificently ringless.

He watched her fold her pale legs into the black innards of the taxi, and marvelled that she was alive and in London.

*

Nothing. Existed. It was as good a way as any of describing how much had happened between Eva going and seeing her again.

Robert ran back in and started to twirl wildly with the first squad of dervishes he came across.

'Down to the whites of my eyes.'

Eva's house was in a part of Tufnell Park he didn't know, a treeless road of Victorian terraced houses. Some had windows that were boarded up or broken. Others were being renovated and had skips outside them filled with torn wallpaper and ruptured mattresses. Hammering came from one house, reggae music from another. A pack of mongrel dogs swung to and fro along the street. They had small, mean heads and black and brown flecked coats that made them look like hyenas.

Robert fingered the address Eva had scribbled, which lay in the inside pocket of his Burton's cream sports jacket, between his heart and his Roger & Gallet L'Homme-deodorised armpit.

The number of the house where she lived was painted on a gate post in white letters that had dribbled before the paint had dried. The garden was littered with old milk cartons and sun-roasted dog turds, and the grass was badly overgrown. He had to push brambles aside to get to the front door. All these things gave Robert hope that Eva was not living a life of impenetrable success.

The door had a beautiful stained-glass window showing trees and flowers in various shades of yellow. He glanced at his hand as it hovered in front of the doorbell like a white bird. He wasn't quite sure what would happen next. His life suddenly felt free and very fragile.

A man with shoulder-length brown hair opened the door. He wore a rainbow-coloured sweater and a badge expressing support for a male curfew in Camden Town.

'Is Eva in?' asked Robert.

'No,' said the man, 'but she won't be long. I'm Nick. Come in. You can wait in the living room, or Eva's room, I guess.'

The first thing Robert noticed inside the hall was a black and white poster of a sun-filled garden, with white italic writing on it which said, 'Sitting silently, doing nothing, the spring comes and the grass grows by itself.' Yes, but it doesn't bloody mow itself, thought Robert. Given the unkempt state of the front garden, he found the poster strangely disturbing and inappropriate.

Another poster further into the hall informed him that 'The hand that reaches for another woman's clitoris has to traverse the centuries and will lose its way many times.' This statement was a great deal more interesting than anything Robert had encountered at work in a very long time. He thought how wonderful it must be to feel such weighty significance in the act of touching, to have a sense that your hand was connected to history itself rather than merely to your own little struggle to be happy.

A long corridor led from the hall to the kitchen. Its walls were covered with information about women's refuges, abortion rights, night taxi services, consciousness-raising groups, Troops Out meetings, Chile and South Africa demonstrations, and lists of Co-counselling phone numbers. At the entrance to the kitchen there was a notice-board with a complex set of matrices outlining rotas for child care, cleaning, shopping and cooking. Robert would not have been unduly surprised to see a rota for mutual masturbation.

Nick asked if Robert wanted a cup of tea, and then whether he wanted herbal or Earl Grey. Robert thought it best to wait in the living room. This was a large room with eight or more chairs pushed back against the walls, making it look like a dayroom in an old people's home. The chairs were deep old armchairs, with the odd spring protruding out of fabric like a badly broken bone.

Nick brought him the tea, which was a thin red colour, and the sort of thing Robert only took if he had a temperature of over 100. He looked at Robert, and smiled, and kept on looking.

'Do you live in a communal house?' asked Nick.

'No,' said Robert, 'I live in a bedsit. I used to live in a shared house a few years ago.'

Nick nodded and went 'mmm' all the time Robert was talking.

'So you live in a bedsit, but used to live in a shared house a few years ago,' he said.

'Yes,' said Robert. He felt disconcerted at the fact that Nick had repeated more or less exactly what he'd said. Nick continued to do this and then asked if Robert wanted to talk about how he felt. Robert retreated to the toilet at the first opportunity. The lock had been removed from the door, and there was a 'Wages for Housework' poster in the place above the basin where he'd hoped to find a mirror.

The front door was slammed shut with a force that made the glass quiver. He combed his hair with his eyes closed, relying on feel and memory, then opened the door and edged out on to the landing, suddenly aware of how much he wanted Eva to love him.

A woman with masses of curly black hair, a white T-shirt and huge ballooning trousers stood in the hall. It was not Eva.

'Nick, I've had a bloody terrible day,' she said, 'and I've got a migraine coming on. Would you mind terribly looking after Clytemnestra tonight?' Robert wondered whether Clytemnestra was the name of a cat or a child, or even some sort of therapy centre.

'Of course. No problem,' said Nick. He introduced Robert.

Andrea looked at Robert's face with what seemed like a hint of weary interest. Her eyes were dark with intensely black eyebrows that almost joined up. They moved quickly down his cream jacket and 100 per cent polyester trousers. By the time she got back to his face she was wearing a look that seemed to him something like contemptuous indifference. She sighed with a quickness and force that made him, for no reason he was sure of, feel vaguely guilty and unworthy, as if he'd once borrowed something from her and not given it back.

He returned to the living room. He felt anxious about meeting Eva. But he was ready to relate to her now, in a way he hadn't been before. He was ready to listen to her for hours, to weep with her, to take risks and make commitments. He wanted to come back into her life, not as a thief or refugee, but as someone who had grown and changed. He would be more honest, open and spontaneous. The only thing he'd done by way of preparation was to recall a few favourite ways she liked to be touched. He was determined that his hand, given half a chance, wasn't going to lose its way.

A white cat, sleek and beautiful, with a chocolate-brown face, leapt on to the sofa, walked along the back of it, wobbled and fell off. Robert had never seen a cat so grossly lose its balance.

And suddenly he felt two hands over his eyes, warm and slightly damp, and a soft voice saying 'Guess who?'; and a kiss, brief and noisy, on his cheek. Then the two hands were hugging him round his chest, which felt as dry and brittle as a wasp's, and the lips were on his cheeks again. No perfume. No patchouli. A scent, if anything, of unscented soap.

He stood, took a deep breath like a skin-diver about to go under the water, and embraced her, letting out a slow sigh which turned into a yearning groan of the type found not infrequently on Roy Orbison records. He pushed his lower body, intuitively, romantically rather than sexually, towards her. He felt her stomach and groin bend back away from him. Cooler air and questions came between them, permissions that weren't yet being given. Certain assumptions he'd made – about melting into each other and never being apart again – now seemed premature. For a second neither of them breathed out and her chest felt hard against his.

'It's wonderful to see you,' he said.

'It's been over six years,' said Eva.

They laughed, almost politely. Robert felt a sudden need to be more careful.

'I'm going to make a cup of tea,' she said. 'We can take it into my room and talk. It really is lovely to see you again.'

What, thought Robert, did it mean when someone said 'really'? That she'd just changed her mind for the better, that she was being kind to you, that she actually did think it?

The phone rang.

'Oh, hi,' she said. 'Great to hear from you. Yes I've been missing you too. Really.'

'No,' she said, 'An old friend. It would be difficult tonight, I think. Yeah, I had a heavy weekend with you know who. I'm trying to get over it.'

Thoughts and questions piled through Robert's mind like a dozen muddy rugby players trying to get to a loose ball. Who the hell were these people? What did they want? What was her history? What web of connections and obligations did she have to others? And what did she see as she glanced over at him now, and gave a little smile that started with the lips turned down, thinner and tighter than he remembered? Did he look dispirited? Did the boredom and disappointment of his life show? Was it in some pattern of creases in his brow or dulling of his skin?

Her face was more beautiful than he remembered, the face of an impressive person. It seemed less rounded now, tapering tightly from her cheekbones to her chin. With her black hair cut short, her face looked lean, focused, stripped of inessentials. Her blue eyes were still and confident, very much her own, doing her business rather than anyone else's.

Her attic room was long and narrow, with lots of square windows, giving it a feeling of being suspended in space and light like the bridge of a ship. At one end there was an oak desk with a marble table lamp and an electric typewriter. He noticed letters in an in-tray from the BBC and the San Francisco Women's Free Press. A magnificent potted palm tree stood next to a white sunlit wall, and further along there was a full-length gilt-framed mirror of the sort he imagined there being in classical ballet schools. It was not, thought Robert painfully, the room of someone about to collapse in tears into his arms.

A cat came mincing across the carpet towards Eva, miaowing and stopping to stretch. It was an ordinary tabby, but quite fluffy.

'This is Georgie,' said Eva. 'Georgie's about the most stable thing in my life at the moment.' She said this quite happily.

Robert reached out to stroke Georgie. The cat bit him on the finger, not hard or painfully, but in a horribly intimate way – some unmistakable bit of inter-species communication about desire and territory.

'She's only being playful,' said Eva. 'It's a sign she likes you.'

'Whose was the other cat, the white thing downstairs? It fell off the sofa.'

'Ah,' said Eva, 'that would be Sacha, Andrea's cat. He's got no instincts at all. He just miaows, looks pretty and falls off things. He's been bred by a lesbian couple. I think he's meant to be some sort of male role model.'

They both laughed. Robert hoped that the laughter might develop and deepen but it stayed thin and tense. He drank his tea carefully, not feeling safe enough to make any noise as he swallowed.

Oh Lord, he thought, what would it be like to live without barriers, to just let my feelings and thoughts flow towards her?

He asked her about her work.

'I've nearly finished a book I've been commissioned to write on women and spirituality, based on my experiences in Asia and America, and some research I've been doing in Europe. And I get by with some freelance articles.'

'That sounds interesting,' said Robert. 'I suppose it needs a lot of concentration.' Oh, shit, he sounded like the Duke of Edinburgh. But he was interested. And impressed. Amazed even. Some part of him didn't believe her, wanted to say, 'Oh, come on, Eva, I know that underneath you're really vulnerable, I remember how you cried and how you couldn't handle your nursing job. People don't change that much.' But then he had another look at her room and realised there was not a single object in it from the days when he'd known her in Lambeth.

Nick tapped reverently at the door: it was the phone, again, for Eva. She slipped out. Robert explored the room like a sneak thief, searching for some sort of intimacy. He rolled back the duvet and sniffed the bed. The cat glared at him. He looked through some photos on her bedside table: there was one of a tall man with broad shoulders and thick, glossy hair. He read some cards that Eva had stuck to the wall above her desk. On one she'd written in large black letters 'You have nothing to lose but your expectations,' and on another, 'All suffering arises through desire.' If all else fails, thought Robert, I can become a Buddhist monk. Or a junkie, haunting the streets outside her house.

On top of the desk was a black lacquered Chinese box with a silver dragon on its lid. Robert peered inside. There was a vibrator (twice as big as his penis, white, plastic, three-speed) and KY Jelly, and a plastic shell-like box that he supposed contained some sort of contraceptive. There were tubes and sachets of spermicide cream, a wooden spatula and a little book on vaginal self-examination. The book was written by someone called Andrea Mitchell: he supposed it was the Andrea that lived in the house.

Eva came back in, and poured more tea.

'So you never got married,' he said.

'I quickly went off the idea. Some of the men I've met, God, I was lucky to get away from them. You, I remember you very fondly – you were always a bit different, not too presumptuous.' She smiled at him, and stroked his hand. With questionable logic, Robert did his best to give her an impressively unpresumptuous look.

'I believe much more in marriage now than I used to,' he said. 'I think it's essential to the wellbeing of children.' As he said the word 'children' he gave a blithe little smile.

'Pah,' said Eva, 'you'd better not go saying things like that round here. We believe in finding alternatives to the nuclear family.'

'Ah, Simone,' he said in a heavy French accent, 'do you remember ze fun we used to have in your room, that time when we spent a whole afternoon in bed pretending to be Sartre and de Beauvoir?'

She raised her head and smiled briefly, but didn't play.

Robert felt worried. It was stupid, this, anyway. He knew that the best form of communication was to stay in the Here and Now. The Here and Now was the smartest of psychological countries, the best of addresses. It was passé now to talk about the past. He winced at how often he used to present himself through little prepared speeches and anecdotes. The secret, he now realised, was to reveal yourself through what you did and felt in the present: to show rather than tell.

Robert looked round desperately for a here-and-now act of communication. The potted palm? The books? The cat? He was conscious of a rather unpleasant smell near him, and wasn't sure whether it was the cat's breath or his own.

Eva suddenly took hold of both his hands in a very here-and-now sort of way.

She said, 'Mmm, it's nice to see you,' and they had another hug. He savoured the smoothness of her hair and the peachy skin of her face. Full of nostalgia, he glanced down, and saw the soft curves of her breasts. Desire flooded in behind his look, like warm sea. From somewhere behind him Roy Orbison strummed the first chords of a very big love song indeed.

Let yourself go a bit more, she used to say, take a few risks.

With a seventh-wave surge of confidence, borne along by a sudden swell of dimly remembered data about the power of non-verbal communication and the way in which memories are powerfully anchored in senses such as taste and smell, and with some wild, Proustian hope that an armpit full of L'Homme deodorant casually brushed against her face might recreate the past, Robert put his lips against Eva's. Delicately, as if it was the daintiest of *pâtisseries*, he slid his tongue into her mouth. Barely a quarter of an inch past the stiffening rim of her lips he knew he'd made a mistake. In an ambiguous face-saving gesture, he ran his tongue along the inside of her teeth as if it were a dentist's finger doing a quick check. His tongue suddenly felt hot and enormous. It reversed out of her mouth in the manner of a car that has just broken another car's lights in a parking space.

'I'm sorry,' he said. 'Um – your teeth are very even, no problems at all.'

She didn't laugh.

'It's OK,' said Eva, 'but you must understand that anything sexual with you is completely out of the question right now.'

So much for the Here and Now, thought Robert. Was his hair that bad? Or his breath? Did his disappointing job show through? But he had to be honest, to acknowledge what she meant to him.

'I look back on my time with you as the happiest period of my life,' he said. 'I never believed I could be so happy.'

'I remember you very fondly,' she said, 'but I was so muddled back then. I was miserable a lot of the time. I remember crying a lot. I realise now that I was having a nervous breakdown.'

'You're joking!'

'No.'

'But we had some great times.'

'Yeah. Sometimes we did.'

'It was incredible how we never wanted to go out: all we wanted was each other's company.'

'Maybe. But I was also afraid of a lot of things back then. I hid from the world a lot. I needed to get pissed or stoned in order to enjoy myself.'

'I wish we'd got married. You said that I was the only person you could ever consider getting married to.'

'What! Did I really? Well maybe you had your chance and didn't take it. I've changed a lot since those days.'

He was silent. He remembered, with fear, a scene in *Nausea* where Anny said that Roquentin had gone through only intellectual changes, whereas she had changed down to 'the whites of her eyes'.

He looked at Eva and realised how much she had indeed changed. He could see it in the way her hair was cut, in such a high, confident arch over her ears; in the irony in her eyebrows and her mouth – the way her smile turned down at first, reflecting inwardly and privately, before, if he was lucky, it would turn upwards into a releasing, grinning smile. All this was different from what he remembered. Maybe he'd been lucky to have known her when he did.

But then she smiled and hugged him again.

'You were very special to me,' she said. 'I don't ever want to lose contact again.'

He felt warmed by her. Maybe he was exaggerating how different she was.

'Do you still have a thing about Sartre?' she said.

'I suppose so, though I haven't read much for years.'

'I read a biography,' said Eva. 'It was quite a shock. For example, his duplicity with women. All that stuff he gave de Beauvoir about essential and contingent loves while he was having passionate affairs with other women. Do you know he even proposed marriage to some American woman called Dolores? And had a special copy of the *Critique of Dialectical Reason* secretly printed with the dedication to his lover Wanda rather than de Beauvoir?'

'What surprised me,' said Robert, 'was that he proposed to de Beauvoir. When they were going to have to work hundreds of miles apart as teachers he suggested they got married so that they'd be given a job in the same town. He didn't make it into a big ideological deal.'

'Of course,' said Eva, 'Simone de Beauvoir now looks a more impressive figure than Sartre. The way she refused to accept a double sexual standard and didn't get married were revolutionary acts.'

'Mmm,' said Robert.

'It's crazy, looking back, that Sartre could lie like he did,' said Eva.

'But we're all human,' said Robert.

'And all that stuff about everyone being free – what a load of bullshit and ignoring of history and nature.'

'But he changed his views on that. He's got a right to change his views.'

Robert felt like he was supporting Sartre in the same way that he supported Spurs, as an act of commitment, for better or worse. He decided not to mention little things he'd discovered, and liked, about Sartre: how depressed Sartre had got at the prospect of going bald, for example; or how his mother used to iron his shirts when he was well into his forties.

'Whatever you say, you have to accept that Sartre and de Beauvoir's relationship has lasted,' said Robert. 'And there has been a lot of equality, honesty and love. It's remarkable.'

'But they've been more like best friends than lovers,' said Eva sharply.

'Why are we talking like this?' said Robert. 'I haven't heard any of your news.'

'Talking like this is my news,' said Eva.

'Everything I know about life, I have learnt from books.'

Eva and Robert began to meet once a week, for a few friendly, brightly-lit hours in the pub or at her home or occasionally the bedsit, which he'd tidy carefully and stress was temporary. He felt ever more attracted to her, ever more certain that this was the person he wanted to spend his life with. But Eva made it clear that, for the time being anyway, she was not interested in anything more than an undemanding friendship. And she also made it quite clear, on the not infrequent and rather serious occasions when he asked, that she did not want to go to bed with him. Robert was left to chew confusedly on his half-a-loaf relationship.

Gradually he heard accounts of the past years: of Eva's passionate, sometimes disastrous relationships; of the death of her father, a traumatic abortion, and psychotherapy sessions about her mother; of travels and turning points and the successful research and writing she was doing on women and spirituality.

He reciprocated as best he could, with news of the department he worked in, and how his mother and stepfather hadn't moved house. He worried that he didn't quite compare now, that he wasn't quite good enough, that he'd let down some view she might have carried of him. He felt that he didn't have the capacity to change and grow that Eva had, and therefore wasn't quite as human.

One day, a week before Easter, as they sat over a bottle of wine in her kitchen, she asked him what relationships he was in at the moment.

'Oh, just a casual one,' he said, 'by mutual consent. A woman called Deborah. An occasional nice time together.' The comment was carefully judged. He wanted to let her know that he was available but not desperate.

'And you?' he said. He tried to be unpresumptuous but his voice went up an octave as he spoke.

'Oh, there's a man called Pascal who I've been madly in love with. He's a French guy I met in Amsterdam when I was eighteen. I met him again and had a wonderful time, but now he's started to be bloody cool towards me.'

Oh shit, thought Robert, the *Being and Nothingness* man.

'Have you ever felt so obsessed with someone that it's like you're losing your mind?' said Eva.

She might as well nail his scrotum to the chair as use words like this, thought Robert.

'Well . . . er, yes . . . with you,' he said.

'Yes,' she said. 'I suppose you were, in your way. Though you didn't always show it. And I was once very much in love with you.'

Robert felt a small, silvery sense of hope.

'I've decided not to trust men as much,' said Eva, 'not to give as much of myself. I don't want to be as vulnerable and easily hurt as I've been in the past. I want to have a lot of relationships, as I want them, on my terms. But he's the one who keeps frustrating me, stirring up all the old problems that I'm trying to get away from. I'm trying to be less neurotic, less dependent.'

Ah, thought Robert, this explains a lot.

'Mmm, I understand,' he said, looking at her pale blue eyes and coal-black hair, and thinking, you're so fucking beautiful, I want you so badly, I want to make love with you, live with you, marry you, cherish you, love you for ever. If only I could work out how.

'You ought to read some Simone de Beauvoir or Germaine Greer,' said Eva. 'I'll lend them to you if you like. I'm going to be busy over Easter, so you might like to take them with you now.'

'Great,' said Robert, thinking, oh shit, I'm not going to see you for weeks, and feeling underneath this a deeper level of sadness because he was starting to deal in disguise and manipulation.

'Oh, and I'm getting quite close, sexually, I mean, to some women as well,' she said. 'Do you know how hard a man's body is? No wonder men are after women all the time. A woman's body is so soft and relaxed.'

Robert now felt not so much disappointed as disorientated. At some level, he knew he was absorbing data for a good bout of disappointment later on.

The cat slunk in, and nuzzled itself between her thighs. Robert thought he was taking on not just most of the men on the planet, but lots of the women, and a good many cats, too.

Good Friday was frustratingly bright, suggesting to Robert a hundred ways in which other people might be having a better weekend than he was. The sun shone with a pitiless light on the threadbare patch on the carpet. He hadn't slept well. There were no clean clothes, and there was a coffee stain on the duvet from a day when he'd felt too low to clear it up. A red bill leered at him from a brown envelope, and there was only one slice of bread left. The room had a temporary quality about it: it struck him as the room of someone who left each morning with the hope that he was about to jump into a new life somewhere else, and would be coming back only to pick up a few books and an extra jersey.

The room smelled slightly – well, if he was frank, more than slightly if one wasn't used to it – of cigarette ash and dirty socks and damp. The damp had been sufficient to produce a small crop of translucent mushrooms on the bathroom carpet, and a towel that, even in the hottest summer weather, never fully dried.

Robert was committed to spending the weekend reading Eva's books. He felt a sense of intimacy and excitement. The books were full of her underlinings and comments: surely they would help him understand how to reach her.

He decided to start with Simone de Beauvoir. It was quite a moment, entering the mind of Jean-Paul's girlfriend. *The Second Sex* was an enormous book, of *Das Kapital* proportions. It was incredible that it had been written in the 1940s. The voice, the sense of the person, was familiar. It was like Anny in *Nausea*: cool and intelligent, with an austere authority. And Simone was fantastically erudite: she seemed to have read everything, and swept Engels and Freud aside as if they were nobodies.

He turned to the section on 'The Woman in Love'. Eva had underlined a statement about the woman wanting to recreate with her lover 'the situation which she experienced as a little girl under adult protection'. She'd put an exclamation mark against another passage, which talked about how sexual 'abandon could become sacred ecstasy and union'. Robert hugged the soft flesh of his pillow. Yes, yes, yes, he thought. But then Eva had written 'NEVER AGAIN' in big letters against a phrase about a woman identifying her whole being with a man. Oh shit, thought Robert. He noticed the smell of damp in the room and the pile of dirty socks and pants in the corner. It wasn't, he felt sadly, a lot for Eva to identify the whole of her being with.

Robert didn't understand much of what he was reading and decided to go back to the beginning of the book. Simone talked about man having a mind which was free

but which had to live in the contingency of a body that rotted and died. Robert fingered his thinning temples, broke
voluminous Tandoori wind and knew what she meant.

In uniting with the woman 'man hoped to reach himself.' Spot on again: Simone was amazing. That was
exactly what it was about Eva when he'd known her
before. She had created within him a sense that his life
was attractive, free and exciting. And that was the problem with Deborah: the true self she saw in him was
dressed in St Michael's summer casuals and aspiring to be
something in management at Brent Cross.

When he woke up next morning, he decided to look at *The
Female Eunuch*. He lay on his back with the book above his
head, but quickly realised that it was not a book to
approach lying in bed naked in a prone position. He got
up, washed every nook and cranny, put on his cleanest pair
of underpants and did twenty press-ups. He momentarily
toyed with the idea of putting on a suit and tie.

The voice of the author was thrilling. He envied
Germaine's confidence and power and ever-present potential for a scathing comment or piece of irony. He had seen
her on TV, radical, beautiful and fearless. To his surprise,
he moved easily through chapters about chromosomes and
curves, and people's ridiculous stereotypes about bodies
and hair. He was enjoying the book, agreeing with it. He
even felt that he would have underlined exactly the same
passages Eva had underlined. He felt more optimistic, that
maybe the differences between him and Eva were rather
small misunderstandings. On the strength of this, he had
some toast and tea, and sponged the coffee stain on the
duvet. But then he was hit hard by reading about how men
used the word 'cunt' as their most loathsome swear
word. 'How true,' Eva had written. Robert was guilty, and
so were all his so-called radical friends. It was incredible
that he hadn't seen it before. Deep in his bowels he felt the

first contractions of a shift in his *Weltanschauung*.

It was a relief to move to Germaine's views about the danger of over-emphasising the clitoris at the expense of the vagina. In magnificent style, she bemoaned the loss of the skills of the Wife of Bath or the 'athletic sphincters of the Tahitian girls who could keep their men inside them all night'. Disappointingly, this section was devoid of any comments from Eva.

Robert briefly considered escaping into a sensual meditation on Tahitian girls, but every time he closed his eyes and put himself on an economy-class flight to Tahiti, Germaine was sitting imperiously in the aisle seat next to him.

He should have left *The Middle Class Myth of Love and Marriage* till the morning and had a good night's sleep first. He recognised it immediately as his own myth. What he'd taken for granted – romantic love and marriage – was laid bare as a particular ideology developed towards the end of the sixteenth century. Marriage was really all about patriarchy, private property and oppression. Eva had put a large tick against a section about the modern nuclear family being about the least successful way of living together ever invented. He stared at the tick, which flicked into him like a Stanley knife. He saw his mother and stepfather, the Genoa cakes and the spaniel farting and the five-times-a-night TV-watching. What kept them together, day after day, year after year, in that overheated room? And how crazy it was that his mother had never had a professional job, that this woman who'd flown planes in the war had then done domestic chores for the rest of her life.

Robert had a pain in his temples and his limbs were starting to ache. What was his *Middle Class Myth of Love and Marriage*? He forced himself to articulate it, enough of a Christian to believe in a bit of crucifixion on Good Friday. His myth had grown steadily over the years since

Eva left – that she was the one, his Miss Right. He dreamed that they'd have a white, sunlit, wedding, with Stephen as best man and a honeymoon in Ibiza. Then he'd carry her over the threshold, and spend his time making love and putting up shelves, followed by children and wonderful Christmases. Of course she could keep her name and still keep working. They would be blissfully happy.

He pushed himself harder. What sort of house? A semi? No, a terrace. Where? Hampstead? Highgate? Too expensive. It would have to be somewhere like Friern Barnet.

And then what? Germaine and Simone said that it might be all right for a year or two, but then it was all downhill. For Eva, life would be trips to the supermarket, endless telly, cleaning the house and resenting him. His mother would come over for a day and stay for weeks. There'd be increasing arguments, tranquillisers and sleeping-pills all round. She'd begin to undermine him socially, through flirting with friends or not laughing at his jokes. And all the while she'd be getting neurotically dependent on her children; and she'd be pleading with him not to go out with his mates, and inspecting his Y-fronts (so de Beauvoir said) for 'signs of his precious seed being spilled on neighbours'. She'd make ever-more destructive attacks on him, escaping through over-eating while he got drunk. She'd lose all her security and independence and reach for tranquillisers whenever little things went wrong, all the while hating him more and more, and making love less and less frequently using contraceptives that either poisoned her or killed all sensation or failed to stop her becoming pregnant. Then, if he was lucky, he'd have an early coronary, and that would be it. His married life.

Robert felt drained. Surely a life with Eva wouldn't be like that. Surely Germaine and Simone were exaggerating.

*

In contrast, Germaine painted an alternative picture of a wonderful place in Calabria where there were extended stem families. Even living in poverty, children weren't neurotic – they stayed up late, mixed with lots of people, and flowed in and out of each other's houses. Germaine talked about having children in a big house in southern Italy, where the kids might not even know who their natural womb-mothers were, and people would come and go in big happy communities. He could see Eva there, in simple flowing clothes, her eyes as pale as silver in the brilliant sunlight; he could see the vine-covered terrace for al fresco meals, the tagliatelli and Frascati. And he could see her talking with Germaine, doing a communal wash together when the mood took them and hanging out clothes on the line while they discussed feminist tactics and felt the sun on their brown, contented backs. They'd glance through the luminous air at the wine-dark sea in which they'd be swimming that afternoon, and maybe they'd talk about these interesting and rather beautiful men who would be coming to stay and with whom it might be amusing to have a loving but totally non-dependent relationship.

And where was he in this picture? He was the annoying obsessive in the C&A shorts, with the peeling skin and greasy Factor 15 sun cream, spying jealously from the back of the olive groves, paunchy and pale, entering into arguments about who she was seeing that evening and the mathematics of how much she meant to him.

He was in turmoil. He'd thought Eva's views on relationships were some sort of temporary posturing. But now he saw that her opinions were based on formidable arguments. There was no reason, at least intellectually, why love should be exclusive or result in marriage. There was, in fact, a lot to be said for women rejecting marriage and going non-nuclear. And it was pretty clear that Robert's dream of security with Eva came from the weakest parts of his personality.

The weekend had stolen up on him quietly and innocuously, and now it seemed to carry some momentous potential, to be quite possibly, in terms of what he believed and hoped for, the centre of his life.

That night he slept fitfully. There was a full moon and he shouldn't have had two cups of coffee.

He dreamed he went to a big mansion above steep rocks leading down to the sea. The mansion was full up and he was told he might find somewhere to sleep near the beach. It was dangerous climbing down the crumbling sandstone cliffs, but he managed to find his way to the sea's edge. There was a narrow jeep track along the sand at the base of the cliffs, just wide enough for one vehicle. At times the track went over dangerous rock ledges, which were washed over by waves. A group of happy Australians, led by Germaine, came and parked a beach buggy on the track and were laughing and fooling around by the sea. Germaine was hauntingly beautiful; Robert felt humble before her.

Then a smart Land Rover bumped along the track driven by a prim grumpy man who reminded Robert of his stepfather. He hooted his horn and tried to get the buggy to move out of the way. People just laughed. Germaine came up, very confident and tanned. They argued. The man said he knew a way through anyway. He reversed and branched off along what looked like a fork in the track but his route simply led into deep sand. He ended up stuck, the wheels spinning uselessly, his face grim and his knuckles clenched white with frustration. A middle-aged woman beside him was crying.

Robert half woke. He recognised the man behind the wheel. It was Jean-Paul Sartre. Germaine had wiped the floor with him. It didn't take much imagining. Sartre would only have come up to her chest, he was ageing rapidly and was poisoning himself with drugs, alcohol and tobacco. No one had taken him seriously since the early sixties: his Marxism was seen as too individualistic and personal, and he was being swept aside, like a tiring full-back, by Lacan, Foucault, Barthès and the rest. And he'd deceived Simone a hell of a lot. There must have been some period, even an exact date, when Simone de Beauvoir's fame and significance, as a result of books like *The Second Sex*, had started to overtake his own – maybe the debate he'd lost to Althusser.

Robert staggered out of bed and fetched his old copy of *Nausea*. He was relieved, as he skimmed through the book now, to see that Anny was still an impressive character in her way, intelligent and independent. But he saw with fresh eyes how Roquentin treated the *patronne* like shit, and banged on regularly about how disgusting women's flesh could be.

Sartre was different now, though, from the man who wrote *Nausea*: he'd changed his views. Robert felt a sense of deaths within him, of the old reader and the old writer. His chances with Eva suddenly seemed absurdly flimsy. He laid his head against the pillow and felt blood and nothingness pumping past his ears.

The next morning his temperature was over 100. His joints ached and his testicles felt as if they had been run over by Germaine's beach buggy. He read some Kate Millett, full of brilliant, researched anger, then slept. In the afternoon he watched *Grandstand* while the sun hurled mockingly brilliant light into the room. It was all the sports he didn't like – horse-racing, rugby league and swimming. And Tottenham lost. He ate a whole box of Mr Kipling's individual apple pies, and smoked his way through ten Embassy. A perfect wasted afternoon.

It was perhaps not the best time for Deborah to come round.

She'd had her hair dyed blonde and piled up, rather att-tractively, on the top of her head. As she sat in front of him, she kept holding out a strand of hair, glaring at it, then stabbing it back into place with a grip. She was wearing immaculately ironed designer jeans and had her full Max Factor face on.

'It's no way to spend a Bank Holiday, sitting here on your own moping,' said Deborah. 'We could be at the spring sales.'

'I don't want to go out, I'm busy reading,' said Robert. 'And I don't feel well.'

She offered to do his washing. He told her she had to stop propping men up, but she insisted on at least making him a hot drink and fetching his Night Nurse. Almost involuntarily, she started to rearrange his hair. It was a ges-ture that reminded him of his mother and he brushed her hand away.

'Look,' said Robert, 'I owe you an apology.'

Deborah's eyes gleamed like those of a labrador being asked to go for a walk.

'I've been reading about feminism.'

Deborah looked disappointed. Feminism for her was worthy but limited, a bit like an Oxfam shop. She might go there for the odd thing, like equal pay for equal work, but not for a whole set of beliefs.

'I've got to be honest with you,' said Robert. 'I'm not after a big dependent relationship. You must know that. I don't want to string you along. And I know I've misused the word "cunt" – I feel ashamed of that. I agree with Germaine that it's time the real cunt came into its own.'

Deborah smiled, kissed him and said it was OK.

He saw her counting the number of tissues in the box near his bed and realised that she might be anticipating making love. Surely she couldn't have interpreted what he'd said as some sort of sexual signal. He felt much too ill, tired and confused. He wanted to be on his own. He reached for the thermometer, and demonstrated that his temperature was over 100.

'The air in this room can't be doing you any good,' said Deborah. 'It's very stuffy and a bit smelly.'

She reached into a Tesco carrier bag, pulled out a large can of lemon-scented air freshener, and sprayed it at various corners of the room, slowly and rhythmically, like a Greek Orthodox priest using incense. Robert thought about how different women could be from one another, and felt a little comforted.

He asked Deborah to tell him about the spring sales. She became increasingly agitated, started looking at her watch, and finally sped off to get an hour in before Brent Cross closed.

Lulled by his Night Nurse, he dozed off and woke hours later, in darkness and drenched in perspiration. A shout and a thump came through the wall. Angry voices and curses. His next-door neighbour was making love. Without looking at his watch Robert knew it would be 10.30. With machine-like precision the man made love at exactly the same time each night. It always lasted for fifteen minutes. If his girlfriend wasn't there, he masturbated for exactly the same length of time. Robert had only seen him once, outside the house, lovingly retouching the bodywork of an old Cortina. They had grunted to each other, and Robert had noticed, chillingly, that the back of the man's hands were tattooed with the names of some of the worst Tamla Motown groups he'd ever heard.

Robert dragged himself back to *The Female Eunuch*. Women had to 'humanise the penis, take the steel out of it and make it flesh again'. A bed thumped against the wall next door, accompanied by a single deep 'aaaargh' sound, like a man being stabbed in a film. His neighbour was having his climax. There were shouts from a pub spilling out into a nearby street, then jeers and a woman screaming. All over the world men were busy hating and oppressing women. Robert felt ashamed.

He looked at his penis with a forlorn nostalgia. It seemed it now belonged, rightly, to women; or was at least like an occupied piece of land, a Gaza strip that had to be supervised and patrolled by a neutral power. He had once seen it in highly technical terms, able to name every part – the glans, the coronal sulcus, the corpora cavernosa and the rest. It had once seemed to carry his main, ontological hopes, to be the vehicle for discovering the magical world of the Beyond, of Heidegger and Husserl and Kierkegaard.

And after Eva, and other experiences, he had seen it as experienced, postgraduate, highly and well commended. Occasionally it was even a cock or a phallus. But now it was being enlisted as a loyal member of the feminist movement. It was being renamed that night; it was like a ship being registered under a different flag. It would now be given a female-determined name. It would be a 'willy', unalterably a willy. 'Willy' was a term much softer, more ironic and possibly eunuch-like, than penetrative words like cock or tool or prick. You wouldn't have found Clint Eastwood or Mellors or Mailer or the man next door having a willy, no chance. A willy was a nice, reasonable career penis, a safe, suburban, nine-to-five organ, conciliatory, and self-deprecating, probably voting liberal or Fabian-type Labour. Most importantly, a willy was incapable of assault or offence. But would a willy transport to delight, would it deal in bliss, would it get women gasping with ecstasy or wobbling exhausted across a room to put 'The First Time Ever I Saw Your Face' on the stereo? And would a mere willy satisfy someone as bold and liberated as Germaine Greer?

By Easter Monday his temperature was 103 degrees, Eva had not rung and he wished he was a woman. Or at least, he wished he could be part of some great historical process, that he could be a member of an oppressed group struggling for liberation. He hadn't ended up with a machine-gun in South Africa or Chile. He belonged to an English southern middle class that had about as much common identity as a box of toilet rolls.

What would it involve to become a woman? How much would it cost? Could you do it on the NHS? Being a woman was where it was at – consciousness-raising groups, building networks and communities, honing self-defence skills at karate classes, experimenting with childcare, going to therapy, starting publishing ventures, organising consumer boycotts, and celebrating each other's growing autonomy and independence. Germaine even recommended the best and cheapest perfume. You were in the business of radical personal change. There was a sense that what you were doing had universal political significance. The men of East Finchley and Tufnell Park had nothing as remotely satisfying as that.

The book ended with a question: 'What will you do?' Robert pondered for a while, then decided.

The next morning, at 8.15, he went to the doctor's.

It was a considerable effort. A whole taken-for-granted future had trundled down the slipway and sunk into the sea. It was hard to raise the energy to get out of bed, let alone to the doctor's.

He had a high fever and a temperature. Through Dr Wilde's thick pipe smoke Robert was agitated enough to say that he believed his symptoms were not merely due to 'flu but also to some combination of excitement, tension and loss, brought on by Eva and by spending the weekend in bed with Germaine Greer, Kate Millett and Simone de Beauvoir. He muttered to the doctor that if ever there was a time in his life when he'd benefit from psychotherapy, it was now. He felt ready for profound personal change.

Dr Wilde stared at Robert, sucked deeply on his pipe,

and blasted out clouds of grey smoke. For a moment Robert thought the doctor was going to say, 'For God's sake, pull yourself together, man.' But then he grunted a few inaudible words and scribbled out a prescription for thirty tranquillisers.

'Existence precedes essence.'

'They were fantastic books,' said Robert. 'I feel radically changed by them.' He was sitting next to Eva on a rickety bench outside a pub in Highgate.

'Oh yeah?' said Eva, raising her eyebrows.

But he did feel changed. He felt sadder but more his own person, perhaps in the way someone felt when they became an atheist or agnostic. And the way he looked at Eva felt different. He was calm as looked at her pale blue eyes and beautiful, intelligent face. His look wasn't flung towards her quite so desperately. It stayed connected to him, almost affectionately.

'I've really accepted something now, about how important it is to respect your independence,' said Robert. 'I'm lucky to simply have you as a good friend.' After reading Germaine and visiting Dr Wilde, he had eventually decided that life didn't have to be catastrophic because he wasn't having a passionate love affair with Eva. He drank his red wine with a feeling of lightness, of celebration even.

'You do seem happier and more relaxed tonight,' she said, and gave him a tender smile. Unusually, she was wearing a dress, black corduroy, almost as dark as her hair. Her bare legs were crossed, rather attractively, a few inches away from his hand. Robert remembered, slightly uneasily, that he'd taken two tranquillisers that afternoon. Was it the tablets, or had he really changed? Did it really matter which?

They strolled across Hampstead Heath under a brown and orange sky. Eva had to be home in time for a house meeting.

'Tell me what you got from the books,' she said.

'I found Simone de Beauvoir puzzling, but very moving. She talked about how we seek to get away from the nothingness we feel inside ourselves by loving another person, how we idealise them because we want them to be a denial that life is risky and contingent and ends in death.'

Eva put her arm round his waist. They walked along on the dark, soft grass, bumping slightly awkwardly against each other's hips.

'It's funny what different people get from the same book,' she said. 'What did you think of Germaine Greer?'

'She gave me massive insights into myths about love, and the extent to which men oppress women.'

Eva let go of his waist and laughed.

'You were a bit sexist, as I remember,' she said.

'No. How do you mean?'

'Well, you did a lot of talking and I was expected to listen. But you always felt free to interrupt me.'

'That's not true. You talked for hours about your mother.'

'Well, at least I was being open. You never showed any vulnerability. You were always a bit embarrassed if I got upset or angry.'

'I'm different now.'

'And I cooked all the meals, and when we went to your mother's you let her do all the work,' she said.

'That's true.'

'And I'm sure I propped up your ego quite a lot.'

This felt more serious. He scanned through his memories of Eva in a new way, almost like a defence lawyer. 'How?' said Robert. They were nearly at her street.

'I probably faked a few orgasms,' said Eva. 'Or was that with someone else?' Her voice was teasing now.

'You said you had your first decent orgasm with me.' He meant to say it lightheartedly, but he sounded like a fastidious record keeper out to win an argument.

'You're kidding,' said Eva.

'No, I'm right,' said Robert. They were now scything their way to her front door through the grass that grew by itself.

'I remember a lot of wonderful times we had,' said Robert.

'We did have some good times,' said Eva, 'but I think sometimes I used to play a role, willing it all to be intense and romantic.'

Andrea was in the kitchen, with dark rings under her eyes, sighing heavily and talking about the difficulties of being a writer and managing childcare. Robert felt instantly guilty. Thankfully Andrea left, saying she'd see Eva at the house meeting in an hour's time.

Eva pulled a bottle of white wine out of the fridge. She made a face towards the door that Andrea had just passed through.

'My independence is important, you know,' she said to Robert. 'It niggles me that I spend so much time thinking about this bloody man Pascal.'

Robert tested his new non-neuroticism, and found it was working. He listened as she described a night when she and Pascal had shared a sleeping bag under the stars in Greece. She said how she now wanted to control her body rather than be engulfed by it.

Robert felt suddenly happy. His sense of himself was lighter. Something had indeed changed since he'd read

Germaine. He accepted that an ordinary friendship with Eva could in its way be fun. He was determined to respect her need for space and independence. Feeling rather mature and democratic, he got up and said he was going to go home.

She walked towards the fridge with the bottle of wine.

He bent his arm behind him to scratch his back. As she passed him she held up his shirt and rolled the chilled bottle across his hot itchy skin.

'You can sleep with me if you want,' she said.

He didn't quite understand her the first time, and she had to repeat herself.

'The hero lived all of the details of that night like annunciations.'

Looking back, it was not so much sexual intercourse he had with Eva that night as an ideological struggle of great complexity. Towards the end it might have appeared that in the right-hand corner of the bed, representing Finchley and the Middle Class Myth of Love and Marriage, was Robert, and in the left-hand corner, representing Calabria, independence and spontaneous association, was Eva. But earlier on that would have been much too simple, and indeed Robert started out determined to make the evening a triumph of Greerian sex: passionate, unpossessive and signifying nothing. He felt deeply indebted to Germaine. If it wasn't for her, he would never have had this sudden opportunity, the chance to look at Eva's room from the longed-for perspective of the high black bed.

'Well, come on then,' said Eva, pulling her black corduroy dress up over her head.

She knelt on the bed. He'd forgotten how attractive her back was. And her breasts looked younger than her face, and more innocent, the nipples small and pre-maternal, delicately pale, the skin as white and smooth as Italian ice-cream.

'Christ,' said Germaine, 'after all I've done for you, you start going on about bloody ice-cream. Stop looking at women as something to be eaten, as ripe melons and red cherries, honey, sugar, peaches and cream, all that stuff.'

Robert felt chastened. He tried to walk towards the bed in a way that was graceful and emotionally independent, Calabrian rather than English. This was easier said than done, and he scraped his shin on the underside of the metal bedframe.

He leaned his face towards Eva's, keeping his body away so that just the surfaces of their lips were touching. Her lips felt cool and aware, like outer sensors of her brain rather than something more sexual. He was conscious of her blue eyes, open, watching him, and felt a change in the shape of her lips against his, a slight, ironic smile maybe. What did all this mean? Why had she suddenly invited him, and what part of her had made the invitation? The social worker who felt sorry for him? The cool feminist, out to prove a hypothesis? The buried romantic? The seductress? She put her arms round him and squeezed him. Fool. He shouldn't be so cynical.

He tried to remember the things she used to like. He stroked the nape of her neck, and caressed her back, which felt soft and relaxed, less guarded or political than he'd expected. When he ran a fingertip along her leg he was surprised by the hair that now grew there: it was funny how fashions, or maybe deeper beliefs, changed. Slowly and lovingly he started to traverse her body with kisses, savouring the warm, slightly salty taste of her skin.

'Robert, I've got a meeting in half an hour so I can't be too long. Why don't we just get down to it.'

Now this was different. A point being made. So practical. They used to spend all weekend making love. It was central to her being. So was this what he was being offered. An object lesson in independent sex, a proof that they could have it without getting bogged down in emotional dependencics and irrational obligations. But then she touched his new willy in a wonderfully getting-down-to-it sort of way, and he decided that maybe things weren't so bad after all.

'I'm going to get my diagram,' she said.

Robert heard this with some amazement. What was she going to do? Was she going to sellotape some map or set of technical instructions – something like a flight-control plan – to her stomach, specifying exactly what he should do? How out of touch he was, how old-fashioned.

'Di-a-phra-gm,' she said slowly: she must have seen his confusion.

She tiptoed across to the mantelpiece. She was beautiful when she moved, graceful and unselfconscious, her body slender and strong, like a dancer's. She brought the lacquered Chinese box back to the bed.

'Actually, I may be able to get away with not using my diaphragm,' she said. 'Screwing is more enjoyable without it.'

She pulled out a small book.

'You take a sample of vaginal fluids,' said Eva. 'Andrea's got some charts in her book: you're looking for colour, texture, smell and so on, to assess the risks of conception.'

She slid her finger across her crotch and raised it to her nose. Then she flicked on a powerful table lamp and held the finger up for inspection.

'Interesting, isn't it?' she said.

Robert had a mild scientific curiosity. He suggested that it was the sort of situation that would probably have felt better if he'd had a certificate in gynaecology and been wearing a white coat. But there was something erotic, too, about her lack of inhibition as she stood there, her cool clinical or cynical style. That labial landscape had once been as familiar to him as a favourite holiday destination, as the harbour at Arenal or the feel of the hot sand at Torremolinos. Soon, soon, he would be touching, caressing it.

He knelt like a supplicant and started to kiss the top of her thighs, but she said this was all a bit intimate for how she felt right now. She decided that they needed to use the diaphragm after all, and suggested that Robert, as a man, should take an interest and learn how to do it.

His hands were soon covered in thick, white spermicide cream. The diaphragm kept popping out. Georgie the cat watched him contemptuously. Robert said that he felt like a contestant having a particularly humiliating time on a Bruce Forsyth game show. Eva laughed and, rather slickly, put the cap in herself.

There was a crisp triple knock at the door. Robert propelled himself backwards out of Eva and across the bed. As always, he half expected it to be his mother.

Andrea's frown appeared round the door, closely followed by the rest of her. She glared at Robert, and raised her eyebrows at Eva. Robert pulled the bed clothes up around his neck, and crossed his legs tightly. 'Avoid loud and aggressive persons, for they are vexatious to the spirit.' It was on Deborah's Desiderata poster.

'I'm sorry to interrupt,' said Andrea in a piping unapologetic voice, 'but I wanted a few words before the meeting. I'm really worried about Clytemnestra. It's the second night running that she's been staring at Tom's willy and saying she wants to have one. Someone's obviously been influencing her.' She rubbed her eyelids, sighed, gave Eva the merest token of a sisterly smile, and trudged out.

Eva put on her red silk dressing gown.

'I'd better go and have a word,' she said.

'But we were just starting to have a good time,' said Robert.

'I'm sorry, but this is serious,' said Eva.

You bugger, thought Robert. If going to see Andrea was

serious, what did that imply about he and Eva being in bed together? He had a quick consultation with Germaine. She told him to calm down. He needed to show Eva that he could make love in a way that didn't threaten her with a cartload of emotional demands.

When Eva came back, she said that Tom was now asking why he hadn't got a clitoris.

'We still have nineteen minutes,' said Robert. He tried not to sound bitter.

A sound came from upstairs, a steady hum, like the sound of a small electricity sub-station: Andrea was using her vibrator. What with this and her Teasmade, she seemed to be moving very close to self-sufficiency.

'Rub against me,' said Eva.

He did as he was told. After a while she began to breathe more noisily. Then there was a moaning sound quickly stifled. He had a brief glimpse of a different person, of the person he remembered calling out, clinging to him, crying for him. He adjusted position and rhythm and alignment, listening to her breath, searching for an angle, a plane, a surface of friction, a word or gesture that would reach her, that would be therapeutic, magical, transfiguring.

All of a sudden, she climbed on top of him. Well, blow me down, thought Robert, people could indeed change. Germaine was right. Eva looked at him for a second in a way that was happy, erotic, unadorned. He felt the bliss of being an object of desire for this person he loved.

And then, suddenly, he was on the ski-jump ramp that led to orgasm, struggling not to slide. Oh, shit.

This was normally the moment to throw everything into reverse, the moment, Robert now realised, which explained why countless generations of men had invented an ideology that denied women's sexuality. It was the Calvinistic moment when, just when you really wanted to let go and enjoy yourself, you had to work hard to stop enjoying yourself. It was the moment when Robert normally summoned his orgasm manager, with his glasses, Austin Reed suit and brief case. The orgasm manager would busily identify some suitable sexual depressants – the picture of Engels, maybe, with its quote about marriage and the domestic slavery of women, or rapid calculations about Robert's risk of lung cancer, or, best of all, Auntie Janet unrolling her pressure stockings and insisting on him kissing her verruca.

Robert paused. The orgasm manager awaited instructions.

'Don't stop,' Eva said in a fierce throaty voice. 'For God's sake let's not stop.' He had a momentary, haunting sense that she spoke not to him, but to some other lover.

They rolled over. Her warm fingers were on his back and pulling him in closer. She was gasping and crying out. He decided to abandon himself to romance, to the wild seas of the Here and Now, to unite, whatever the risks, with his own desire.

A high-pitched voice started groaning, 'Oh my sweet baby, my sweet darling, I love you so much, I've missed you so badly, oh my sweet baby.'

Robert realised with horror that the voice was his. He was having a kind of leakage of interior monologue, a premature ejaculation of words.

Eva giggled. Germaine had given up and was covering her eyes in horror.

'Robert,' said Eva, 'what's going on inside your head? You sound like Diana Ross.'

He carried on making love. But she had stopped moving. He felt a slight push of her chest against his.

'You're a little bit heavy,' she said, and kissed his shoulder.

'That was really nice,' she said. Past tense, he thought.

'What? Have you come?'

He said it with the air of someone who was ringing up

the local sorting office to see when a precious parcel was going to be delivered, and was being told it was already on his back doorstep.

'Yeah. A while ago. It was nice, though, still feeling you inside me.'

Well, that's one of her orgasms out of the way, thought Robert. If you believed Masters and Johnston there were only twenty-nine more to go.

'It was wonderful,' he said.

She suddenly sprang up and sat on the side of the bed. Robert had been looking forward to a long hug. How much Eva had changed. Clearly Simone didn't get it right all the time. She'd written in *The Second Sex* about how distressing the separation of bodies was for women as they lay 'in their position of defeat'. It might have been true for her and Jean-Paul, but not for the whole world.

'Do you want me to toss you off?' asked Eva, looking at her watch. 'I'm sorry, but I've got to go to the house meeting in a few minutes.'

She was bluffing him, surely. She was making a point. They didn't have to be that precise about meetings: they often sat around at the start making cups of tea and chatting.

'Um, no,' said Robert. 'I'm not into having it every time. I'm happy with the lovely time I've had, and don't feel some phallocentric orgasmic imperative.' He wasn't absolutely sure what this meant, but it sounded sufficiently like the title of one of Andrea's articles for him to feel on safe ground. He felt pulled into bluff and counter-bluff, rather than whatever else, possibly love, had been going on between them.

Eva laughed.

'That was really nice,' she said.

'It was blissful, magnificent,' said Robert.

'It was a nice little fuck,' said Eva, 'with someone who is an old and very special friend, whom I do still feel a lot for.

Now don't you start getting possessive about me or my body just 'cos we've had a nice little fuck.'

She leaned over and kissed him, warmly, he thought. His first experiment in how to get Eva to love him had been, at best, a partial success. But he could build on this and move forwards. He felt absolutely determined to marry her.

She padded across to the door, opened it, then turned back towards him.

'If you felt really heroic,' she said, with a teasing little smile, 'you could empty Georgie's shit box.'

'In each privileged situation, there are certain actions which have to be performed, certain attitudes which have to be assumed, certain words which have to be said.'

From that night on, despite all his good intentions, Robert was madly in love with Eva. He thought about her all the time. He spent hours daydreaming about the way her dimples showed when she smiled or how her blue eyes clouded over as she became aroused. A surprise phone call would leave him high for days. A cancelled meeting would empty him. His was the simplest of psychologies, the most obvious of causations. She was in his life like a heatwave, affecting everything.

But Eva's view of their relationship remained the same. Robert, for the time being at least, was simply one of a network of close friends with whom she had intimate but totally non-dependent relationships. She seemed content to carry on meeting once a week or so, for a meal or a drink, and sometimes to follow this with an hour in bed and occasionally to have him stay for the night. There seemed no cumulative effect to these meetings. Their relationship began afresh each time: that was as much as she offered. He had to keep his dreams secret, his fantasies about weddings and children and happiness. It was simply not the done thing, emotionally or politically, to want a person in this way.

Like a rat in one of Marshall's experiments, his desire for Eva was subject to the most powerful of behavioural influences, intermittent reinforcement. Eva was unpredictable. She might be pleased to see him or she might not. She might end up falling in love with him again, or she might not. Loving Eva was a foolish, addictive religion.

Robert knew he had reached a stage in his life where a few bourgeois certainties would not go amiss: a house, promotion – above all, Eva. Increasingly, like the despised middle class in *Nausea*, he, Robert, didn't want to die 'unwed, childless or intestate'. Wanting things like marriage and career success was reinforced by news of Stephen. Stephen was getting married to Fiona: indeed, Robert was invited to be best man. Stephen had a detached house now, bought partly with a slightly embarrassing inheritance from a rich relative. He had a study with floor-to-ceiling bookshelves on which rested copies of his own *Sunday Times*-reviewed book on trade union history. And he was a university lecturer. Stephen sailed into his future like a boat through easy water.

But Robert's future felt more uncertain. His main uncertainty, about what would happen with Eva, was compounded by anxiety about his work. The grant had nearly run out on the electricity project. He'd never believed in it anyway, which only made things worse. He was getting to work late, he didn't care, and no one appeared to notice. Setting the alarm clock each night seemed increasingly pointless. He woke up shapeless, the parts of him, limbs and thoughts and plans for the day, felt like objects floating weightlessly in space. Nothing seemed to hold him and his actions in place any more. Nothing except Eva.

'Change often feels like that,' said Eva, when he explained how he felt one day. 'You have to find security inside yourself, you can't just look to me.'

Part of him believed that she was experimenting with Germaine's world, role-playing it, and that, deep down, the old Eva was still there. He had, for example, high hopes that going together to Stephen's wedding might alter the views she now held on love and marriage. But he acknowledged, too, that it might be possible to change himself, to become the sort of unpossessive spontaneous person that Eva wanted him to be. Eva and Germaine and Andrea believed in a certain sort of freedom, that people possessed the capacity to refute aspects of how they'd been so far and begin again. Existence preceded essence. Even a man like Robert, working steadily through his second bottle of tranquillisers, might be capable of change.

It was clear to Robert that one prerequisite for getting closer to Eva was to be respected by the women in her house. The house summed up her hopes for a life beyond the oppression that families and men had caused her. If he didn't meet with her friends' approval, then he wasn't even on square one of the relationship.

There was a lot that Robert admired about Andrea and the other women in the house. They were unsentimental, tough-minded, independent; they didn't smile at men unless they meant it, and they didn't drape themselves in cheap sexual signals. They sometimes smelled of sweat, only burst into tears for very good reasons, and always knew the score.

When it came to dealings with Eva's household, there was a word which Robert knew he had to keep in the very front of his mind: the word 'alternative'. 'Alternative' was a magical, legitimising word that flew above their lives like a banner. It implied superior insight, integrity and ideological position. It could be applied to any area of life – to newspapers and theatre, to printers and food shops, to places to go in cities, to medicine and politics and relationships and childbirth. And if he was to get anywhere with Eva, 'alternative' was a label that he needed now, like a *Good Housekeeping* seal of approval, to be firmly applied to him.

The eight people in Eva's house were dedicated in particular to finding an alternative to the traditional family. Children, of whom there were currently two, both Andrea's, were to be brought up communally, able to rely on any adult in the house for support, learning right from the start to trust in structures beyond patriarchy and the nuclear family.

Because Andrea was finishing her novel, much of the structure beyond patriarchy was in practice supplied by Nick. He spent early mornings and most evenings looking after Tom and Clytemnestra. Tom didn't fully understand the attempt to move beyond the nuclear family and spent a lot of time wandering about with a bottle in his mouth asking where his mummy was.

Nick was also allowed to contribute to the house much of the income from his rather ideologically suspect job as a town planner. As Robert was a regular visitor it seemed only fair for him, too, to put some money into the kitty. And he started to help with the childcare. In time he grew to enjoy the kids' company, their friendliness and the games they played, which were so much more inventive than anything he could remember as a child.

One day, it was suggested by Andrea that Robert's name should go up on the cleaning rota, and that he ought to take a turn at cooking a communal meal. He accepted these opportunities gladly.

It was hard to explain the concept of 'alternative' to Deborah. She and Robert met one day for an early-evening half-pounder and relish, and then went back to Robert's bedsit for a coffee. Deborah soon made it clear that she wanted to talk about US.

'Fiona told me you're going to be Stephen's best man. I was wondering whether we were going to go to the wedding together – it's about time I knew where I stood.'

Robert was silent. She sat on the carpet, between him and the door, pink and expectant. He felt trapped in his own untidy room. 'I want to know where I stand,' she said again.

Her eyes looked different, dark and glistening, almost soulful. Robert thought gloomily that even Deborah was capable of personal growth and change. But then, to his relief, he realised that she looked like this because she was wearing her new tinted contact lenses.

'I'm in another relationship,' said Robert. He hadn't slept with Deborah since meeting Eva again.

'But you're not giving US a chance. I sometimes think that I'm just some sort of insurance.'

Maybe she was right. Perhaps she was there like the Norwich Union, just in case the alternative future with Eva didn't work out, just in case his mother had been right all along.

Robert hated the inequality in power, the sense that she wanted him more than he wanted her. It made him feel attractive and independent in a useless, contorted way. He was struck by the uncomfortable parallels with Eva's relationship with him.

'The most we could have would be a very casual friendship. We must be careful about establishing dependencies. In any case, love and marriage is a middle-class myth, bolstering up patriarchy.'

'I don't believe you. You don't sound at all convincing. You're kidding yourself,' she said. 'You're not that far short of thirty. Who are you going to meet who really wants to settle down with you. If you don't watch out, you're going to get left on the shelf.'

'What nonsense! What shelf?' said Robert, trying to suppress an image of 151,329 surplus men filling Wembley and White Hart Lane. Nearly all of them were bald.

'I'm not going to hang around,' she said. 'I'll dump you and settle for someone else. There's a man in my office who's asking me out. He's an assistant buyer.'

Deborah took out a small mirror and reapplied some

lipstick. There were, thought Robert, several things he rather liked about Deborah: her total lack of introspection, her en-suite vision of the future, her shopper's sense of practicality and getting on with life; and the way she dressed, the red mini and shiny high heels.

She brushed back the hair on his neck in a way that felt like she was looking for his St Michael label. He thought at times that he'd been chosen as a good bargain: that she might say to her friends, 'I found him on the shelf in the sale – he's polite, middle-class and completely harmless.'

'You can't look after yourself,' she said. 'You live on baked beans and can't even organise clean clothes for yourself.'

Robert began to reply but was interrupted by a confident knock at the front door. He inched it open, and there, oh God, was Andrea.

'I was passing this way,' said Andrea, 'and Eva asked me to drop in the kitty money for the meal you're cooking. I've also brought the wholefood book that we usually cook from.'

Andrea stood on the doorstep looking into the house with a mixture of curiosity and distaste, like a journalist researching an article on some unpleasant social problem. To his horror she accepted his mumbled invitation to come in.

Robert led the way into his room, the whole house suddenly feeling like a giant pair of dirty underpants. Why did the only *Daily Telegraph* he'd bought in the past month have to be lying on the stairs? And why did she have to call round when Deborah was there?

Deborah stood in his small kitchen, his little Miss Selfridge with her full face on. If his fairy godmother had appeared at this moment, Robert would have wished, with all his being, that Deborah be turned, in a puff of smoke, into a black bisexual intellectual.

He introduced them and set about making coffee. Andrea commented quickly on Deborah's high heels.

'Those shoes look very pretty . . .'

Deborah smiled, not realising that 'pretty' was one of the most pejorative terms in Andrea's feminist lexicon.

'. . . but high heels are very uncomfortable and bad for your feet. I mean, who on earth are you wearing them for?'

Deborah looked a little confused. For God's sake, thought Robert, I'll die if you say you're wearing them for me.

'My boss likes secretaries to be smartly dressed,' said Deborah, 'and I enjoy wearing them anyway.'

Robert breathed a sigh of relief. He stirred the Nescafé more calmly.

'And Robert likes them too, I think.'

His hand started trembling. He knocked over a bottle of milk. Deborah rushed to the sink for a cloth, but Robert, with a dramatic hop, step and jump, got there first. Then Deborah dropped a contact lens and as Robert knelt stiffly down to join the search, Andrea made an excuse and was gone.

Preparing a communal meal provided an opportunity for Robert to demonstrate to Eva and her friends something new about who he was; that beyond conventional appearances, there was a capable, alternative person. Cooking raised a number of challenges. The meal had to consist of wholefood from the most politically acceptable countries; it had to be cheap, ideally costing only a handful of coins from the kitty; and it had to be cooked and served without fuss, particularly if you were a man.

And so, whilst it was therapeutic for Robert to fantasise about serving them a Kentucky fried chicken with Chilean red wine, he knew what he had to do, and conscientiously worked his way through the Kentish Town Wholefood Shop *Alternative Food Book*. He was planning to cook a meal of perfect ideological purity yet subtle individuality.

He went round Safeway with extreme care. He avoided

all food which had any possibility of being phallic-shaped, and kept a careful eye out for Cape Produce signs. He rejected anything which said ambiguously that it was a product of more than one country or from the 'sunny countries of the world'. He stared long and hard at the Rioja wine. What was the position of Spain these days? Just what sort of progress had it made towards full parliamentary democracy? The pièce de résistance was to be his Tanzanian coffee, bought from a non-exploitative co-operative with which Andrea was involved.

He queued at the check-out behind two women with sad, bowed bodies, and next to a stack of romantic novels which seemed quite brave in their way, like flags for a different, more idealised, or idealistic, world.

He glanced up and saw his next-door neighbour coming down the aisle with his trolley. He wore a black weightlifter's vest and strutted along with his chest puffed out and every muscle tensed, aiming, it seemed to Robert, to keep the whole of his body in a state of permanent erection.

His neighbour stood at the express check-out a foot away from Robert's queue. They couldn't avoid acknowledging each other. Robert said hi and gave his name in a deeper voice than he'd normally have used. The other man grunted that his name was Ron. Robert noticed the tattooed hands, the spiders and Motown bands. On most of his fingers, Ron was wearing gold sovereigns which looked like the shields of some miniature mediaeval army.

'Can't find any Wonderloaf,' said Ron. 'There's no decent bread these days, it's all this bloody food for lefties and queers.'

Robert nodded ashamedly and tried to hide his trolley from Ron's line of vision. He glanced into Ron's basket. It was full of metal and flesh. His pack of six stainless-steel beer cans looked liked the cylinders of a car engine, and next to them was a huge tray of pink and white mince, like smoothed vomit, and a dark red rump steak. In contrast, Robert's basket was filled with mounds of fruit and vegetables, in russets, yellows, and greens, as if composed for a still-life painting. Everything looked round and vulnerable and easily squashed. And Ron had hard St Izal toilet paper to Robert's soft Andrex.

Then Robert noticed a packet of Morning Coffee biscuits at the back of Ron's basket, and felt a ridiculous sense of hope that his neighbour stopped each morning to nibble a biscuit and read Jane Austen.

'The tart's away this weekend,' said Ron. 'Got to shop for me fucking self.' He paid, muscled through a swing door and was gone.

Robert felt troubled. Here he was, at twenty-eight years old, worrying about what was in his supermarket trolley. What did it matter? Why did it bother him? What would it take to finally think for himself?

The kitchen at Eva's house was a large L-shaped room with bare floorboards and a pine refectory table. All the breakfast debris was still there, congealing muesli dried as hard as concrete on the edge of the cereal bowls, a small lake of spilled milk, a half-drunk mug of pink tea. Whose turn had it been to clear up? He looked at the rota board. There was a note clipped on to it. 'Robert, Sorry. No time to clear up. Meeting on book. And migraine. Luv, Andrea.'

With a sense of valuable credit being earned, Robert tidied up the mess. Then he measured out brown rice from a large sweet jar that stood with a dozen others on a wooden shelf which ran the length of the wall. He laid out his vegetables and fruit. His individualistic touch was to be his curry sauce, no mere paste from a jar, but his own, made from a dozen fresh spices and herbs. He felt a moment of pride that he doubted Ron would feel as he hurled his steak into the blackened Trex of his pan. Robert's meal would be cheap, ideologically sound, and yet expressive. It would sit inside people with a solid but lively presence, and an interesting array of after tastes. As their stomachs and bowels bubbled and tweaked into the night, but never catastrophically, they would know he'd been there.

Eva sat three people away from Robert at the meal, next to Terry, a woman with a shaven bullet head and huge tartan shirt. Terry was trying, for ideological reasons, to give up men in the way other people gave up smoking. She hadn't yet succeeded, and her latest bloke, a motor mechanic in a donkey jacket, sat next to her.

Andrea came in. Her face looked pinched and she had dark rings under her eyes. She smiled weakly at Robert: she had a weak smile like some people had a bad back. She glanced at the carefully selected CND and Male Curfew badges on his jacket, then put her arm round him and gave him a little kiss. She thanked him for clearing up.

Robert heaved up the old metal saucepan containing the spitting lentil sauce and laid it in the centre of the table.

'Put a mat under it, for Christ's sake!' yelled Terry. Robert felt a small electrical jolt inside his bladder. He brought over a casserole dish full of his curry, with splendid colour contrasts provided by red, yellow and green peppers. He'd got little bowls of Greek yoghurt and plates of pitta bread. He suddenly worried that it all looked too twee and indulgent, like a typical once-in-a-blue-moon man's meal. Nick nodded appreciatively and went 'Mmm, mmm, mmm,' but Robert was increasingly aware that Nick did this all the time – he could hear him doing it even when he was on his own, as if he were permanently trying to appease some invisible person.

Eva looked particularly cool and contained. She raised her eyebrows and gave Robert a quick semi-private smile, but he sensed slivers of judgement, little questions about what he was up to, of caution at him moving further into her house and its mealtimes and conversations. At times like this she felt heartbreakingly distant, connected to him by just a few thin strands of irony and the occasional glance.

They began to eat.

Terry's new man sat opposite Robert, spitting out fragments of brown rice as he spoke and regularly slapping Terry's thigh. Robert could only wonder at the motives that led her to this choice in men. Perhaps it was a type of aversion therapy.

Terry began to pick through her curry, minutely inspecting it and dissecting it for evidence of culinary or ideological flaws. She grunted and said it was not bad.

'You shouldn't use baby sweetcorns, though. It's a terrible waste, growing them to that size and then picking them. And they often come from Thailand, which is shocking in its exploitation of women.'

Robert blushed. Then Andrea cleared her throat. Everyone stopped talking and looked at her, aware that she stood at the top of the house's hierarchy, which was as elaborate and uncriticisable as a wedding cake.

'It's lovely, Robert,' said Andrea.

People relaxed a little after that, or rather the power people did. They relaxed enough, God forbid, to have a conversation. This was the most uncharted and dangerous part of the evening. Clytemnestra's father, a thin, bearded man who lived in a commune a few streets away, started talking loudly about Nicaragua, Grunwick, and a speech by Margaret Thatcher on stricter immigration controls.

When it came to conversation, Robert thought it safest to restrict himself to bursts of eloquent silence. As he busied himself with the fruit salad he nodded in the animated, appreciative way that Nick had mastered.

When Clytemnestra's father stopped talking, Andrea said grimly that she could think of hardly any men who really, really supported feminism. Could they think of a man who didn't try to get his own ego in there, control conversation, achieve some kind of phallic dominance? As the women started to run down a list of the men they knew, Robert's genitals shrank to a level of detumescence he'd never previously thought possible.

Most of the men, including Clytemnestra's father, were quickly dismissed.

'What about Nick?' said someone.

'Some men find it difficult to be phallic even when you want them to be,' said Andrea. 'Nick gets attention in other ways.'

Robert knew what she meant. Nick had a face that always looked on the verge of bursting into tears.

Robert crouched over the sink, craving invisibility. What had happened to his politics? What did he, if challenged, believe in? When it came to the crunch did he believe in anything as passionately as Deborah believed in Marks? He hoped he wouldn't have to speak: words at this moment felt out of reach, clumsy and submerged.

'I think Robert's an example of a man who's trying to be non-sexist,' said Andrea.

Robert gripped a pineapple so hard that its needles penetrated his hand.

'Maybe I seem like that because I don't feel very confident about speaking,' he said.

'But that's part of it,' said Andrea. 'You give people space, you don't push your ideas and ego at them the whole time. And you've also cooked a beautiful meal without any fuss or bother.'

He felt thrilled and grateful. He'd been included in an alternative vision by one of the most powerful members of the feminist aristocracy. He had a sudden glimpse of a new alternative identity, of 2CVs and lentil bakes and running crêches. He looked at Eva. She winked at him. Surely she was impressed. Things were looking up. The future seemed better. At this moment, his mother would be washing up, his stepfather watching the news. Ron's incisors would be ripping into his steak. Deborah would be nibbling at a Ryvita and reading *Good Housekeeping*. If he wasn't here, he'd be back in that lonely bedsit eating baked beans because he couldn't be bothered to cook anything else. But Stephen? Ah, that was more painful. He'd be in his detached house, at his desk, writing, some friends expected, Pouilly Fumé chilling, Fiona wondering whether to wear a magnificent lacy dress. Put Eva and himself in that scene. No don't. It hurts too much.

'I hear you're interested in joining the house,' said Terry. 'I'd like to hear why.' She stared at Robert and waited. For a brief moment, some tiny part of him wanted to shout, 'Because it ups my chances of meeting some new chicks,' but he quickly pushed aside such madness and concentrated on what he needed to say.

'Some of it's because I know Eva, and want to be closer to her, but only on the basis of mutual respect and independence,' he said. 'And I like the idea of supporting each other with domestic chores and childcare, and exploring alternatives to nuclear families and monogamy. I was impressed when I read Germaine's alternative vision of Calabria, and I really liked what I read of de Beauvoir.'

Terry's bloke made a noise that was somewhere between a belch and the word 'bollocks'. Robert wondered if what he'd said was a bit over the top. Was he speaking the truth, or dealing, like Nixon, in PR and credibility? He looked at a bowl of oranges, clean, round and innocent, shining like harvest moons. He remembered simple meals at home in his childhood, the pre-ideological joy of Golden Syrup on Wonderloaf bread.

'I was reading an article,' said Terry, 'by someone who thought de Beauvoir had been too heavily influenced by

Sartre, and was too dependent on him as a sort of fatherly mentor.'

But people ignored her. There some warm nods and smiles in Robert's direction. He felt more confident and made a small joke about needing to ring Reuters to check the latest situation in Tanzania before he served the coffee.

While the kettle boiled he put the fruit salad onto the table. He scraped a few remains of the vegetable curry into the organic bin. He'd never seen anyone in the house spread any compost onto the garden, but he supposed this wasn't the point.

Eva came over and helped him.

'Have you ever been to Calabria?' she said. 'It's full of the most disgustingly sexist men, lots of *mafiosi*, filthy children, bloody boiling hot, the drains stink, double standards everywhere, everyone genuflecting at confession then going and sinning again. You'd hate the lizards and the insects. And the heat. You'd get a red back on day one and bloody hate it.'

Over coffee she came and sat next to him. His thigh touched hers. It gave off a stillness and heat like sun-warmed rock. Her breathing was even and slow. He thought, someone who can breathe like that can save me, heal me. For a minute he wished he could be inside her skin, protected by that heartbeat and the peaceful weight of her. It was foolish. His stomach creaked and bubbled with the anxiety of the meal, with the risks and stupidity of attachment and loss, and how fragile and tender it all was.

Andrea asked Eva to tell them some more about her research.

'I'm interested in mysticism,' said Eva. 'It's one of the few areas of life where men find it difficult to compete with women. An erection and a logical mind get you absolutely nowhere.'

That's not what I remember from when you used to meditate in Lambeth, thought Robert. He had a sudden sense of what it used to be like when they were together, of warmth and incense and delicious desire.

'But don't you think it's appalling for women to go bowing down before male gurus?' said Terry. 'Half the time the gurus are screwing everybody behind the scenes.'

'Meditation is about the dissolving of subject and object,' said Eva. 'It's to do with paradox rather than logic.'

People looked bemused but respectful. She was very cool when she talked. Robert thought about how she researched meditation these days rather than actually doing it.

Then Terry asked him about his work.

He was sweating. His eyes hurt: they felt braced against the 150-watt bulb and the threats the room held. He explained as briefly and vaguely as he could.

'I'm thinking of leaving my job anyway,' he said. 'I fancy something more socially useful.'

'Like what?' said Andrea.

'Like helping with an alternative paper, or organic gardening, or repairing push-bikes, or typesetting at one of those printers that has TU in brackets after their name, or helping tenants to organise.'

Andrea looked worried.

'If you were to join the house,' she said, 'which I really hope you will, the money you earn could be very useful. You could see your job as a type of social and political contribution in its way. It's the sort of thing that could make the difference to people like me finishing our novels.'

There was a silence.

'Robert wants me to go to a wedding with him,' said Eva. 'He's going to be the best man.'

You bugger, thought Robert.

He felt sufficiently good about the success of his meal to offer to wash up, scrub down the work surfaces and feed the cats.

When he went through to the living room, it was in near-darkness, lit only by a distant streetlamp and an occasional red glow as someone sucked in hard on a joint.

As his eyes became more used to the darkness, he saw Eva and Andrea kissing on the settee with the broken springs, and then Andrea cupping and squeezing Eva's breasts. When Eva saw him, she smiled and blew him a kiss. Nick was massaging Clyt's father's back. Terry was perched on her bloke's knee with a tilted, ironic expression, while he rolled one of his own and sipped a Long Life. Robert sat on the floor, and assumed what he hoped was the benign expression of someone who approved of democratic, non-possessive sexuality. But inside he felt like a small, fatherless child, filled with a frightening sense of uncertainty, a feeling that nothing seemed to hold his life in place any more. His future with Eva might suddenly empty through a black hole and disappear.

It was a relief when he heard Tom crying upstairs and, as the nearest person and the one with his hands least full, so to speak, could run upstairs and comfort him.

Nick drove Robert home and crashed his Morris Minor on the way. He'd been enthusing about a recent encounter group and the need to spend more time in the Here and Now, which he made sound like a particularly good country pub. He kept turning towards Robert to give him plenty of good quality eye contact and didn't see a traffic light changing. A car hit them with appalling mechanical violence, and all Robert's thoughts about alternative futures crystallised into one simple wish: to see and hold Eva again.

It was 1 am. He lay curled on his bed, relieved to be alive and utterly exhausted. He felt small and weak. The bed for once was home, a warm and simple womb.

He heard a misfiring 2CV engine outside the house. Eva's car. Normally, he'd have rushed to put on the right music and tidy up. But tonight, he just felt numb.

'Shit, I was worried,' said Eva. 'Nick told me. How are you?' She sat on the bed and hugged him.

'Ouch, my ribs hurt.'

'That'll be the seat-belt. Where else does it hurt?'

'My chest, when I breathe in.'

'You ought to go to the hospital. You might have a broken rib.'

'No, I'll go to the GP in the morning.'

She hugged him delicately and kissed him. Tears streamed down her face.

'Robert, I do care a lot for you, you know. I love you dearly. You mean as much to me as anyone I've ever known. I'd have been devastated if you'd been killed. I think I'm over my neurosis with Pascal, I really do.'

She looked into his eyes and squeezed both his hands. Robert felt the quiet satisfaction of having had just the right sort of car accident.

'I know I put a lot of emphasis on being independent. It's not because I don't love you, it's because I don't want to end up like my mother,' said Eva, 'embittered, sacrificial, repressed.'

She made him a cup of tea, and offered to hold the mug for him, but that would have felt just a little too powerless.

'I feel tired,' he said. 'All I want to do is go to sleep.' He would need no tranquillisers tonight.

She insisted on staying.

'I've been thinking,' said Eva in the morning, 'about having a baby, about whether it might after all be possible to trust some man enough to be the father, to be in at least some form of relationship as parents, for a few years anyway, even if we don't live together.'

Robert felt the onset of a rare starlit moment of bene- diction, like a hitch-hiker in an isolated spot for whom a beautiful car is slowing down, a sense that the universe and its forces were coinciding with his own life, going for once in roughly the same direction. 'Mmmm,' he mumbled, 'mmm . . .'

'And you,' she said, with a dimpled grin, 'you're one of only four people I think I could do that with.'

'You have to have energy, generosity, blindness.'

Robert had been aware for some weeks of the difficulty of making a best man's speech that would command consensus support, and this feeling intensified as he looked around him at Stephen's wedding reception.

Mr and Mrs Duvalle's relatives and friends looked resolutely Conservative in Austin Reed suits and Jaeger dresses. Stephen's side had a mix of clothes that seemed to convey something about the confusion of contemporary socialist thinking, cream flares and brightly coloured velvet jackets being every bit as popular as business suits. It was good to see Stephen's father there. Robert loved his authority and sense of history and slightly grumpy way of dealing with social occasions.

There were other groupings as well: several radical feminists wearing bomber jackets and militarily short hair, some lone men cuddling pint glasses, and the usual outcasts, notably Auntie Janet, who had presumably been invited to snub his mother.

Robert faced choices that politicians had faced through the ages: to go for a speech that was short and non-controversial, to appeal to a broad popular front, or to say something more radical aimed at a small, committed vanguard. In the end he knew there was really only one thing to do: he had to use his speech to influence and inspire Eva. He had tried to reach her through making love, he had tried to reach her through becoming an alternative man, and now was the moment to open up a third front and present the case, such as it was, for the Middle Class Myth of Love and Marriage

He sat with Eva on the sweet-smelling lawn of the large cottage in Sussex to which Mr and Mrs Duvalle had retired. A marquee in a field beyond the house looked as white and glistening as an iceberg. Fiona and Stephen stood on the lawn for a final set of photographs. Fiona's dress, seen against the emerald-green grass, was achingly, mystically white, like a cone of sparkling virgin snow.

Eva was wearing a black silk flapper dress that she'd found in an Oxfam shop. She hadn't put on any make-up, and the dress combined with her short hair and pale skin to give her a scrubbed, almost nun-like quality. She and Robert had a bottle of chilled Moët and Chandon to themselves, trickling with condensation in the sun. He stroked her warm, silk-covered back. A lark sang close by, and beyond this Robert could hear the laughter of friends and relatives. Given that they were attending the chief ceremony of patriarchal oppression, everybody seemed to be bearing up remarkably bravely. He commented on this to Eva and she gave him a teasing little kiss.

The wedding trip thus far had gone well. They had stayed in a country hotel with a view over the downs and had talked and made love with an intensity that reminded Robert of the Eva he'd once known. The marriage service had been in a twelfth-century village church surrounded by yew trees and ancient graves. Eva had whispered that she was finding the service strangely moving, and that it stirred up deep feelings that she wanted to work on with a therapist.

And Robert too had been full of feeling as the vicar

talked about the mystery of love, and being joined by God as one flesh, and how marriage was a gift of God and a means of his grace. Take that Calabrian commune, Robert had thought, take that Simone. Stephen had stayed resolutely upright and atheistic during the prayers, his body raised above the bowed heads like a pinnacle sticking up out of mist. Robert and Stephen had managed a couple of quick pints before the service, and Stephen had told him that as long as Fiona never voted Conservative or opposed Miners' strikes, she could indulge in whatever ceremonies she wanted. He'd also said that he loved Fiona, and wanted her to be his partner for life.

Beyond a general requirement to smile inanely, Robert's best man duties were finished for the time being. He picked up another bottle of Moët and headed for an El-san toilet to review the notes for his speech.

He had worked long and hard on it. He would start traditionally, by giving an account of Stephen's life, but then establish his radical credentials by referring to patriarchy and sexual slavery. This done, he'd move on to the heart of his speech, which was about commitment and love.

He would lighten it up again then, by appreciating Fiona in a spirit of equal opportunities. He didn't know a lot about her these days, but he could at least mention her 2.2, her promising career in teaching, her beauty (if this wasn't too sexist – she was stunningly beautiful in, what was it called, a pre-Raphaelite type of way).

As a precautionary measure, in case a bit of ritual was expected, Robert had written down a fairly safe joke about how many women with PMT it took to screw in a light bulb.

He had a last quick look through his notes and decided to leave out a quote from Kate Millett about how a hundred years ago women could be burned to death for killing their husbands because the law defined this as treason.

Suddenly this didn't seem quite the thing for a wedding party in a peaceful Sussex village.

He felt confident enough to engage in a long, celebratory swig of champagne. His speech would show Eva he understood her criticisms of love and marriage but then inspire her with a new vision.

He met Marshall and his second wife Lizzie on the way back across the grass. In the bright sunshine, Marshall looked pleasingly older than he did indoors, ruddy and slightly corrupt, like Robert Redford might look after fourteen pints of lager. His wife was drunk and upset in the melodramatic way that people seemed to reserve for weddings. It appeared that she'd just discovered that Marshall did not attach quite the same value as she did to the concept of fidelity. Marshall said that she was stupid to have had illusions: the idea that she was the last person he'd have a shag with was an affront. As Robert edged away, Marshall shouted that he'd give Robert a thumbs-up or down as to how the speech was going at various points.

Robert smiled his way round more clumps of guests on the lawn. A semi-proprietorial hand was placed on his shoulder. It was Deborah. His speech seemed an ever-more complex task. 'Isn't it wonderful? Doesn't Fiona look radiant?' she said.

'Um . . . er . . . you'd better come and meet Eva,' said Robert.

The two women shook hands. Deborah immediately admired Eva's dress.

'I wish now that I'd put on a little make-up,' said Eva.

Deborah took this as a cue to talk about how the world was about to enter a new chapter in the History of Lipstick. Eva gave the sort of attention that a therapist might give a difficult new client.

Seeing them together Robert realised that Deborah was

attractive in her way. With her dyed blonde hair and tinted contacts she had a pretty if slightly bland face. But Eva was beautiful because she was her own person. It showed in the solid graceful way she stood, and the stillness and self-possession of her eyes.

Deborah started, possibly in a joky way, to ask Eva if she didn't think Robert would look better if he had more of a suntan and invested in a hair-weave. Robert deep froze his anger: if he ever needed to be cruel, the energy for it would come from moments like this.

An hour later, he walked along the far side of the house, rounding up stragglers for the wedding meal. Eva had gone for a walk on her own. The first red signs of sunset were appearing on the horizon, along with a crescent moon and a bright planet that was probably Venus. Procol Harum's 'Whiter Shade of Pale' started to play from somewhere inside the house. Stephen and Fiona came out on to a small lawn and swayed slowly round, locked in embrace. A blackbird started to sing its head off.

It was all too much for Robert. Unless Stephen and Fiona both had piles, it was unquestionably a Perfect Moment, one of his visions coming true, the manifestation of his sweetest Eva-dreams. He felt dizzy with grief, envy, longing. Germaine, he thought, Germaine, help me, what am I supposed to do? The Middle Class Myth of Love and Marriage has got me in its grip. I want it, I want the kitsch, I want Eva to wear white, I want to dance on a lawn to this music. Help me.

And there was Deborah at his side, her arm round his disappointed body, whispering that they could still make the US work.

The guests squeezed into the marquee, which smelled of mown grass and tepid white wine. People had been drinking for a good part of the day and there was a well-oiled, slightly boisterous atmosphere. This made Robert feel nervous – they'd be hoping for a speech that was a bit of a cabaret turn.

Eva had chosen, not in any hostile way, to sit with some women near the back. Deborah was horribly near the front. Fiona's father was finishing speaking. Robert had never liked him, and didn't like him now. He reminded him of the bourgeois men in *Nausea*, convinced of their own accumulated worth. He was talking smugly about his good lady wife, and what a pleasure it had been to give his daughter away. Robert saw Eva make a face. She'd no doubt tell the anecdote at the next house meeting. Robert realised that he was saddled with a kind of Cabinet collective responsibility for whatever was said by people at the top table.

Mr Duvalle stared at Robert over half-moon spectacles and muttered something about the best man saying a few words.

Robert got to his feet. His body felt unpredictable, as if it were capable, like a cargo ship in heavy seas, of sudden redistributions of weight that might make him dramatically lopsided. He unfolded his notes and took a deep, steadying breath.

'It is one of the traditional duties of the best man,' said Robert, 'to paint a brief picture of the bridegroom for those not well acquainted with him.'

He talked about Stephen's family, his wonderful relationship with his father, his first-class honours and PhD, his book on trades union history that had been well reviewed in the quality Sundays, the lectureship attained at the age of twenty-three, and the detached, double-fronted, gas centrally heated house.

The words as he spoke them didn't sound nearly as lighthearted as he'd intended.

'Now, I guess we should look at, um, marriage for a moment,' said Robert. 'A lot of people think that it's an institution that should be killed off as soon as possible.'

Someone whistled and a couple of people jeered. Robert ignored them, and read directly from his notes.

'It is said by many that marriage and love are a middle-class myth. Indeed, there is probably no one who hasn't pondered on that sort of question today. A wedding brings to the surface our hopes and dreams, our memories and betrayals.'

This seemed much too solemn, more for the Vicar than the best man. Was that a sniff he heard from Marshall's wife? Well, there was nothing for it but to press on. He looked towards Stephen's family.

'With at least some people here I will have no need to excuse myself for quoting Engels . . .'

He paused. It was essential to say the next bit with as much tongue in cheek in possible.

'"Marriage is a variety of prostitution . . . um . . . er . . . that has traditionally involved the exchange of the female's domestic and sexual services in return for financial support."'

Someone shouted, 'Show us your knickers Robert,' but behind this, he was thrilled to hear a low cheer from Eva and the feminist group.

He then became aware of Mr Duvalle tugging at his jacket and whispering that he should pull himself together. Robert was concerned. He'd meant to use the Engels quote only for dramatic effect, and Mr Duvalle was, after all, paying for the champagne.

'Of course,' said Robert quickly, deciding to move away from his notes, 'things are different today; of course, in Fiona's case she's educated and capable of getting a good job,' and, he added, with an obvious teasing wink at Stephen, 'they've got enough money for a cleaner.'

'And of course her sexual services were offered many years prior to marriage,' said Marshall, in a horribly noisy aside to a couple of blokes near him. They whistled and laughed. This was bad news. Robert was losing control of his audience.

Mr Duvalle half raised himself from his chair.

'I'm sorry,' mumbled Robert, 'and, please, guys don't make insulting comments.'

'Services' was the wrong word, anyway, it was the sort of trap that Engels fell into, assuming that women got married because they had a low sex drive and could restrict all the hassle of sex to just one oppressive man.

Robert paused, thinking, firstly, that he might well be pissed, and, secondly, that Engels had made the sort of comment that belonged to an era that systematically denied the clitoris.

'Engels made the sort of comment,' said Robert, 'that belongs to an era that systematically denied the clitoris.'

He became aware of a swirl of movement to his right, and turned his head in time to see Auntie Janet faint dramatically, falling heavily backwards and collapsing a trestle table containing a bouquet of pinks and some of the best remaining bottles of champagne.

Robert realised that he'd reached a stage that psychologists might term 'disinhibited'. Whether through alcohol, tranquillisers, or a desperate anxiety to communicate with Eva, his power to censor or control his language was becoming, at best, erratic. It was as if boundaries between himself and the outside world were dissolving. Who he was felt weightless, transparent, almost non-existent. He might do or say anything. He didn't dare look at Mrs Duvalle. But then again, he wasn't making this speech for her. She hadn't even invited his mother.

He returned to his notes.

'It is so hard today to sort out what believe in when it comes to love and marriage . . .

'My own view is that we need a bit of commitment. Freedom is useless unless you commit to something. It's not the dream of love and marriage that's wrong, it's our cynicism and lack of faith in our own capacity to love.' He turned towards the bride and groom. 'Stephen and Fiona, I know you will be really happy.'

Deborah had a tissue in front of her face. Marshall was making a vigorous thumbs-down gesture. Robert realised in a new, existential way that it was impossible to please all of the people all of the time.

But Eva had moved nearer. She looked less cynical, more like the Eva he remembered. She was listening.

Looking back, with all the benefits of hindsight, this would have been a good moment to finish. But Robert was now in full, champagne-inspired flow.

'Some people don't even believe that people fall in love. Or they see it as an oppressive, psychologically immature state. But, please, let me quote you something from Sartre's *Nausea* . . .'

He glanced down at his notes, with a sudden sense of himself as precious and vulnerable.

'"To love,"' said Robert, '"you have to have energy, generosity, blindness. There is even a moment, right at the start, when you have to jump across an abyss."'

'Well, bloody jump then,' someone shouted. He suspected it was Marshall. There were a few jeers and laughs from the lads.

But Stephen got up, muttered thank you to Robert, and looked touched.

Love, thought Robert. He looked towards Eva, beautiful in the black silk dress. Then towards Marshall and the lads. 'Love . . .' he said, 'Love . . .' His mind suddenly went blank. He felt as if he were trying to start a car. What the hell was love? He'd thought about it so much. The only words that came into his mind were 'love is not having to go to the bathroom to fart' – or was it the other way round? – but he couldn't say that. He was aware of his heart, and that blood, like his speech, didn't flow in a smooth linear way but in dramatic pulses.

He felt flimsy, giddy, engulfed, like someone trying to stand up in the midst of strong waves. He had to find a way to finish.

Fiona, he thought, he'd forgotten to mention her at the start of his speech.

'I'd like, er, to pay tribute to Fiona,' said Robert.

Fiona looked worried. In a foolish moment Robert decided to change her 2.2 into a 2.1, but mentioning that didn't make her look any more pleased. He moved on.

'Anyway, from everything I know about you, Fiona, you're a tremendous person, and you're absolutely made for each other.' Oh shit, his voice now sounded like a third rate disc jockey's. 'As we can all see, Fiona, you are looking wonderfully beautiful in . . .' Robert paused and looked at her dark tumbling hair and her tense, pale face.

'Fiona, you are looking wonderfully beautiful in a really pre-menstrual type of way.'

An elderly man sitting at the top table said 'Hear, hear,' in a very loud and parliamentary fashion, and banged the table several times with a spoon.

It was terrible. He was cocking it all up. He'd meant to say 'pre-Raphaelite'. His head was awash with warm champagne, scattered notes, ideological confusion.

'Give us a joke Robert,' Marshall shouted out. One or two lone blokes said, 'Hear, hear.'

He wondered about his PMT joke, but Stephen got up and came towards him with his arms outstretched. He gave Robert a hug and said that it had been a great speech. Robert felt tears pressing against the tight discs of his eyes. And then he felt a melting, milky sense of relief as Stephen eased him back into his seat and the speech, he presumed, was over.

'But the end is there, transforming everything.'

As far as Eva was concerned, their relationship improved in the months after the wedding. She remained committed to her emotionally independent lifestyle, but was touched that Robert had cared enough about her to show his feelings and risk making a fool of himself. She still considered a baby at some point in the future and whenever an opportunity occurred, Robert tried to queue-jump the list of possible fathers by inserting her diaphragm as incorrectly as possible.

Robert still found it hard to live in the present. He couldn't stop himself trying to change Eva's beliefs about relationships. He was increasingly fond of Simone de Beauvoir and quoted her regularly.

'Listen to this,' he said one day as they sat in Eva's room. 'Why do we fall in love? Nothing could be more complex . . . because it is winter, because it is summer; from overwork, from too much leisure; from weakness, from strength; a need for security, a taste for danger, from hope; because someone does not love you, because he does love you . . .'

'That's rather nice,' said Eva. She was kneeling on the carpet, with just a towel round her, drying her hair by the gas fire. The curtains were drawn, a bottle of red wine was open, and The Cars were playing 'You're Just What I Needed'. The room felt intimately warm: even in shirt-sleeves he felt a slight, slippery sweat.

'You see, she doesn't reduce falling in love to some sort of power game or neurosis,' said Robert. 'Germaine Greer and the people in this house are so cynical about it.'

'But when you say you're in love with me,' said Eva, 'you say it like a line in a story. I can see you're wanting me to respond in certain ways. I feel I'm being manoeuvred.'

She bent her wet hair towards the fire. He stroked the smooth, white beach of her back.

'Well, I want to know where it's all leading,' he said, 'what sort of story I'm in.'

'You should trust life a little bit more,' she said. 'You don't need to know the end of a story to decide whether or not you're enjoying it.'

But he did. He did.

If anything his confidence in the future had, since the wedding, been decreasing. He'd had one particularly nasty trip to Burton's Menswear. He'd taken some clothes into a brilliantly lit cubicle, stared into the mirror and seen six hairs on a part of his temple where he'd expected to find hundreds. He was older and more worn than he'd imagined. He wrestled his head into a polo-neck, determined to restrict himself to questions like 'does this jumper fit?' But when his face popped back into view, so did the question, 'So what are you doing with your life, you ugly bastard?' He suddenly saw that the future was not just a hoped-for place lying out in front of him, it also came from inside him, biologically, entropically, the dissolution of what he was, a bombing and crumbling and decay.

He stroked Eva's back again and sighed.

She turned round and looked at him with her blue eyes and lean, fine-boned face. Her cheeks were red from the fire.

'You take things too seriously,' she said.

'Well, what about you?' he said. 'The way you talk about that man, Pascal, as an obsession that you're trying to get over. You make being in love sound like an illness.'

Her lips turned down into the frowning stage of her smile. Then she grinned and the dimples showed at the corners of her mouth.

'I feel very good when I'm with you,' she said, 'very healthy. I'm more able to relax and be myself with you than with anyone else.'

Robert wasn't sure how much of a good thing this was. People said similar things about their dogs.

'You can relax because I'm in love with you,' he said. 'I feel tense half the time. It's a question of differences in power.'

'Everything could change,' she said. 'At times I do almost feel like I'm in love with you again.' She picked up a pair of scissors and started to trim her toenails.

'I really do like what Simone says,' said Robert.

'De Beauvoir and Sartre never got married,' said Eva. 'She's never even lived with Sartre. I don't think she even had much of a sexual relationship after the first few years. They were more like best friends, supporting each other, telling each other absolutely everything – well, nearly everything.'

'We could be like that,' she said. 'It's what I value most in you.'

Oh, no, thought Robert. What was she trying to say now?

One night a few weeks later he lay in her bed listening to her write a letter. It was late and he was desperate for her to join him.

He looked at her through one half-closed eye. She was sitting at her desk, bent over an oval of yellow light from a table lamp. Who was she writing to? And what was she saying? The pen made a scratching sound that was separate, distinct and sharp. She paused, stayed very still, then the writing began again. He felt that he didn't exist for her at this moment, that she was totally directed towards some other. He felt on the edge of a sea of chaos and non-being.

Robert couldn't bear to sit on the edge of a sea of chaos and non-being for too long. He sat up and sighed.

'I thought you were asleep,' she said.

'It's one o'clock. I wish you'd come to bed.'

'You sound angry,' she said. 'I won't be long.'

But she was still deliberate and unhurried as she carried on writing, absolutely in her own time. It wasn't fair on him. She ought to apologise or at least feel guilty.

When he closed his eyes he felt shapeless. He longed for nearness, for this marvellously independent woman to lay her warm body alongside him. He knew exactly what Simone meant when she talked about the impossibility of trying to possess a free person.

A few minutes later he heard the dry crackling of the writing paper being folded, and Eva's nail making a crease, like the sound of a skate across ice, then a sucking and swirling as she collected a little pool of saliva in her mouth and licked the flap, and soft thuds as she patted the flap closed against the surface of the desk.

There was the minutest of brushing sounds as she crossed the carpet, the creak of the wardrobe door, the metallic chime of two wire coat-hangers touching, a rustling and gasp of breath as she pulled her dress over her head, and a pause while she smoothed it down on the hanger, taking her time: then a slight crackling as she took her tights off. She clicked the light switch and his head was filled with healing darkness. Then she was next to him, and a single electrically charged finger stroked his neck.

She held his hand while she slept. Her hand was warm

and friendly and squeezed his own hand tightly if he experimentally tried to detach it. Surely, thought Robert, this hand belonged to her original, real self. Surely, despite everything, theirs was a story of true love.

A week later there was a message at work. To ring Eva. Urgently.

The message had been there since 3 pm the previous day. Robert should have been in his office then, but had slunk off early, work being as demoralising as ever. Marshall didn't seem to notice. He regarded absence as a sign that someone was out and about doing what he called 'networking', which in his own case nearly always involved women.

'Hi,' said Eva. 'Look, I'm sorry, I forgot to tell you that Pascal is coming over from France this weekend. I tried to ring you yesterday.'

'Oh.'

'You know, that person I told you about,' said Eva.

Too bloody right, thought Robert. Six foot two, long thick hair. And going back a hell of a long time, to even before he'd met her. The Frenchman she was neurotically and obsessively Still in Love With, the *Being and Nothingness* man. This was different to her casual sexual relationships.

'I know you'll understand,' said Eva. 'I'm feeling a bit depressed about the whole weekend. It's probably all over with him, it would be healthier if it was. But I'd be letting myself down if I didn't see him. I just had such feelings, you know.'

Shit. Fuck. Oh, no. Oh, no. Think Germaine, quick, think Germaine.

'I understand,' said Robert. 'The last thing I want is to create a whole lot of neurotic, possessive demands on you.' Who was he kidding?

'Robert, you're very special, maybe the most special person in my life, there's not many men would say something like that. I'm really thinking very seriously about us now, you know.'

'You'll sleep with him, of course.'

'I don't know. I'll have to see. I know it's a bit touchy for you, but it's actually none of your business.'

Oh fuck you, thought Robert. Bitch. Shit.

'Anyway, he's coming on Friday evening. It was important to let you know. We can all three of us meet up if you like.'

'You must be joking. I don't want to be part of some threesome acting out that hell-is-other-people play.'

'Look, I know this isn't easy.'

'I feel hurt. I feel jealous. I can't help it.'

'I know,' she said, 'and I realise it's taking a risk, but that's what we have to do sometimes.'

'Are you going to change the sheets?' said Robert. Then he added, 'And I bet you're going to shave your legs.'

'That, too, is none of your damned business,' said Eva.

'He smiles ... right up against my face.'

Work was the only place where he could think of spending the Friday afternoon. The secretary was shocked to see him.

He lay almost horizontal in his swivel chair, picking his nose and flicking the bits on to the carpet. He felt drained, furious, despairing, jealous, terrified. He looked at a photo of Eva on his desk. 'It's over,' he thought, 'my baby doesn't love me any more.' And tears began to gather behind his eyes, round and wet and insistent, like miniature Roy Orbisons trying to get on stage.

His door opened. It was Marshall. 'How are you?' said Marshall, putting the emphasis on the second word in a way that subtly suggested that Robert was ill or inadequate in some way.

'I'm OK,' said Robert.

'Doing anything special this weekend?' said Marshall.

Well, crying, shouting, thought Robert. Looking through the window feeling depressed. Hatred, jealousy, self-loathing. A packet of individual apple pies in front of Racing from Haydock. The usual sort of things.

'Eva's seeing some other bloke this weekend,' said Robert. It was best to be honest.

'You're joking. I wouldn't bloody stand for that. What a bitch,' said Marshall.

'But it's part of our relationship, our understanding.'

'Well, Christ, if any woman did that to me . . .'

'You do it to them.'

'Double standards,' said Marshall. 'Part of our culture. Take away double standards and the country would collapse.'

Marshall glanced at a swaying tower of reports on Robert's desk. It was a monument to depression rather than hard work.

'You've got two options,' said Marshall. 'Put a brick through the window and tell the bastard to piss off, that's probably what she's really hoping you'll do . . .'

'Or?'

'Or make her as jealous as possible by screwing someone else; make sure the bitch knows all about it.'

There was no way Robert was going to renew things with Deborah. He owed her that much, not to use her as some sort of pawn.

'I don't want to be a sexist bastard,' said Robert, 'I've got to try not to be so possessive.'

Marshall punched him on the shoulder.

'Men and women have been screwing each other for a lot longer than feminism's been around,' he said. 'Life obeys deeper laws than people like Germaine Greer will ever understand. It's basically biological. Males need to be aggressive because it's their role to hunt and defend territory. Females need to be sensitive because they have to bring up the babies. Feminists are operating as if nature didn't exist.'

'And anyway, lad,' said Marshall, putting on an exaggerated Nottingham accent, 'Women's lib's a bloody middle-class southerner's thing.'

Robert was silent. He didn't have the morale to take Marshall on.

'Cheer up,' said Marshall. 'Things aren't that bad. I've just completed my research on the ten most painful human emotions, and jealousy's only number three.'

It was past six o'clock. Only Robert and a cleaner were left in the building: he could hear her vacuuming the corridor. He sat motionless in his chair, trapped in the cinema of his jealousy. Pascal would have arrived by now. Right now, at this second, Eva would be greeting him. She would be running across the floorboards, her feet bare, her face shining. The room would be immaculate, the bed lit by a single spotlight, Georgie's shit box newly cleaned, and the cat shut outside.

Eva was looking at Pascal, her eyes sparkling. 'The First Time Ever I Saw Your Face' was being sung by Roberta Flack from somewhere near the bookcase.

'I've missed you so badly,' she says.

Zoom in to the kiss. She thrills him with that sudden shameless push of her tongue into his mouth. His face is obscured by tumbling rings of thick black hair. They embrace as tightly and gracefully as lovers in a Rodin sculpture. Being-in-itself and for-itself.

'I want to spend the whole weekend in bed,' she says. Her voice is husky with desire.

'Well, it's fucking unfair,' said Robert out loud. 'All I ever got was the odd hour here and there.'

'What did you say, dear?'

He looked up and found himself staring into the eyes of the office cleaner.

'You don't look at all well,' said the cleaner. 'You're very pale and a bit trembly.'

Pascal's manicured hand was moving down from the beautiful dimples on Eva's back to caress her silky, waxed, gleamingly glossy, feminine rather than feminist leg.

'*Je t'aime,*' he was saying. '*Je t'aime.*'

Cue Serge Gainsbourg and Jane Birkin, organs, violins

and heavy sighing as they move towards the bed.

The cleaner emptied out his waste bin: twenty goes at the first draft of a report on ECT, two banana skins and an empty packet of Embassy Kings. According to Simone de Beauvoir, work was the place where he found a transcendent justification for his existence.

Let s face it, thought Robert, let's face the fact that, apart from Sartre and de Beauvoir, I have always had problems with the French. It's nothing personal. I like the idea of going to France, and look forward to croissants and nervy artistic women and hanging out in Les Deux Magots, but within a few minutes of getting there, the main experience is humiliation. I thought it was blue jeans but they've gone back to black, and, what with my red shirt, I look like I'm on a pub darts trip to Margate. I go to a café and open my notebook to capture a compelling insight. It's then that I notice that my pen's leaked in the heat and left an inky blue ejaculation all over my carefully ironed shirt. I realise that to the French people in this café, I am different in only a few irrelevant details to the fat Englishwoman in the tight pink T-shirt with 'Très Chic' emblazoned across the bust. I might as well be done with it and get my own 'Très Chic' T-shirt, and start moaning to her about how a country with a toilet like the one downstairs can call itself civilised. I want to talk about their useless Johnny Halliday pop music and how easily they surrendered to the Germans, and to get pissed and kick tables over and frighten all those smoothies and poseurs.

And, specifically, he wanted to do these things to Pascal.

Eva had hooked her legs around him, pulling him in. Her body was dramatically white against his bronzed torso, and her head was thrown back in abandon and surrender.

Robert trudged to the bus stop as the splendid Parisian phallus cruised in. Eva was arching her back in stretched ecstasy, like a pole-vaulter clearing the bar. She was crying and calling out, in a semi-mystical sort of way, like those times when he knew her before. She was enraptured. She was de Beauvoir's Woman in Love, dreaming of attaining supreme existence through losing herself in the Other.

Robert crept up to the back of Eva's house. For once the alley was free of the pack of hyenas. Eva's curtains were closed save for a tiny vulva-shaped opening.

The worst thing was not completely knowing. What if they were not making love? What if, by some miracle of the type for which Robert had been fervently praying, Pascal had just had a particularly embarrassing and unGallic premature ejaculation? But that conjured up a yet more frightening image. What if they were talking, with a melting sense of understanding each other in ways no one had ever done before? Or looking into each other's eyes and experiencing an ecstatic sense of oneness?

He slipped into the shed at the bottom of the garden and felt for the ladder. He placed it against the house, then found a brick and laid it ready at the foot of the ladder. A brick through the window would do wonders for their ecstatic sense of oneness.

Georgie the cat was sitting on the windowsill. She spat and hissed at him. He swept her off. She fell gracelessly through the air and landed with a satisfyingly disappointed yowl. He climbed higher.

A chorus of shouts like a French revolutionary mob suddenly came from behind him. Robert heard ragged chants of 'Free the night,' 'Reclaim the night.' It was Andrea's male curfew march.

'Andrea, there's a man breaking into your house,' said a piping voice.

Robert pulled his jersey over his face and swung down the ladder. He jumped the last few feet, landing in an old cucumber frame. He leaped over a brick wall, then ran down a track and some side streets, and into the entrance to Tufnell Park tube station. As he sat panting on the train, he noticed that he was wearing a horribly clashing orange sweater and blue jeans. The French had won again.

'You could have sworn that things were thoughts ... which forgot what they had wanted to think and which stayed like that, swaying to and fro.'

Robert stayed the night at his family home for the first time in nearly a year. Cracks were appearing along the walls of the lounge. His mother made Madeleine cakes but forgot to put the coconut on them, and his stepfather slept through the news. But they seemed happier than he remembered.

Early the next day he ran to the library and got out books on de Beauvoir and Sartre. He had to know more about the relationship that Eva held out as a possible model for their own.

Robert admired Sartre and de Beauvoir's alternative lifestyle, and the way Sartre lived in cheap hotel rooms and had no possessions other than a few books. But before he'd read very far, he realised that he could never have a relationship like theirs. For all their talk about having an 'essential love', Sartre and de Beauvoir were committed to a combination of sexual freedom and transparent honesty that Robert found bizarre. They sent each other letters detailing every nuance of their affairs. Sartre spared nothing: he went into the precise details of some virgin he was seducing, and the traumas of her subsequent breakdown, and the way in which another woman's kissing was so powerful it was like having his tongue sucked by a vacuum cleaner. And Simone, in turn, shared all her feelings about her lovers. How could they not suffer appalling jealousies? There was something voyeuristic and cold about it all. Was that really the sort of life that Eva wanted?

His stepfather helped his mother make lunch. Robert was surprised at how much he appreciated the house, its sense of order, the absence of rotas and stinking milk bottles in the fridge. There had been things they'd achieved that Jean-Paul and Simone never had. They'd done their own cleaning and brought up a child and not made young girls suicidal with jealousy.

His mother served up a kedgeree as Pascal glided once more into Eva's hot, beautiful body. Mr Webster hammered at the same fenceposts he'd hammered at years ago. With *Grandstand* on in the background, Robert went back to the book. Ah. Here was the answer to why Sartre and de Beauvoir put themselves through all that trauma. Their absolute commitment was to Know Life and Express it. To capture every detail, and turn all their experiences into Literature. They weren't so much looking for love as looking for words. All their affairs were instrumental to this overarching enterprise. Well, yes. To Know Life and Express it. It was all right if you were French, that sort of thing, but it wouldn't even get Pascal a job as a lavatory cleaner in North London.

Later that afternoon Robert sat in his room, surrounded by the vintage-car curtains, the El Cordobes poster and the plastic Vulcan bomber.

He picked up his old copy of *Nausea*. Part of him felt stupid being here like this, like a kid again in his bedroom, moping about with words. He saw more clearly now the way in which Sartre wrote, the way he banged on about tongues becoming huge centipedes, and mirrors being traps, and parks smiling. It was poetic in a way. But any analyst worth his salt would say that Roquentin had the mind of someone with severe early-life problems, the mind of a narcissist unable to sort out what was him and what was the world.

Robert, though, still had a grim empathy with Roquentin. Like Roquentin, his own reasons for living were collapsing: he'd buggered up his career, he was living in a mushroom-infested bedsit, and Eva was, at this very second, in love with a beautiful, dandruffless genius. And once your world started collapsing, it was then that the Nausea set in. Things started to exist in a new way. A coin stared like an accusing eye from behind the *Telegraph*, his hand was a disgusting pink crab moving its claws in and out, the saliva in his unloved mouth became a 'permanent little pool of whitish water'.

Robert felt that if he didn't breathe carefully he was going to throw up. He sat down on the bed until his head cleared, not quite sure whether he was on the brink of a massive insight or whether it was the kedgeree.

He read his favourite chestnut tree passage again. Nausea had once filled him with visions of mystical experiences and café *patronnes*, but now he suddenly recognised another language in the book: a buried language of grief and loss. The park in *Nausea* was a place where people's worlds 'collapsed' and 'emptied' and 'disappeared'.

'For fuck's sake,' he could hear Marshall saying, 'get yourself out for a few pints with some mates. Leave the morbid introspection to the French. With any luck, Pascal's getting some lower back pain by now, or finding Eva a bit too bloody neurotic.'

But it felt gloomily, hurtfully appropriate to go to the local park. It was wet and deserted, and the trees gave off a familiar slow-moving sense of time. He remembered when he'd been here last, with Eva when they visited his parents. He sat on a swing and started to sway to and fro, his head pulsing with the single overwhelming fact of her and Pascal being together. Then he imagined his father pushing him on the swing, that clever jazz-playing man, the sense of lightness at the top of the arc, then plummeting warmly back, his father unseen and laughing behind him, out and back, to and fro, in suspended movements between being held and being released.

A tube train accelerated into the tunnel with a familiar rhythm of electrical hums and clicks. Marshall was right, it was fucking stupid, this. He should lighten up. Put a brave face on it. But then, it was as if the very motion of the swing was thinking for him, remembering, creating images.

Was it here, he wondered, that his mother told him about his father? Was it here that she finally got exasperated with his endless questions, and screamed that his father was never coming back? Was it here, as *Nausea* said it was, that the park 'suddenly emptied, as if through a big hole, and the world disappeared'?

He was grateful when he got home for the warm fire and the telly. His mother said he looked as white as a ghost. He was filled with a new curiosity about his childhood, and started to ask his mother questions. She was filled with an equally unexpected burst of curiosity about *Match of the Day* and Sheffield United's goalless draw. But Robert persisted. Could she remember a time when she'd told him about his father? Maybe it was a time in the park?

'You did get very upset there once,' she said. 'You had your first asthma attack there, you got breathless and started panicking. But I can't remember whether it was anything to do with your father.'

She looked grey and strained. She still said the words 'your father' reverentially.

'But what was it like for you at the time, mum, were you depressed?'

'I had to go away for a little while,' she said. 'That was what upset you most. But you coped very well, really. You were such a perfect child.'

He decided to stop, fearing that they might reach some awful level of intimacy where family roles collapsed and events escaped from their proper places in time.

Later, as he went upstairs to bed, she said that she'd like to give him his father's diaries.

'That "I" . . . a dough which goes on stretching and stretching.'

On Sunday night Eva rang him at the bedsit.

'I was wondering whether you wanted to come round.'

'I don't know,' said Robert quickly.

'If it's any consolation,' she said, 'we only made love three times, and none of them was particularly wonderful.'

Three times, thought Robert, the Gallic cock had crowed three times and she had betrayed him.

'I could only see you for a few minutes,' said Robert. 'I've a lot of things I have to do.' It was a bitter, carefully planned tactic.

She sounded disappointed. He felt a sweet, righteous sense of anticipation. She owed him something now. She might not be madly in love with him, but she owed him something.

Eva looked tired, in a private, lover's sort of way. Her face was pale and silvery and there were dark crescents of shadow under her eyes.

The sheets on the bed were new and as smooth as a billiard table. The waste bin had been emptied of any offending tissues and the cat's shit box had several large new turds in it. All the little sexual accoutrements were back in the lacquered box.

'I really wanted to see Pascal again,' she said. 'We go back a long time. You know, there was once a time in Greece, I think we were rather stoned, we slept out under the stars . . .'

'We're not Jean-Paul and Simone,' said Robert. 'We're not turning all this into some novel. I don't want all the details. I've been feeling really devastated.'

A silence. She looked serious, and concerned, but not nearly as guilty as he'd assumed.

'I feel . . . he said. 'There's something I have to . . .'

'I know it hurts,' said Eva, 'but it was no different when you had that affair with that American woman.'

'What affair? Barely anything happened.'

'Well, that's not what your friend Marshall told me.'

'Nothing much happened,' said Robert. What a bastard Marshall was.

'I do think about what you say,' said Eva. 'I don't dismiss the possibility of us living more closely together, sharing more time. Pascal gets me really mixed up. He turns me inside out emotionally. I make myself vulnerable and then find he's cool and detached.'

She came and sat to next to him, and gave him a little nudge with her hip. He briefly touched her leg. It had a bristly feel to it. She was letting the hair grow again. He wasn't sure what this meant.

Robert was aware of another feeling that was hard to name, possibly shame. What was he doing listening to her like this, why wasn't he furious? If someone like Marshall or Ron had been listening through the wall, he would be saying that people like Robert wouldn't even have managed to colonise the Isle of bloody Wight, although Robert wasn't sure whether the Isle of Wight should have been colonised in the first place.

'I've been feeling terrible,' said Robert. 'I need time to

think things over. I'm madly in love with you, I can't help it, and I don't know if I can stand the stresses of you having weekends like this. I find it hard to know why you are so against us giving it a go together.'

She stroked away a strand of black hair that had fallen across her face. Her eyes looked smoothly into his. 'I know it upset you,' said Eva, 'but I don't feel guilty. It was a risk, but sometimes you have to take risks in relationships. If it causes you so much pain, then maybe it's better not to see each other or sleep together. I like you, I love you, but I will have lots of other friends and no doubt some lovers. I want my individuality and independence, and nothing will take them from me.'

Robert felt his face blanche. It was one of those frightening moments when he realised that he was responsible for creating what happened next in his life. In the briefest of seconds, almost arbitrarily or proudly, all he had to say was 'I agree,' and whoosh, their relationship would be over. He'd get the 104 bus back to the bedsit, and his life with Eva would collapse into nothingness. There'd be no sense of commitments made, or vows sanctified in heaven, to slow them down: it would be straight out to the bus stop. A phrase came back from *Nausea* about the future waiting out in the street, 'hardly any paler than the present'.

'No,' he said quickly, 'I don't want that.'

He'd gone to her house feeling that he was the victim of a crime. And now he realised that all she'd done was to see her old lover; in a clear and honest way. He'd given himself ridiculous, neurotic rights that his life must never be painful or unfair.

He hugged her, not quite in the way a defeated boxer hugs an opponent at the end of a fight, but with some complex mixture of love, powerlessness and relief.

The next evening he wanted to be out, in case Eva called round: for it to seem like he had his own, independent life.

He went to the Cosmo Club in Hackney to have a drink and listen to the live reggae.

A woman sat at the table next to him. She had honey-blonde hair and bright red lips, and wore a white V-neck jersey and a black mini-skirt. Her eyes held his for a little longer than was polite.

'Do you fancy a dance?' she said to Robert

They tried a reggae dance, attempted to bump groins and rhythmically sway, a task Robert found impossible. The music was disorientatingly loud. He could smell cigarette smoke on her hair.

They sat down again. She leaned forward to stub out her cigarette. Her breasts swung forward in the V-neck sweater, a memory slid into place, and he realised, with a swelling historical thrill that he had been dancing with Betty, formerly the barmaid at the William and Victoria and regular star of the night-time fantasies of his youth.

They had a couple of drinks, and another dance, and then he offered to give her a lift home, to a block of council flats in Highbury. It was only fair to escort her through the unlit entrance halls and stairways, and then into a room with a double mattress on the floor, a pile of clothes in a corner, and a pleasant absence of books.

She took out a bottle of Pernod. Its aniseed taste reminded him of sweetie bags in childhood playgrounds.

She leaned towards him and he found himself kissing. She sucked at his tongue in a wet, rhythmical way, and the image came to mind of Jean-Paul's vacuum cleaner. Then her hand was on the top of his zip, in what was, unquestionably, a phallocentric act.

'I like you,' she said with refreshing simplicity.

Events started to accelerate, moments that were normally unhurried and separate started to bang into each other like cars in a motorway pile-up. He registered few details: some knickers so tight that they left a red ring on her bottom, a distant chorus of disapproval from Germaine and Andrea, a sense of natural justice with Eva, and then Betty's voice shouting, 'That's how I like it . . . go on, give me one,' and then, 'Ram it in, ram it in,' as if she were not so much in bed with him as a spectator at a boxing match urging a fighter on towards a knock-out.

She put the centre light on afterwards. Her face looked waxy and tired.

She told Robert that what she liked about him was that he was sensitive. He could listen, unlike that bastard Ron, whom she was trying to get away from with the help of the women's advice centre. Ron thought she was his exclusive bloody girlfriend and insisted on sex whenever they were together, no matter how she felt. Robert started to recall the research Marshall was doing on the ten most painful human emotions:

1. Anxiety
2. Guilt
3. Jealousy
4. Grief

He couldn't remember the rest. Some of number one was creeping into his system, alongside number two and a tiny bit of number four. He'd forfeited a lot of his rights to number three.

'This bloke of yours . . .' said Robert, reasonably calmly, thinking that there must be quite a lot of unpleasant Rons in North London. 'A real bastard,' said Betty helpfully. 'Threatens to kill me or anyone that touches me. Doesn't accept I've left him.' Robert felt a definite twinge of anxiety.

'Er . . .' he said, 'he doesn't by any chance like Tamla Motown, does he?'

She started to nod.

'Has he got, er . . . you know . . . tattoos . . . said Robert. His voice sounded extraordinarily small and thin.

She was nodding. 'Crap bands, all Tamla.'

He saw how Marshall had got the deputy head of department job at such an early age. He was right. Anxiety was definitely number one. It was the inescapability of it, the sense of being locked into some awful future event, its utter seriousness. Emotions like jealousy seemed luxurious in comparison.

Robert began to collect his clothes. What a bloody idiot he'd been. He'd betrayed something with Eva and given away some precious sense of himself. And for so little.

At first he was too dazed to hear Betty muttering about him giving her a present, and that she'd make sure she kept quiet. But then she repeated herself. He handed her ten pounds and staggered into the street.

'I met someone, you know, nothing much, totally casual, one thing led to another. I really regret it,' said Robert to Eva later that week.

'I don't want to know,' she said. 'Spare me the details. I understand and I don't want to know the gory ins and outs.'

Robert had a sudden tactical insight into their relationship.

'It was funny,' he said, 'but I lay in bed with her and she was all over me—'

'Look,' said Eva insistently, 'I don't fucking want to know. It's OK. It's fine. But don't go on. I don't want to start feeling angry or jealous. As you said the other night, we're not trying to write a bloody novel.'

Jealous, thought Robert. Oh wonderful word, magic word. The details, real or imagined, suddenly seemed important allies, capable of working with immense narrative power in Eva's imagination.

He started to think of a perfect, nippled detail, but then Eva swept out of the room saying that she was sick of relationships and all the hassles they caused.

*

'It's not the fact that you had sex,' said Andrea. 'That's fine. It's the fact that Betty is a very troubled person.'

They were having a house meeting in the kitchen. Robert was one of the agenda items. He was very relieved that Eva wasn't there.

'Of all the people you could have chosen,' said Andrea, 'you chose someone who's been in a very oppressive relationship.'

At the mention of oppression, Robert's right leg started to tremble.

'She's got a drink problem,' said Andrea, 'And other health problems.'

Robert's left leg started to tremble.

Some radical friends of Andrea's had seen them leaving the Cosmo and had then had a quiet word with Betty at the women's centre. Andrea had been fully briefed.

'My only defence,' said Robert, 'is that it just sort of happened. It was a bit like Camus's Outsider. I got swept along by events, her body, like the Arab's knife, just sort of flashed before me, and I reacted, got taken over by it all.'

It was an unfortunate cultural referent. He was given an impressive lecture on how the Arab and the girlfriend had been given no individuality in Camus's book, they'd been treated simply as objects. Robert was amazed that he hadn't seen this before.

'Couldn't you see that she was pissed and desperate?' said Andrea.

'I was pissed and desperate. I can't tell you how much I regret it.'

'I think we're being too hard on him,' said Terry, to Robert's surprise. 'The lad made a mistake. She probably egged him on. You know what she's like.'

'Well, I think Robert should do something to raise his awareness of sexuality issues,' said Andrea. 'He needs to do some work on himself if he's ever going to fit in here.'

'How about going on the encounter weekend with

Gerry Mortensen and Martha Cromwell?' said Nick. 'I'm going, Andrea's going, it should be fantastic. Gerry's groups have certainly helped me raise my level of consciousness.'

As Nick talked about his consciousness, Robert had an image of a crane straining to lift a very heavy weight. In some ways, though, the weekend sounded like a good and creative idea.

Two days later he was sitting in Eva's room. She seemed worryingly calm. She was talking about a possible opportunity to go to a conference in Heidelberg. Maybe she would stay on afterwards to do some research. Her eyes were luminously clear. She seemed to look through his face, past him.

Just as she was explaining that the trip would only be for a few weeks, the front door exploded open and there was the sound of a man's voice shouting in the hall.

Robert's heart went into arrythmic contortions. It was Ron. What was more terrifying was that it was 10.45. He'd broken his routine. All order had broken down, the world was spinning into chaos.

'Where's the fucker who messed with my Betty?' roared the voice.

Robert's legs were shaking. His bladder and bowels and stomach and kidneys started bubbling with fear.

He considered taking off his clothes and going downstairs naked. Marshall had once recommended this after being caught red-testicled in the bedroom of someone else's wife. Confronted by an enraged husband, Marshall believed that his swinging scrotum had mesmerised the man for just long enough to enable him to jump through a window and save his life.

This is horribly unfair, thought Robert. He peered over the top of the banisters. Ron's eyes were as black as an Aberdeen Angus bull's. The veins on his huge head-butter forehead throbbed like electric fencing. The Tamla tattoos glistened with sweat and rage, the snakes writhed and the daggers twitched. He wore the gold sovereigns, one on each finger, and all intended for Robert's consciousness-being-raised, liberally educated, agonisingly soft-tissued brain. He felt like one of the cats that Andrea's friends produced, all instinct bred out of him, soft and vulnerable, unable to defend his territory.

Robert never needed to go down the stairs, and half an hour later they were having an impromptu party. While Nick hid in his room, Terry had appeared with an axe and swung it furiously towards Ron's groin, screaming at him that he was a disgusting, violent, oppressive abusing rapist. Her garage mechanic bloke had appeared behind her with a crow bar. 'Magnificent,' was the only word Robert could mutter, again and again and again.

The party began at midnight. Nick made a bowl of rice and a curry with green beans and fleshy chunks of fish. They drank large amounts of French table wine. The kids got up and ran round jumping with delight. They moved Eva's stereo into the living room, and leaped about to the Police, Joe Jackson and The Cars. The music seemed to Robert like the heartbeat of the house, and he had a glimpse of a life beyond the nuclear family, beyond fear and obsession. He suddenly felt excited about the prospect of the encounter group.

But Eva looked tense and private and danced on her own.

'Something's changed,' she said later. 'I'm frightened something's changed.'

'Existence precedes essence.'

It was a surprise to see Marshall at the encounter group. Robert had mentioned that he was going but Marshall had shown little interest. His being there made the event feel safer but less satisfying, like meeting a next-door neighbour on the Khyber Pass.

It was most definitely not a surprise that Andrea took Marshall on, or in the language of the group, 'confronted him'. For hours afterwards, the more experienced participants said that, of its type, it was one of the most interesting events they had ever witnessed in a group.

The weekend started on the Friday evening. Sixteen people sat on a pale green carpet in the large Victorian room that constituted the Camden Town Centre for Personal Growth. The room was empty except for a record-player and two table lamps. People had been asked to bring their own cushions, along with a sleeping bag, some favourite music or words, and food (vegetarian only) to share at mealtimes.

Robert knew three of the participants: Nick, Marshall

and Andrea. Andrea was representing a feminist magazine and because of the potential publicity had been offered a free place. She had brought a black beanbag that rose behind her head like a throne. There were rather more women than men. Robert noticed in particular a shaven-headed woman who glared at him whenever he made even the briefest eye contact. Next to her sat an incongruous-looking middle-aged man in a striped blue business shirt and maroon club tie. His leg moved rhythmically to and fro with the relentless mechanical efficiency of a metronome. It was his former schoolfriend, Jonathan Creighton, spectacularly aged.

The facilitator wore a cream velour tracksuit and introduced himself as Gerry. He had tiny ears, virtually no neck and a glossy suntan, the whole effect combining to make him look rather like a seal. He gathered people into a circle, said 'I'd like to begin now,' and then appeared to go into some sort of trance. Robert sat cross-legged on the floor, feeling his legs go numb and trying to control the sense of panic he felt. Each moment of silence gave birth to an even more tense silence beyond.

Gerry explained the purpose of the weekend. He talked in a soft, hypnotic voice about raising awareness, confronting ego and encountering other people 'without our usual masks and public personae'. He talked about this being a place to learn, take risks and experiment. Robert listened carefully, fearfully; he was here hoping to change, to become less neurotic and possessive. He was here hoping to find a way out of the bind he was in: that Eva would only really love him if he was emotionally independent, but that he would only feel like this if he knew she really loved him.

Gerry talked about trying to live in the Here and Now, whether it was tasting the food they ate, experiencing emotions, taking a shower or defecating. Even things like defecating, said Gerry, should be done with awareness and integrity. Robert wondered what on earth all this meant.

The first thing they had to do was to team up with a partner, and say something that they saw, felt and imagined about the other person.

Robert paired with Jonathan, who smelled rather strongly of brandy. Marshall bounded manfully across the room to Andrea. Robert called after him as loudly as he dared, but he was gone and there was no way of warning him of the risk he was taking. Robert played it safe with Jonathan.

'I see that you're wearing a tie.'

'I feel sorry that you never made it as a concert pianist.'

'I imagine you're in banking or something.'

Marshall was taking appalling risks with Andrea.

'I see you're not wearing a bra.'

'I feel quite randy.'

'I imagine . . .'

Robert couldn't hear the rest, but he could see Andrea's shoulders stiffening with anger.

The next morning, Gerry gave a 'lecturette' on something he called the Transparent Self. What they all had to aim at, it appeared, was a state where they were completely open about how they felt and received plenty of 'feedback' about themselves from others. Gerry asked for comments. Robert talked about the parallels with Sartre and de Beauvoir, and their ideal of transparent honesty. He was told to stop 'intellectualising'. It was just as Robert had thought. To open your mouth was highly dangerous: you might get wiped out.

Gerry asked if anyone wanted to 'work', and Marshall, hesitantly for him, let out a deep sigh, and said yes, he wanted to work on the difficulties he had in relating to women

'Particularly with regard to attraction and sexuality,' he added helpfully.

Robert wondered what he was up to: whether this was a cunning ploy, or some Road to Damascus turning point brought on by his wife Lizzie having abandoned him shortly after Stephen's wedding.

'That's great,' said Gerry. His quiet voice sounded more American than it had when they started. 'Why don't you go look at the women in the group, and the men too if you want, see who you feel attracted to, and tell them.' He turned towards the rest of the group and added: 'It's important to own our feelings, to really hear people's reactions, and to deal honestly with feelings of acceptance and rejection. In short, it's vital to have integrity.' Gerry made 'integrity' sound like a state-of-the-art hi-fi system.

'Marshall,' he said, 'I want you to give yourself permission to look, to really look, at whoever and whatever you like.'

It was difficult to read Marshall's expression as he looked round the group – was that a nervous twitch at the side of his mouth or a suppressed smirk

Marshall padded across the room, stopped in front of Andrea and sat down. Andrea rolled her eyes towards the pink-painted ceiling rose. 'Andrea, I want to be honest.'

His eyes shone bulgingly blue. You could see the whites all round, spattered with red veins.

'The thing is, Andrea, I really fancy you,' said Marshall.

Andrea grimaced, the shadows under her eyes turned darker and red spots appeared in the centre of her cheeks. She sighed with the slow expulsion of breath used by a karate dan about to break a stack of slates. A thin young man with a blond bouffant hairstyle nervously retied a red silk scarf around his neck.

'Go on,' said Gerry.

'I'm trying to be open and honest,' said Marshall. 'I really fancy you, Andrea. I don't know what you feel about me, I know you may be a lezzie or bisexual, but I fancy you. I'd like to . . . I'd like to . . .'

Marshall coughed and looked less at ease than Robert had ever seen him. 'I'm sorry, I'm not putting this well, I'm struggling for the words,' he said.

'Be authentic. Say what you need to say,' commanded Gerry, sitting up straighter in his cross-legged position, as if assuming take-off position for some yogic flying.

'Andrea, I think you're beautiful,' said Marshall. 'I'd like to . . . to, you know, make love. Poke you. Shaft you.' As he spoke he lapsed more and more into his native Nottinghamshire accent.

Gasps and tuts ricocheted around the room. Some older feminists looked at each other and held hands like colonial nuns facing attack by bandits. Robert would not have been surprised if they had started singing hymns.

'Andrea?' said Gerry, with impressive simplicity.

She was controlled, measured, taking deep breaths before each phrase.

'Marshall. I don't like you. I find your manner offensive. You disgust me. Repulse me.'

Marshall had a goatish, grinning look to him now. Robert had seen that look at his parties. He was not easily discouraged.

'I read somewhere,' said Marshall, 'about, you know, about attraction of opposites, sexual tension.'

'Marshall, listen to me. It's quite simple. I don't like you. And I don't fancy you. You revolt me.'

Gerry suggested that she offer Marshall specific feedback about what she didn't like about him. 'If you must know,' said Andrea, 'it's everything: it's your grossness, your sexism, it's . . .'

She started to tremble slightly. Her voice was unsteady.

'Can you be more specific?' This was from Martha, Gerry's co-facilitator.

'I know it's unfair, I know it's not behavioural feedback, but alongside everything else, your nose reminds me of . . . of . . . a penis. In fact my ex-partner's penis. I know you can't help it, but . . .'

It was the first time Robert had ever seen Marshall look truly surprised. Andrea's use of the word 'penis' gave what she said a weighty, almost clinical, tone.

Marshall's eyes swivelled and squinted as if he was trying to perform the impossible task of seeing his nose from several feet away. A wave of new energy and interest surged round the group.

Robert saw it instantly. How had he not noticed before? The glistening bulbous glans that was the tip of Marshall's nose, the groove running through the middle of the tip, with a little dent like the opening of the urethra, the long, tubular way it lay against his face, the red and purple tension of its surfaces.

'And Marshall, it kind of erects, changes colour, stiffens when you get excited. It did that as you were talking to me during the first exercise,' said Andrea. 'I felt . . . I felt . . .'

People assumed earnest expressions. Whenever someone mentioned feelings and started to struggle with words, it was a sign that they were being authentic.

She managed to continue. 'I felt . . . I felt . . . nasally raped.'

She gave a grim, ironic little laugh. Robert wasn't sure whether she was joking or not. A woman near him giggled and said to her friend that Marshall's nose was the very manifestation of patriarchal oppression.

'I know it's unfair, but it just seems absurd. It kind of makes me angry, furious. It's in the wrong place,' said Andrea.

Marshall's eyes were completely vacant. He looked catatonically still.

'What does it take to make you feel anything?' shouted Andrea suddenly. 'What does it take to get you to *hear* me?'

Robert was sweating. Every time he adjusted his position his clothes stuck to him. He doubted whether he'd get through the weekend in one piece.

Andrea asked Marshall why he hated women. He still stared ahead without expression.

Martha, the co-trainer, held Marshall's hand. He was quiet for a very long time. Sixteen pairs of eyes locked relentlessly and silently on to him, creating a force-field of intense expectation. After what must have been many minutes, he bent over double and let out several long groans. Dry sobs broke from inside him with a sound like a piece of wood being slowly sawn in two. Kleenex tissues were passed at regular intervals and held expectantly under his nose, but no tears came. Occasional words were mumbled about childhood and school.

Gerry looked pleased. One or two women yawned and exchanged cynical glances. But Robert was impressed, awestruck and moved. And deeply grateful that Marshall was taking up so much time.

After twenty minutes or so of this, Gerry started to press various parts of Marshall's back and legs. 'He's doing bio-energetics,' someone whispered reverentially. Marshall let out an enormous roar and starting writhing on the floor.

Afterwards, a plump woman in a knee-length cardigan said confidently that it had been a primal scream, a rebirthing. Others felt that it was merely a deep level of cathartic discharge that you could have got on a cheaper co-counselling weekend.

The shaven-headed woman, who was called Jude, glanced at her watch and tutted. No doubt she saw Marshall as a man who was, typically, taking away her space to work in the group. Nick was weeping openly and had joined a small knot of people massaging and hugging Marshall.

Robert found the whole event quite incredible. He'd seen Marshall as static and unchanging. And now he'd witnessed him in a state of catharsis, change and growth. Germaine was right: it was possible to start not by changing the world but by changing yourself. It was a truly revolutionary act. He remembered Sartre's epigram that existence preceded essence. He, Robert, had started to see himself as mainly essence, as having an unalterable set of characteristics: like being anxious, introspective and the rest. And now, here was Marshall, of all people, showing him that we might after all have the freedom to refute how we'd been so far, to begin again, and change. He had a glimpse of himself returning to Eva as a different person. It was exhilarating. The flag of Personal Growth, Liberation, was being hoisted aloft in front of him.

'I think you've had a major breakthrough,' said Gerry, with the touch of self-congratulation that a surgeon might use in talking to a patient after a particularly successful operation. Martha added comments about how Marshall had faced his own vulnerability, the exact same vulnerability that he seemed to despise in women.

Marshall finally sat upright. His eyes were blinking as if new-born. He looked exhausted but clear. In fact, all things considered, he looked remarkably well.

Gerry suggested that, because they didn't have time before dinner to get into all the issues that had been triggered by the Piece of Work, they had a round of what he called Appreciations. Nick told Marshall how moved he felt. Then Marshall staggered across the room until he was opposite Andrea.

'Thank you,' he said. 'I've gone deep inside myself. You've really helped me to see something.'

Andrea managed a tense half-smile. She stood up and briefly held both Marshall's hands.

Robert saw some light come back into Marshall's eyes

'I'd still . . . you know . . . I'd still like to . . . you know . . .' muttered Marshall. He put his arms round Andrea and hugged her to him in what seemed to Robert a decidedly over-optimistic embrace.

'We'll have an hour's break,' said Gerry, 'and after that I suggest we come back in and take our clothes off.' He gave the smallest of winks to Martha. The veterans, Robert guessed, knew that the weekend had been building up to this point.

The thought of nudity, of being stripped of yet another defence, acted like a laxative to Robert's bowels. He tip-toed towards the toilet door, which led off from the kitchen in contravention of all hygiene regulations. The toilet had, literally, been deconstructed: the bottom of the door had been sawn off and the lock removed. Robert supposed this was all part of the workshop, part of helping the emergence of the Transparent Self.

He tried to keep one arm pressed against the toilet door, and, as a precaution against splashes, placed a thick cushion of toilet paper on the surface of the water. He raced along as quickly as he could, wondering what it meant to defecate with integrity.

He flushed.

The water climbed steadily up the bowl, past the high-tide mark and on towards the rim. It stopped at the very edge of the rim, and looked as calm, he supposed, as a mill pond.

He'd blocked the toilet. Fool. And there was nothing to prod it with. He gazed at the evidence of his appallingly over abundant use of toilet paper, the sheets floating like lilies on the surface of the bowl. Shit, he thought, I can't get anything right. I'm nearly thirty and living in a rented bedsit, my job's futile, Eva doesn't want to live with me, and

I can't even flush a toilet without blocking it. The strongest
feelings of the weekend started to build like storm clouds
inside him. He leaned his head against the door and felt
like crying.

He'd been more disappointed than he cared to admit
when he finally read his father's diaries. They'd been stag-
geringly ordinary: 'New term starts', 'house insurance
renewal due', 'piano lesson for Peter H.', 'golf', 'the
Williams, drinks', 'Robert's birthday'. Well, what had
he bloody expected? Evenings in the Café des Arts?
Roquentin?

Someone pushed the door. He braced his shoulder
against it.

'Are you OK?'

It was Martha's voice. 'I'm feeling a little sick,' he said. 'I
won't be a moment.'

'You may be having what we call a Healing Crisis,' said
Martha. 'It's quite common on our weekends: you have to
see it as very positive. Do you need some support?'

Robert did not.

He found a comb in his back pocket, knelt down and
scooped away a few pieces of blocked paper. The water
level slowly retreated, then stopped halfway down the bowl.
To risk or not to risk? He flushed again. With frightening
speed the water raced back up to the rim and lapped over
the top. He felt close to the total and unconditional
surrender of his ego.

Then there was a huge sucking sound from deep below
the S-bend, a whoosh, a vacuum of air, and the bowl was
empty, filled with disappearance, non-being, nothingness.
It was gone. Robert felt a sense of elation, almost a peak
experience.

He eased his way into the kitchen, trying to look relaxed
and uninhibited, to look like someone who had indeed
defecated with integrity. He felt alienated but not completely destroyed. He knew something more definitely now

about Who He Was; some new piece of self-awareness had dawned. He knew that not all aspects of the Transparent Self were for him. A certain amount of secrecy and privacy was essential to his life. He was part of an English tradition which valued reticence and reserve, and preferred long-drop toilets with doors three inches thick and locks that wouldn't disgrace a bank vault.

'The Dream Companion.'

'Talk about your bodies with a partner of the same sex,' said Gerry. 'Give them a guided tour of your body and what it means to you.'

Gerry looked less naked than everyone else. He had a soft, sleek body, so deeply and evenly tanned that it looked covered in some way.

Robert once again paired with Jonathan, who now smelled rather strongly of whisky.

'This discriminates a bit against us heterosexuals,' said Jonathan. 'I came here hoping for a bit of a sensual massage. Pairing with you is a bit of a sodding anti-climax.'

Robert, inevitably, tried to describe his body as Eva would have seen it. He talked about his thinning hair, and how much pain it had caused him, the agony of picking hundreds of hairs off Eva's pillow before she opened the curtains in the morning. But then there were his green eyes, which Eva once said were beautiful and reminded her of the sea, and she liked his body, even if his legs were a little short, and . . .

Jonathan was ignoring him. He was crouching down, using Robert's body as cover to peep at the rest of the group.

'Christ,' said Jonathan, 'look at the knockers on that Linda. You'd never have guessed how luscious they were, would you? It's the loose clothes she was wearing. You'd never have guessed what was underneath.'

Robert didn't play. He pointed out that Jonathan was treating her like a sex object.

Gerry instructed people to come into the middle of the room and form a circle.

'Allow yourself to look,' said Gerry, 'at whoever and whatever you want to look at. Let it happen. This is an existential moment.'

Robert stole glances at Jude and Andrea, or rather bought them on hire purchase, feeling there'd be a price to pay for his slow traverse over the previously dungaree-clad Jude's elegant body. And despite the risk, he was hypnotised by Andrea's pubic triangle, by the danger signals it seemed, like a radiation warning sign, to transmit. Other glances felt like acts of charity or commitment to equal opportunity. He gave a carefully measured twenty seconds to a former nun whose stomach was as creased and white as the crevassed surface of a glacier. He suddenly felt tender towards her, as if a barrier had indeed been removed.

Jonathan had an erection. Unmistakably. The silence in the group itself erected, suddenly became tight and focused and directional.

'I feel he's making an aggressive patriarchal statement,' said Jude. 'He should apologise to the group.'

'I feel helpless. It's like a buried sub-self taking over,' said Jonathan. This man is learning fast, thought Robert.

Taking an embarrassingly long period of time, and with leg actions similar to those of a hurdler, Jonathan managed to perform a movement that could only be described as stepping over his own penis. He succeeded in pinning it away behind his legs. With his genitals out of sight, he looked remarkably like one of the more assertive lesbians in the group. What, thought Robert, when it really came down to it, was the difference between men and women?

I'd like to go round and have each of us say one thing we really appreciate about our bodies,' said Martha. 'We get so used to putting ourselves down. So many of us have a negative body image. We need to reaffirm our bodies as a beautiful creation of God.'

Robert found this rather moving.

'Linda, why don't you start?' said Martha.

'I like my luscious big knockers,' said Linda. Jonathan looked triumphant.

Robert played safe. 'I like my face,' he said.

They moved on to Jude. 'I like my back.'

'Marshall?'

There was a sudden swell of curiosity as people looked to see if Marshall's penis resembled a nose. Was it going to be snub, Grecian, Roman, retroussé?

Incredibly, but somehow appropriately, Marshall's penis had some sort of black and white barcode on it. It appeared to have become, literally, a consumer product. But then Robert realised that it must be a tattoo of some kind.

Marshall looked solemnly, somewhat bravely, around the group before speaking.

'My nose,' he said, 'I like my nose.'

'Mmm. Mmm. Mmm,' said Nick.

A few minutes later the women decided to have their own group. As the minority, the men had to move through to a different room.

Still naked, they trooped out under the gaze of the women, Robert feeling like a member of the sort of New Guinea tribe he used to see in *National Geographic* magazines at school: it did not, somehow, seem the right time to debate issues of separatism and equality. With rhythmic shouts of 'You bastards,' coming through the wall, Marshall thought the men had to go back in and 'make a stand'. Robert was horrified. But then, to his great relief, Jonathan insisted on talking about the fall in his unit-trust prices.

Reclothed, the group came back together. Jude said she needed to do some work. Her face looked even more tense than usual. Martha suggested Psychodrama.

Jude selected Robert to act as her partner. Moments later he was sitting on a cushion staring into her glittering angry face as she shrieked, 'You shit, you shit,' at him over and over again.

Robert felt a mixture of fear that she might start hitting him and a profound, almost spiritual pleasure at the fact that he wasn't, in reality, obliged to her in any way, shape or form.

After a few more minutes of screaming, Gerry asked Jude what she wanted from her man.

'I want him to feel something. Anger, passion, love, something, anything. I don't want all that cool, calculating defensiveness every time I talk to him. And I want him to take me seriously as a woman.'

Dozens more 'You shits' hurled into Robert's face like grit against a window.

Gerry nodded at Robert and muttered about improvisation. Robert leaned uncertainly towards Jude. Her anger came up from her body in hot thermals of sweat and perfume.

'Darling,' said Robert, and hesitated. He'd not had to role-play anything since primary school.

He put a hand on her back, and felt the damp, grainy surface of her tartan shirt and the tense cogs of muscle underneath.

He wasn't sure what to do next. He sighed.

'That's exactly what my bloke does,' said Jude, turning round to face the group. 'He sighs.'

'Tell him how you feel,' said Gerry, pointing at Robert. 'You shit. You don't respect me as a woman. You don't support me in my work. You're not helping me to grow. You don't try to understand how I feel. You don't really care about me, do you?'

'Do you?' she shrieked again. A fist hammered on to Robert's chest, which made a disappointingly hollow sound.

Robert was uncertain what to do. But then Gerry, whispering into his ear like a boxing second between rounds, suggested that he tell her precisely where to get off.

'Fuck off,' said Robert quietly and politely. He hesitated. 'Fuck off,' he said more firmly. 'Fuck off.' The words were coming more easily now. 'Fuck off,' he shouted. 'Fuck off, you oppressive, overpowering, spoiled, selfish bitch. I'm not fucking putting up with your humiliating behaviour any fucking longer. I'm sick of your negativity. I'm sick of your lack of commitment to any sort of life together. I'm sick of your joyless pessimism about marriage and children. Fuck off, fuck off, fuck off!'

Jude held her breath for an extraordinary length of time, then burst into what were later agreed to be large floods of tears.

Some time later she thanked Robert for helping her come to a major insight, then they hugged each other in a way that seemed to Robert respectful and almost comradely.

He was, of course, asked how he felt. He was a little shocked at the ease with which he'd role-played anger: he'd had a glimpse of a different way of behaving, felt what it might be like to let go and say how he really felt, and not care about the risks.

'Who were you so angry with?' said Martha. 'Who were you talking to back then? It wasn't just to Jude.'

Robert went to bed early. He was glad to escape from something that the trainers were calling a party, but which was in

fact a demand for everyone to perform spectacularly uninhibited dances and improvisations. He wished he was with
Eva. His anxiety about the future had been heightened by
the possibility of her going to Heidelberg.

His sleeping bag smelled of spilled bacon fat and
unwashed feet, but at least it was private. He wondered
what on earth he was doing with these people. He thought
about Stephen. Stephen didn't oppress people like
Marshall did, but nor did he humble himself like Nick.
Stephen would never need to sit in a circle talking about
how he fucking felt. He simply didn't need it. He was OK.
He had a humorous, tough-minded respect for himself
and others that enabled him to get along with just about
anyone, with an Andrea as much as a Deborah.

Robert lay in the darkness, listening to the music and
laughter downstairs. How often in his life he had dreamed
of closeness and love, but how difficult he'd found it in
practice. He wasn't very good at letting go or trusting
people.

That night he dreamed he was running through woods
in an autumn storm. He suddenly tripped on something
hard. He looked down and saw grey, bloated flesh protruding through a covering of leaves. He woke up shaken
and desolate.

He was kept awake by someone having sex in a way that
reminded him of Thomas the Tank Engine going up a
steep hill. She then had the sort of yelpingly noisy and self-
advertising orgasm that was born of years of
consciousness-raising. It was all very familiar. The only
interesting question was who was Andrea with?

It was the start of the final morning. The more experienced participants had lungfuls of feeling to express about
the end of the workshop. They appreciated the group, felt
challenged by the group, and wanted to thank the group.
Increasingly, they referred to the group as if it was a

person: a tough, empowering and ultimately loving Mother.

'Who wants to work?' asked Martha.

There was a long pause. This was the point at which someone usually lurched towards the middle of the group, bringing a problem with them like some invisible dog on a lead. Robert held his breath and looked down. He was one of only a couple of people who hadn't worked on themselves. He tried to keep his face light and composed, but he knew his shoulders were sagging. I am sad, he thought, almost arbitrarily, but then he couldn't get the thought out of his mind.

After moving backwards and forwards across the room in diffuse exchanges, some, then a majority, then all of the eyes swivelled their barrels on to him.

'Robert,' said Martha, 'what's going on for you?'

'Um . . . er . . . I'm just feeling a bit tired and heavy.'

No one else, for once, leaped into the ring with a cushion. The invisible matrix of the group, the net woven from all its subtle interactions and possibilities, settled over him and him alone. Oh shit, thought Robert. It was, by default or need or natural justice, his turn.

'I think I'd like to work. Just for fifteen minutes, please.' This was what the experts did, estimate how long they needed, in the manner of an experienced auctioneer valuing an antique.

Robert knew the basic rules. You trudged into the centre of the group with a cushion, and sat down facing the facilitator. It was then appropriate to say 'I want to work on my feelings about . . .' For extra marks you burst into tears at this point, or went pale and started shaking. At all costs it was important not to be composed or articulate.

He fingered the small fawn Habitat cushion he'd brought.

'I feel blocked,' he said. If in doubt, like pawn to king four, it was a good opener.

'I'm really worried about my relationship with Eva, about what the future holds, whether we're ever going to live together, make commitments and settle down.' This was not so good. It was too specific, more a counselling than a therapy issue.

He quickly corrected himself.

'It opens up a lot of feelings I have about myself, from childhood, and about being a man.' Better.

'Let this cushion be Eva,' said Martha, throwing a splendid Liberty-print specimen into the middle. 'Tell her what you really want.'

This wasn't too difficult. He could remember a conversation from a couple of weeks back. All he had to do was put lots of 'ums' and 'ers' and silences and eye-blinks into the telling of it.

'Eva, I love you, I'm in love with you,' he said as sincerely as he could to the cushion. 'I want to marry you, and have children with you. OK, maybe marriage is not as important as it was – I accept Germaine's criticisms. But I'm sure we could live together and make it work. I know you've got reservations about me, about whether you could fall in love with me again. But falling in love's a myth or an illness anyway: people like you and Germaine keep telling me that. You can see that other bloke Pascal, if you have to. We can invent our own way of relating, just like we used to talk about Sartre and Simone de Beauvoir doing. We just need to give it all a try.'

Robert was not sure how well this was going. He felt as far from being natural as he'd ever felt in his life. It also seemed like a small betrayal of privacy and intimacy with Eva. But at least he'd used up a few minutes of his time.

Martha asked the group for any suggestions.

'I think Robert's struggling to find a way through Ego,' said Linda of the luscious boobs. She made Ego sound like a town in Scandinavia with a particularly complex one-way system.

'It's not a relationship you've got with Eva, it's a drag,' said Marshall. 'You're betraying yourself, humiliating yourself, and not doing Eva any good, either.'

'When you said "I'm in love with you" it sounded rather abstract,' said Jude. 'Your head and body didn't move at all while you spoke. It was as if you were reading out a weather forecast.'

'Well, it is bloody abstract being here,' said Robert. 'It feels like play-acting, trying to do the done thing, trying to fucking please people.' Robert was surprised at his anger. He wasn't sure whether it was real or role-playing. It was as if he back in yesterday's session with Jude.

'That's good,' said Gerry, 'there's some real feeling starting to show. Why don't you tell us all what it is you want right now?'

'I want to get out of here, buy a Sunday paper, read the football reports, and have a bloody strong coffee and a couple of pints. That's what I want, and I don't care what you think.'

'Stay with that,' said Gerry. 'Get a sense of what it would be like to talk like that to Eva.'

At Gerry's suggestion, Robert practised saying to Eva that from now on he was going to care a lot more for himself and his needs, but it sounded flat and ridiculous.

Then Gerry thought he should sit on the Liberty cushion, pretend to be Eva, and talk to the other cushion as if it were him.

'Listen you fool,' he said to his small fawn Habitat. 'Can't you get it into your head? I've changed. I'm not the mythical perfect girl you lost. I've changed. I look back on our relationship when we first met and see that I was lost, vulnerable, naive. I've got myself together. I like you. I enjoy making love with you. I enjoy being friends. I'm not trying to hurt you. I'm not trying to piss you around when I say I want time for myself, and other relationships, and my work. Unlike you, I like my work. I'm not trying to oppress you when I talk about Pascal and trying to sort things out with him. I've struggled through a lot. I've been hurt a lot in the past. And I've got to a point where I feel in control of my life for the first time. The idea of ending up in some dull, monogamous relationship in a semi somewhere appals me. I can't give you security: you have to find it in yourself.'

It was good being Eva. Robert felt wiser, clearer, and more powerful. Just as he'd suspected, it was better these days to be a woman. Or at least one like Eva.

Martha looked at the group, inviting feedback.

'You seemed much more alive when you were being Eva,' said Andy, the man with the bouffant hair.

There was a long pause, during which Robert's mind went rather blank. It was a shame. Lots of people were struggling hard to help him and he was letting them down.

Martha said, suddenly, 'What were the words you brought with you?'

'It's silly really. I've brought some words from Simone de Beauvoir, about her relationship with Sartre. Probably just to mock myself with.'

Martha asked him to read them out.

'"Together we set forth to explore the world. My trust in him was so complete that he supplied me with the sort of unfailing security that I—"'

Martha interrupted. Robert was relieved. For a second his insides had, in the language of the group, felt rather wobbly.

'Say "she". Read it as if you're talking about Eva.'

'She supplied me with the sort of absolute unfailing security that I had once had from my parents, or from God . . . there was nothing left for me to wish, except that this triumphant state of bliss might continue unwaveringly forever.'

Feeling increasingly absurd, Robert moved on to other quotes. 'She corresponded exactly to the dream companion I had longed for since I was fifteen: she was the double in whom I found all my burning aspirations raised to the pitch of incandescence. I should always be able to share everything with her . . . my life would be a beautiful story come true, a story I would make up as I went along.'

'When you were speaking, your shoulders were very bowed. It was as if you were carrying a heavy weight,' said Gerry.

'It feels stupid reading this stuff out,' said Robert. 'Maybe my relationship with Eva once offered all that. But I didn't trust her completely. I didn't set forth with her to explore the world, literally or in any other way. I was too stupid to see what she was giving me. Too cautious. It's all so bloody special, that stuff about dream companions and bliss. It's not for me. I'm just ordinary, that's all I am' – he suddenly thought of the diaries – 'an ordinary wally.'

'The notion of a dream companion is probably a pre-Oedipal thing,' said Andrea. 'It might be useful for you to read some Lacan.'

Robert was very quiet. Was this it, the major insight he'd reached, that he was just an ordinary wally? Could he go back to his place now? Or maybe he should tell them about his dream. He was unsure whether the body in the woods had been his own or his father's.

'"Finally one must take one's life into one's arms,"' said Andy. 'It's a quote from Arthur Miller.'

'Aye, but he took Marilyn Monroe as well, didn't he?' said Marshall.

Robert felt Gerry's hands on his shoulders, massaging them frantically. Gerry was becoming increasingly desperate in his efforts to get Robert's feelings started, like an AA patrolman in pouring rain at a car breakdown. But Andy's words had affected Robert in some new way.

'You seem small and sad,' said Martha. 'How old do you feel right now?'

The faces of the group faded. Robert saw a beautiful autumn day, and a park filled with chestnut trees, and a father holding a little boy's hand as he scuffled through leaves. Together we set forth to explore the world, thought Robert. My trust in him was so complete. The father was pushing him on a swing now. An ordinary vulnerable man. Together we set forth to explore the world . . .

'Why are you gripping that cushion so tightly?' said Martha. 'Who are you holding on to?'

He kept hugging his cushion, swaying forwards and backwards, and trying to speak: about his father, Eva, himself; but the words were filling up like water inside him. He felt an awful quivering compassion for his own life.

They said afterwards that he sobbed for twenty-seven minutes. It was, Robert realised with a touch of pride, the record for the weekend. Two whole boxes of tissues were held under his dripping nose. He couldn't stop. Marshall blamed it on the vegetarian food and thought that Robert needed to get a 14-ounce steak down him as soon as possible.

Robert felt a new and slightly bitter respect for himself. His voice sounded different, his own voice rather than something to please someone else. He felt himself tentatively on the inside of his life for the first time, as if in an undiscovered room that was his alone, where he could find his own independent thoughts and listen to his own voice.

With a slight hint once more of self-congratulation, Gerry reminded Robert to listen to his own needs, to love and care for himself. He had to remember that he deserved some good things in life. Then he suggested that Robert wrote down three words that described some parts of himself that he could now leave behind. Robert thought for a minute, then wrote down the words that Kate Millett said Freud had used to describe female sexuality: Passive, Narcissistic. Masochistic.

To a rather patchy round of applause, he tore the words into tiny pieces and threw them into the bin. As soon as the group ended, he ran without looking back to the nearest pub.

Three hours later, filled with five pints, ten Embassy Kings and a sense of exhausted excitement about the weekend, he went round to see Eva, and, in a scene reminding him strongly of Roquentin meeting Anny in *Nausea*, found out that his relationship with her was over.

Part III
1979–1986

'Nothing. Existed.'

He'd gone to see Eva after the group with a sense of breakthrough, of his psychic waters having finally broken. He felt a new relationship to himself: maybe he didn't quite love himself as yet, but he felt a sort of dogged loyalty, a growing friendship and interest. He would think more for himself, say what he felt, stop being so nice, be miserable if he wanted to be. And his relationship with Eva would have a new spontaneity and vigour

She was in the kitchen washing up. The room was full of the smell of chicken giblets being cooked for the cats. As she bent over the sink he could see the bumps of her spine through her T-shirt. He loved her pride and independence and lean, beautiful face. But, he thought, I don't need you to save me any more. I have brought you what you wanted, not quite my head in a charger, but myself changed.

He was preparing to tell her about the group, but she turned round from the sink and spoke first.

'I spent a lot of time thinking last night,' she said. 'And I've definitely decided to go to Germany for a month or two. I want to do the work, and I need a break from relationships for a while, especially with men. It's all got so complex, so much hassle. I'm sure we can sort things out after I've been to Heidelberg. We'll both be clearer then about what we want.'

'I'm sick of ambiguity,' said Robert. 'I'm sick of feeling humiliated, I'm sick of being pissed around.' It was as if he were still in the group, talking to Jude. Martha and Gerry were almost tangible presences in the room, urging him therapeutically onwards and upwards. For the first time in years, he felt a sense of excitement in being with *himself*, almost like a child with a new toy.

'Tell me whether you're giving me the boot,' he said. 'Are you choosing to leave me? Is it over or isn't it?'

'For goodness' sake, don't be so melodramatic,' said Eva. 'Is this what the group taught you?' She turned back to the sink and started to rub a saucepan with a Brillopad.

'I'm through with being messed around. Tell me yes or no, *now*!' he shouted. Right then he didn't care what was destroyed. He was speaking as he felt, with a thrilling sense of power and independence.

'If you want to be ridiculous, yes, I want to be on my own for a while.'

'You always deal with things by fucking going away,' said Robert. 'You can't commit yourself to anything.'

'I feel as if you've just come in and invaded me,' she said. She looked pale and grim.

He walked past the posters in the hall. There were tears in his eyes. He felt new; transparent.

'From now on I'm going to love and care for myself,' he said to himself. He kept repeating it as he walked to the 104 bus stop, through streets piled high with Winter of Discontent rubbish, and then all the way back to the bedsit.

She wrote from Germany saying that the evening they'd spent had been heavy and negative. She'd been in a lousy mood, but as well as that, she'd missed seeing Robert's gentleness and humour that night. He'd been full of some sort of aggressive high. Maybe he was right in some of what he said, but, what with this and the hassle with Pascal, she was getting fed up with spending all her energy on relationships. She'd had enough of all the confusion they created. She was going to drop everything for a while and go to India. If anything changed she'd write.

Robert felt desolate but not wiped out. What was happening didn't seem absolutely final, and he had too much pride to grovel to Eva now. And being on his own felt better than it had done before: he was grateful to the group for the way it had helped him to restore some self-respect.

He took some of what he had learned from the group into work as well. He attended a meeting on research funding chaired by the deputy director of the polytechnic. The deputy director ignored the research item and spent hours rambling on about office allocations at a new building. Robert decided, in the language of the group, to confront him.

'I feel angry,' he said, 'at having to sit through a meeting that is so disorganised, and I feel angry that you have discounted the item that matters to me. I feel very . . . er . . . angry.' He went quite red, slapped the table and breathed out hard. Martha would have been proud of him.

The deputy director said it was one of the most immature outbursts he'd ever seen in a meeting. Days later, the funding was axed on Robert's job and he was on the dole. Well, cheers Gerry and Martha, thought Robert. I've lost Eva and I've lost my job. There didn't seem a lot left to his life now except defecating with integrity.

Marshall said that expressing feelings was getting to be a bit passé. Feelings were a temporary Californian import that didn't suit English culture. And it was no bad thing for Robert to be out of the poly: Thatcher was going to win the coming election and the future was going to lie in the private sector. Marshall was spending most of his time setting up a management consultancy business. 'The direction for psychology,' he said, 'lies in things you can put the word "executive" in front of: executive recruitment, executive psychometric testing, executive stress, redeployment counselling, and the rest.' He invited Robert, for an income only slightly greater than his dole money, to work as his assistant in setting up the new business.

A year after the group Robert married Deborah. They'd drifted back in contact after her relationship with the Assistant Buyer didn't quite work out. He was sitting with her one day in a café outside Lord John in Brent Cross and she started talking about the car insurance discounts they could get if they were a married couple. He suddenly couldn't see any overwhelming reason not to. It was clear now that Eva wasn't coming back, and he liked Deborah's sense of order and pragmatism; and the way her tan faded into the whiteness of her bottom, and the fact that she didn't wear badges saying women needed men like fish needed bicycles. An ordinary life suddenly seemed attractive. It would be nice to have someone to say hello to when he came in, to watch telly and have kids with. He realised these days that life wasn't about perfection. Deborah's businesslike approach to life and marriage had considerable appeal.

They had a honeymoon in Ibiza and bought a semi in Friern Barnet. Mrs Thatcher got elected. Deborah passed exams. She was accepted for a job in Marks and Spencer. She made love that night with an intensity Robert had never known in her, and his head was filled with green St Michael logos as he came.

Deborah ran the house on Total Quality Management principles, like a miniature M & S department store. Right first time, every time. The sheets on the bed smelled menthol-clean. There was never a cardboard bog-roll tube or dirty sock to be seen on the floor. She waged war on house dust mite, and banned cats on the basis of allergy articles in magazines. She believed that having a child had to be done in a quality way, too, and thought it best to wait until she'd reached a higher management grade and they could afford a live-in nanny and a four-piece en-suite bathroom.

Robert started to become successful in his own right. He felt more competent and confident. Marshall's management consultancy was doing well. It was fun to get up early for a change and work hard.

The company had what Sartre might have called an essence view of people. Their psychometric questionnaires would specify the precise unchanging essence of someone's personality and the types of job this suited them.

One day Nick came to be tested. He wore a sweater showing a herd of cows with prominent pink udders grazing in a luridly green field. His profile described him as 'Amiable. Sensitive. Uncompetitive. Idealistic.' It was hard to tell him that he had a personality that made him virtually unemployable – who in Maggie's Britain wanted to be described as amiable? Nick was upset. He spoke in a voice that was now unfashionably slow and inarticulate. It was painful for Robert to see Nick slouched unhappily in front of him. Robert felt guilty about his work but there wasn't an alternative he could see.

Shortly after Charles and Diana got married, Deborah began to change, or maybe it was merely that certain characteristics that had always been present intensified. She acquired a big sculpted blonde head, and solariumed her skin into the sort of colour a paint manufacturer might call Saharan Bronze. She began to look at people with a smiling, wide-eyed gaze, which reminded Robert, in his darker moments, of Nancy Reagan.

Then she went on Assertion Training for Managers and was taught how to disagree with people effectively. She put this into action with Robert. She challenged his soft views on urban riots and unemployment and Cruise missiles – if he was really worried they could even be like American people and build a bomb shelter. She told him not to be sentimental about competing with others, and compared him unfavourably with Marshall, who looked after his appearance and had a thrusting four-wheel-drive personality.

Sex at some point became bonking. She was promoted on to something called a fast-track career path. Mrs Thatcher got re-elected. They bought a bigger semi. Robert sat on the first en-suite bog he'd ever owned, and felt deep within him the satisfaction of property-owning democracy.

So many questions and preoccupations were changing. Dreams were changing. Definitions of success were changing: money, work, houses were the things to be taken seriously, the rest didn't matter. Even Andrea was different. She announced she was visiting one day and Robert went round systematically untidying the house and removing aerosols from toilets and frilly nylon covers from boxes of tissues. He needn't have bothered. Andrea arrived in a brand-new silver Volvo and broke bread with Deborah by talking about how her flat had doubled in value in eighteen months.

Only Stephen and Terry didn't seemed to have bought into any of it. Stephen was only interested in his politics and his ever-expanding family. Terry was at Greenham.

And Eva. Robert heard nothing of her, but he still missed her in a way. He'd say her name to himself, an image of her pale blue eyes would come, and he wouldn't be able to blink it away. Spiritually she still lived next door to him. He conversed with her, reminisced with her, shared things, argued. She looked at his life and said, 'Well, here you are, married and secure, with a nice little job. Who was right,

you or me?' He'd tell her he was more practical about his
life now; maybe it was a little dull and orthodox, but he felt
less neurotic, more independent of the things that had
once drained him. 'But what's happened to your spirit?'
she'd say. 'You've lost the things that matter most.'

'We could have been happy,' he'd reply. 'We could have
had children by now. Your ideas about relationships were
far too rigorous. Your ideology got in the way of you seeing
me clearly.'

'But you were so desperate, so needy,' said Eva. 'It was
frightening what you were hoping for. You could have
drowned me.'

His desire to see Eva only really intensified after his
mother died. His mother kept making light of increasing
pains. She lost weight but said this was a good thing: her
pains were in embarrassing women's places and she didn't
want doctors fussing around with her body. She was stoical
in the way that her generation was expected to be: she was
accustomed to sacrifices and felt lucky to have survived the
war. She died after a long useless labour and much genuine nausea, on a hot, smelly summer's day, while Mr
Webster hammered feebly outside.

The whole world seemed soulless after that. He grieved
for his mother, and then, as in the encounter group, for his
father, too. He let himself go, eating more and more, taking no exercise and not bothering to floss his teeth. At
work he had periodic shaking fits. Increasingly, he became
obsessed with security.

Bit by bit, he did the lot. Burglar alarm, infra-red
outdoor lights, steel bars, higher BS standard mortices,
chains, spy holes, and a panic alarm by Deborah's side of
the bed (after some discussion of the relative increases in
homosexual and heterosexual rape). Stephen kept telling
him that it was Friern Barnet, not Beirut, that he was para-
noid. 'You're building yourself a prison,' he insisted.

In any case, it was violence rather than burglary which

was the problem. More and more people were finding it easier to reach for a Stanley knife than to struggle with the complexities of sentence-formation. It was becoming the norm to be forced to eat your own little finger for breakfast, or to be shot dead in front of your family in the fully en-suite master bedroom.

Of course Robert knew that the only real security and freedom was internal. It was spiritual. It lay in accepting your own life and your own death. This was something that Eva knew, and which gave her a particular grace and self-possession. When he'd first known her he hadn't been afraid of death, because he was in love with her and living in the present. Whereas now he was so keen to last a bit longer, to get enough time. He had years of nothing very much happening, of 'days being tacked on to days without rhyme or reason', and then, all of a sudden, in 1986, things came to a head.

'...But it was really out of politeness.'

It was a Friday evening in June. He was lying in bed waiting for Deborah to emerge from the bathroom, looking at the house, as he usually did, through a burglar's eyes and noticing small security flaws: if a burglar was under five feet tall and swung on his hands along the sill he might just be able to climb head-first through the toilet window . . .

Deborah came out of the en-suite in her Friday night cream St Michael basque, perfumed, bony and tanned. It was almost like a stage entrance in a long-running play.

They embraced on the orthopaedically firm mattress and began a familiar erotic routine.

A few quick grunts, and the bonk, at least for Deborah, seemed to be finished – surprisingly quickly, from which Robert surmised that she was not thinking about him.

She'd done enough assertion training to insist on his right to reciprocal satisfaction, and started to tug at him conscientiously. He scanned through his library of erotic images.

Her left hand stretched for a tissue from a large pink box. She held it between thumb and forefinger, like a nurse, ready for Robert to do his business.

'It puts me off, you holding that tissue,' he said.

Squashed against her, the air filling with the smell of his gingivitis, this was threatening to become a humiliating end to the day.

'Well I don't want to mess up the bed,' said Deborah. 'I was reading an article on house dust mites. The average bed has tens of thousands. They live mainly off our dead skin, but what they like best is sperm: it's far higher in protein content and can keep them going for days. I don't want to get it on the bed. It can set off asthma.'

'It seems so clinical,' said Robert.

As a concession to reassure him, she pulled the box closer, laid the tissue across the top of it, sighed heavily and carried on.

'Are you going to be much longer?' she said a minute or two later.

Among other things he was, if he was honest, struggling to keep his will pointing upstream against a tide of troubling, neurotic thoughts. What if the alarm wasn't switched on properly, the window locks not secured? What if, at this very moment, the escaped bisexual rapist called the Ferret was sloping along their street, seeing their light on, and sensing their vulnerability with his extraordinary animal instinct? Or what if at this furthest extreme of being caught with his trousers down, some drug-crazed gang was swaggering towards his door, it being nearly midsummer, which apart from Christmas, was the most violent time of the year.

But finally he relaxed, finding himself with Betty all of a sudden. And as a first twitch announced itself, Deborah snatched up a tissue, and started talking, right in the middle of his climax, of the Saturday-morning task list. And at this very moment, as he stood, so to speak, on the receiving end of a less than St Michael quality hand-job, well below British Standard 5750, now, at this very moment, as if being shafted by his own expensive electricity and sensors, the burglar alarm went off.

'You're the man,' said Deborah. 'You'd better go and have a look.'

'Ring the police,' said Robert. 'No, don't bother, they'll have cut the wires.'

There was a banging on the front door. Would they have pangas? Baseball bats? Sawn-off shot guns? Sulphuric Acid?

'Everything is in the box file, second drawer down in the filing cabinet,' said Robert. He looked fondly and forlornly at his little finger and put on his pink fibre-pile jogging trousers.

'The tax return and life insurance are up to date. Thanks for everything,' said Robert. He walked bravely and stickily downstairs, almost with a sense of relief.

'But the end is there, transforming everything.'

Robert flung open the door, his chest bare, like a Christian martyr, and found himself facing an elderly neighbour. He switched off the alarm.

'I tapped on the window,' said the man. 'Couldn't find the buzzer. Must have set something off.'

'Our new infra-red vibration detector,' said Robert, 'Just in from the States.'

The neighbour held a letter.

'I know it's late,' he said, 'but it seemed important. A letter from India, delivered to us by mistake. Someone's sent it on from Finchley.'

Eva's writing was still recognisable: what hope the remarkable care and roundness of the characters had once inspired.

Inside was a postcard of two lovers sitting across a Parisian café table, and on it was written 'De Beauvoir needs Sartre. Love Eva.'

Robert spent the next week in one of the more exciting types of turmoil. Why was she contacting him, summoning him into her life, after all these years of silence? And in talking about need surely she was being ironic?

He thought of the times he'd known Eva. When he'd first met her, he'd been a ridiculous adolescent, living completely in his mind. She'd transformed his life into something thrilling and sumptuous. She'd raised his flag of independence, made him feel free. And then he'd left her. Looking back, this seemed forgivable, natural enough, just a stage. Her intensity had at times been overwhelming. He'd needed to go off and meet other people.

And the second time he'd known her, he'd loved and desired her more than he'd thought possible. But he'd wanted to possess her, institutionalise her. He'd been dependent and neurotic, though it was her unpredictability that had helped make him like this. At times his self-esteem had been zero. Then he'd gone to the group and found a different sense of himself, but too late and too explosively.

His life with Deborah was a bit soulless, but it was also ordered and businesslike: he got up in the morning and achieved things; he was not a pushover; he felt periodic outbreaks of self-respect and confidence.

At times life seemed like a goalless draw. But maybe there was something to be said for the goalless draw. If he managed to make it to his deathbed without hating Deborah too much, losing his job, or having his little finger cut off, then whilst that might not be an ideal result, neither could it be dismissed out of hand.

And yet. And yet. Robert thought about how he'd once been to Paris with Deborah and spent the whole time comparing prices in different department stores. How could they have made Paris into such a boring place? What had happened to the ridiculous dreams of childhood and adolescence, to falling in love with snowy mornings and French novels and girls wearing patchouli? He and Deborah didn't seem to believe in anything except steadily rising house prices and an occasional bonk. Germaine, when it came down to it, had been right about a lot of things.

He'd once seen a Personal Ad in *Time Out* that said simply, 'De Beauvoir seeks Sartre.' His life had felt suddenly weightless. What magic the phrase had created! What a contrast it was to the endless 'attractives', and 'younglookings' and 'GSOHs'.

'De Beauvoir seeks Sartre. Sartre seeks de Beauvoir.' What would it be like for two people to come towards each other along the ley-lines of those phrases?

'De Beauvoir seeks Sartre.' It was above all a dream of how this other person would see him, with a look that would confirm his existence and create a certain sort of love story, about equality, spirit, humour and intelligence. And now Eva wrote that she needed him.

In the end Robert gave up trying to put his thoughts into long letters and sent her a postcard of the London Underground with a few things scribbled on the back. In the days that followed, he felt hugely hungry. He ate more and more, gorging himself on Mr Kipling's Individual Apple Pies. Deborah said it was passive aggression towards her, a concept she'd learned on a Psychology for Middle Managers course. She was angry that Robert was going to let her down at Stephen's house-warming party by waddling out pasty and overweight.

Three weeks later, on the day before Stephen's party, Robert found an airmail letter from India curled on the doormat like a scorpion.

Dear Robert,
When we met after your 'group', I felt it was very melodramatic, very either/or. I felt sad, but going to Germany seemed like a good natural breathing space. I needed time on my own, and I think you did too. I went off to India, to an ashram, then I met friends and went to the States and published my

book, and did some teaching. I kept in touch with Nick for a while and heard you'd married Deborah. I had this image of you sitting in your smart semi, with the TV, on, and Deborah looking *très chic* in the corner. It seemed very comfortable and secure. But I wanted to take the risk and contact you.

I think, looking back, that some of the times when I knew you were very good. That first time we were together, there was something about myself that I love now. I was very neurotic and unhappy at times, but I was also struggling, joyful and passionate. I giggled a lot. I lost my giggle, but didn't seem happier.

I think that intellectually and in other ways we are equal and good for each other. There are lots of criticisms of de Beauvoir and Sartre, but I still have some faith in what they sought in a relationship. Above all, that we must invent our own way of relating. I believe again, like I once did, that in some deep way we are suited to each other, that we have the same idiom. I feel we needed to go off on separate trajectories, you exploring marriage and convention, me wanting to be independent and free of any attachments, and now it's time to move towards each other. It seems quite obvious and simple now, doesn't it, how to relate?

Things have got clearer for me since my mother died a year ago. I found her death very traumatic, despite all my psychotherapy. At times when I was in the communal house my main preoccupation in life was avoiding the mistakes my parents made. Like a lot of women, I struggled to get clear of the shit about relationships and marriage and motherhood, maybe at a price that other women after us won't have to pay. What I see since my mother died is that I've been hiding deeper pain about how hard I tried, as an only child, to hold their relationship together. And I've felt a lot of pain about how I was never allowed to be an ordinary, needy child. It enrages me that women spend so much time nurturing men and are then accused of being emotionally dependent.

What I realise now is that it's at the times when I've felt most loved and supported that I've been able to be most independent. It's one of the real paradoxes of relationships, I suppose. I think Sartre and de Beauvoir found, for all their faults, a brilliant way of handling that sort of dilemma.

I really wanted to write to you when I read de Beauvoir's account of Sartre's death. She overheard his doctors talking and found out that he had a particularly painful disease, uremia. She burst into tears, and begged the doctor to never let him know that he was dying, never to let him suffer any pain. He'd have taken it so badly. She knew she was taking a risk: their relationship hadn't been easy and she'd been accused of being possessive and protective.

I found all this very moving. I wept and wept. After all their commitment to honesty, she could make her judgement there and then, freshly and anew, trusting in herself. De Beauvoir remembered how Sartre said he always wanted to be a call to life, for death never to enter his life. She was fantastic, the greatest. I am trusting my judgement now and getting in touch with you. I'd love to meet up. You might even want to come out here for a little while. *But you must think carefully about what you want.* And I wouldn't want to do anything to oppress Deborah. (Does she need some adventures in life, too? You should think about that.)
Eva

Robert hid the letter in his desk. The next morning, after a minor argument with Deborah about whether he should put on a fake tanning cream, he was off to Stephen's party, carrying a Baby Boomers Trivial Pursuit as a present, a copy of *Nausea* to read by the pool, and a spectacular question about what he wanted. It was a question that was so preoccupying that he completely failed to notice his left testicle protruding from the side of his trunks as he made his way along a warm concrete path to Stephen's swimming pool . . .

It was a relief for Robert to arrive back from Stephen's party and enter the cool privacy of his empty house. He poured himself a glass of Sancerre, looked at Eva's letter again and lay back on the settee to read *Nausea*.

He approached the book with a strange feeling. Sartre and de Beauvoir were dead. He'd spent the last years of his life blind, unable to write and preoccupied with worries about money. In many ways their generation had died. Their particular concept of what a life was and how to live it, the grandeur and self-importance of some of that, had gone. People didn't live like that any more.

More details were emerging about how bizarre some aspects of Sartre's life were. To a quite incredible degree he had wanted to be in control of himself. He didn't like penetrative sex and mistrusted orgasms because they threatened to engulf his mind. He hated raw food, shell-fish, the countryside and anything else that reminded him of nature unmediated by the mind. He never wanted to submit to the notion of contingency, or to accept that his body rotted and died. It was sad, his failure to trust the world, nature, himself. Robert now saw more clearly the parallels between Sartre's life and aspects of his own: the loss of a father, the lonely childhood, the pressure to become a perfect, false person for someone else, and the refuge taken in words.

Many of the questions with which Sartre tussled had died as well. Who agonised much now about freedom and contingency, or whether existentialism was a humanism, or whether to join the Party? De Beauvoir's feminism had kept her more contemporary than Jean-Paul, but she had been increasingly criticised for the weird existential pains that it took two philosophy degrees to feel, for her nega-tivity about motherhood, and her rejection of psychoanalysis.

It was sad how things didn't last. Even their relationship had ever more flaws exposed. It seemed that they deceived each other more than they let on, and managed their pub-lic images carefully: what they did in the Resistance and her sexuality and all the rest. And people rightly asked whether Sartre would have looked after de Beauvoir in the way she looked after him when he was ill and dying. Yet for all this, they remained faithful to each other in their way. It was a committed, passionate, creative relationship.

Robert turned to *Nausea*.

It was much clearer to him now that the book was about someone who didn't manage to love, let go, or lose himself in play. It was about someone who was trapped in a lonely narcissistic world. Roquentin had so little trust in anything that he was forever fearing that objects were going to swallow him, engulf him.

And the book was so adolescent, the way it railed against the bourgeoisie and promulgated its got-to-be-moving-along Eurorail sense of freedom. It seemed so foolish now to have treated it as a manual for how to live.

When it came to politics, Robert saw that Roquentin could have been right-wing just as easily as left-wing. He could have ended up pushing someone off a train platform just to prove he was free. And he was an academic snob who was contemptuous of the self-taught provincial man. Roquentin never referred to having parents or looked at how life had made him what he was, and why, for example, he needed to reject an ordinary life. He arrogantly assumed that he was his own cause, in absolute control of his destiny, and the language he used. And women weren't treated that well: some were just used for sex, and lots of disgust was expressed about women's bodies. And, as Eva used to say, his accounts of perfect moments and the mind showed no awareness at all of other cultures.

Robert had always felt ambivalent about the end of *Nausea*, where Roquentin talked about accepting himself, at least in the past, through writing a novel. Robert sometimes toyed with the idea of writing a novel one day, about Eva and himself; it might help him hold on to the reality of the time they'd had together. All in all, however, he found it disappointing that Sartre's hero said he was going to be saved by writing a book. It devalued what had happened, made it less universal. It was as if Lenin had got to the Finland station at the start of the Russian Revolution and suggested everyone went home and had a stab at a first novel. Secretly, of course, Robert was angry that Roquentin hadn't lived happily ever after with Anny.

Christ, thought Robert, pouring another glass of wine, you could if you wanted to, find your criticisms of *Nausea*.

Why, then, did he smile so warmly as he read it? Why did he keep putting the book down to let feelings of delight spread through him? It was the joy of recognising himself in the book: his idiom, his neuroses, the dreams he'd had of a life to come. How well he knew the way in which Roquentin had tried to approach the world through his careful, mistrustful mind. How well, too, he knew Roquentin's desire to be loved and saved and transformed. And how much he'd wanted to have Roquentin's cool, intoxicating sense of freedom, his feel for mystery and poetry, his spirit of adventure and belief in the possibility of change. Robert had liked and loved Roquentin, and through this found some possibility of liking and accepting himself. The book had been his first psalm.

But Robert wasn't as naive as he used to be. He'd changed, grown up a bit. And so, too, would Roquentin have changed, in the years beyond the end of the book. Sartre said that the thing he most regretted about *Nausea* was that he hadn't come closer to his character's pain. Eventually Roquentin would have faced this pain and learned to trust things beyond his mind. He would have developed his relationship with Anny. He might even have wrestled with his conscience and applied for Telecom shares.

Robert lay back, letting the book dream into being once more a particular, free sense of who he was. What should he, Robert, do now?

That evening he wrote to Eva, and left a note for Deborah saying that he'd gone to bed early and taken a couple of sleeping-pills. It was almost with relief that he heard Deborah come back with Marshall. He heard the curtains being drawn, and Deborah finding the note and saying that Robert would be out like a light for ten hours. A while later, he heard Marshall admiring her M & S lace basque, and Deborah commenting on Marshall's tan and the good shape his body was in. Then there were the sounds of Marshall pressing himself towards her, and, after a long pause, while Deborah no doubt checked her box of tissues, there was a lot of grunting and groaning, and beyond all this there was an earnest conversation about Total Quality Management. Marshall even started to say how he was trying to respect women more. Alongside some sadness, Robert felt a small, almost aesthetic, type of satisfaction. They could have been manufactured for each other.

*

He started reducing weight in the morning. Deborah had probably been right about passive aggression. He hadn't consciously planned things, but, then again, becoming a fat, pasty slob for a little while had probably made change easier for everyone. It was great to have a light breakfast and go for a run again, in an early-morning sun like dry white wine. He was very understanding with Deborah when she raised her relationship with Marshall. They both agreed that things had been slipping into the red for quite some time. 'Even Marks and Spencer sometimes stock out,' she said philosophically. Marshall was surprised that Robert was being so reasonable about everything, and agreed it was only fair to give Robert a couple of weeks immediate paid leave to help him get over the trauma.

At 30,000 feet, grey clouds spread out below him like a giant cerebral cortex, his decision felt as good as it had felt at home. He sat on a 747 watching *Paris, Texas* while dozens of Indians were served contemptuously with low-grade vegetarian food.

It wasn't so much that he was sure things would work out with Eva. For all he knew, they might find that too many years and people lay between them. It was more a feeling of being true to some sense of himself, that he was free to choose and change.

Bombay was chokingly hot. He spent a night in a windowless hotel room where something with claws scuttled across his feet in the dark. He hid under the sheets, sweating. When he left the hotel in the morning he had to squeeze past a pile of dead rats four feet high. He caught a train up into the hills, sweltering on a hard wooden seat and taking tepid fizzy drinks at every station. There was a delay for two hours over a cow that had been injured on the line. Then the train climbed higher, into cooler air. He finally arrived, via a three-wheeler taxi, at a hotel where the owner lay on a bed in the sun, next to a freezer full of

Cokes, and told Robert to calm down, that it was impossible to change anything.

The ashram next day was an oasis of shady trees and zen rock gardens. And there was Eva, with her fine-boned face and pale blue eyes, as slender and graceful as he remembered, giving a little jump of excitement as she saw him, then hugging him fiercely. He let himself fall towards her, savouring her warm skin and the sweet spicy smell of patchouli. They sat on a bench and looked at each other nervously, wary of ghosts and changes. Then she put her arms round his neck and her mouth came hotly against his. Over the next few days they began to talk and make love with a new type of availability and abandon.

Later that week, they sat one evening in an outdoor restaurant, underneath red and green fairy lights, and surrounded by the sounds of Indian music and bicycle bells. Eva was wearing a thin silk dress. She periodically smoothed it down so that it followed the curves of her thighs. They talked about their mistrustful childhoods, and attempts at relationships, and experiments in being alone. Robert realised that they now looked at each other not with desperate neurotic need or calculation or separateness, but with a relaxed look that confirmed each other's existence and created a certain sort of love story, about equality, spirit and humour. He mentioned all this, and she giggled and told him to stop being pretentious. But for a long time afterwards, she agreed that it was there, sitting in that restaurant, with the warm night air gliding about their legs, chatting and laughing, and clinking their glasses in a toast to Roquentin and Anny, Simone and Jean-Paul, Deborah and Marshall; it was there that they knew they came towards each other now as reasonably free people, and that they trusted each other enough to create, through all the possibilities and uncertainties, some sort of life together.

THE DEAD HEART

Douglas Kennedy

That dumbshit map. I'd been seduced by it. Seduced by its possibilities. That map had brought me here . . . That map had been a serious mistake.

The map in question is of Australia, stumbled across in a second-hand bookshop by American journalist Nick Hawthorne, en route to another dead-end hack job in Akron, Ohio. Seduced by all that wilderness, all that *nothing*, Nick decides to put his midlife crisis on hold and light out to the ultimate nowheresville – where a chance encounter throws him into a sun-baked orgy of surf, sex and swill, and a nightmare from which there is no escape.

'Pulls off that most difficult feat of being hilariously funny and frightening at the same time'
Independent on Sunday

'Fluent and entertaining ... a highly accomplished début'
Sunday Telegraph

'A comic triumph, culminating in a high-temperature, high-tension attempt at flight which has the reader sweating almost as much as the character'
Time Out

Abacus
0 349 10645 2

THE ICE STORM

Rick Moody

'One of the wittiest books about family life ever written'
Brendan O'Keeffe, *Guardian*

Nixon and 'Nam, pet rocks and shag rugs, wife-swapping and
party-hopping. Suburban New England, 1973, and the Hood family
are looking for ways to spend a Friday evening as far from one
another as they can get. But with the weather about to turn
dangerous, they're soon going to wish they'd stayed home...

Acutely acerbic, painfully funny, *The Ice Storm* is an astonishing
novel of the decade that taste forgot.

'A blackly funny and beautifully written novel ... [Moody] is
clearly a writer to watch'
Isabel Wolff, *Sunday Times*

'A huge '70s nostalgia trip, a litany of kitsch, a mountain of
memorabilia as the backdrop to a bitter-sweet story of
suburban America ... Excellent'
Time Out

'Vibrates with period detail ... *The Ice Storm* is frequently
farcical, but what makes it also heart-rending is not the fact
that its characters are dots in a landscape that will exist long
after they have gone; but people who must endure beyond the
ephemera that serves to diminish them'
Independent

Abacus
0 349 10641 X

☐ The Dead Heart	Douglas Kennedy	£5.99
☐ The Ice Storm	Rick Moody	£5.99
☐ Up North	Charles Jennings	£6.99
☐ The Virgin Suicides	Jeffrey Eugenides	£6.99
☐ The Moon Rising	Steve Kelly	£5.99

Abacus now offers an exciting range of quality titles by both established and new authors which can be ordered from the following address:

Little, Brown and Company (UK),
P.O. Box 11,
Falmouth,
Cornwall TR10 9EN.

Fax No: 01326 317444.
Telephone No: 01326 372400
E-mail: books@barni.avel.co.uk

Payments can be made as follows: cheque, postal order (payable to Little, Brown and Company) or by credit cards, Visa/Access.
Do not send cash or currency. UK customers and B.F.P.O. please allow £1.00 for postage and packing for the first book, plus 50p for the second book, plus 30p for each additional book up to a maximum charge of £3.00 (7 books plus). Overseas customers including Ireland, please allow £2.00 for the first book plus £1.00 for the second book, plus 50p for each additional book.

NAME (Block Letters) _____

ADDRESS _____

_____

_____

☐ I enclose my remittance for £ _____
☐ I wish to pay by Access/Visa Card

Number ☐☐☐☐☐☐☐☐☐☐☐☐☐☐☐☐☐☐

Card Expiry Date _____